JACK HIGGINS

THE JUDAS GATE

HARPER

Harper
HarperCollins*Publishers*
77–85 Fulham Palace Road,
Hammersmith, London W6 8JB

www.harpercollins.co.uk

Published by HarperCollins*Publishers* 2011

8

Copyright © Harry Patterson 2010

Harry Patterson asserts the moral right to
be identified as the author of this work

A catalogue record for this book
is available from the British Library

A format ISBN: 978 0 00 732047 9
B format ISBN: 978 0 00 738560 7

Set in Sabon by Palimpsest Book Production Limited,
Falkirk, Stirlingshire

Printed and bound in Great Britain by
Clays Ltd, St Ives plc

For Ian Williams

WASHINGTON, D.C.

___

THE OVAL OFFICE

1

The Washington day in August had been almost sub
tropical, but by late evening an unexpected shower had
cooled things.

The Hay-Adams Hotel was only a short walk from
the White House, and outside the bar two men sat at
a small table on the terrace, a canopy protecting them
against the rain. The elder had an authoritative moustache and thick hair touched with silver, and wore a
dark blue suit and Guards tie. He was General Charles
Ferguson, Commander of the British Prime Minister's
private hit squad, which was an unfortunate necessity
in the era of international terrorism.

His companion, Major Harry Miller, was forty-seven,
just under six feet, with grey eyes, a shrapnel scar on
one cheek, and a calm and confident manner. A Member
of Parliament, he served the Prime Minister as a general
troubleshooter and bore the rank of Under-Secretary of

State. He had proved he could handle anything, from the politicians at the United Nations to the hell of Afghanistan.

Just now, he was saying to Ferguson, 'Are you sure the President will be seeing us?'

Ferguson nodded. 'Blake was quite certain. The President said he'd make sure to clear time for us.'

Sean Dillon stepped out on to the terrace, glass in hand, and joined them, his fair hair tousled and his shirt and velvet cord suit black as usual.

'So there you are.'

Before Ferguson could reply, Blake Johnson appeared from the bar and found them. He wore a light trench-coat draped over his shoulders to protect a tweed country suit. He was fifty-nine, his black hair flecked with grey. As a boy, he'd lied about his age, and when he'd stepped out of the plane to start his first tour of Vietnam, he'd been only eighteen. Now, a long-time veteran of the Secret Service, he was Personal Security Adviser to the new President, as he had been for several Presidents before him.

'We thought we'd been stood up,' Dillon told him, and shook hands.

'Nonsense,' Ferguson said. 'It's good of him to make time for us.'

'Your report on Afghanistan certainly interested him. Besides, he's wanted to meet you for some time now.'

'With all the new blood running around, I think that's very decent of the man,' Dillon said. 'I thought we'd have been kicked out of the door along with the special relationship.'

Ferguson said to Blake, 'Take no notice of him. Let's get going.'

For those who didn't want to make a fuss, the best way into the White House was through the east entrance, which was where Clancy Smith, a large, fit black Secret Service man assigned to the President, waited patiently. He had met them all over the years.

'Great to see you, General,' he told Ferguson.

'So you're still speaking to us, Clancy?' Dillon asked.

'Dillon, shut up!' Ferguson told him again.

'I'm only trying to make sure there's a welcome for Brits these days. I seem to remember there was a previous occasion when they burned the place down.'

Clancy roared with laughter. 'Dillon, you never change.'

'He doesn't, does he?' Ferguson said bitterly. 'But let's get moving. If you'd be kind enough to lead the way.'

Which Clancy did, escorting them through many corridors until he finally paused at a door. 'Gentlemen, the Oval Office.'

He opened the door and led the way in. The President was in his shirtsleeves, working his way through a mound of paperwork.

*　　*　　*

The President and Blake were sitting on one side of the large coffee table, with Dillon, Ferguson and Miller on the other. There was coffee available on a sideboard and they had all helped themselves at the President's invitation.

Ferguson sipped some of his coffee. 'Trying times, Mr President.'

'Afghanistan troubles me greatly. The casualties mount relentlessly, yet we can't just abandon them,' the President said.

'I agree,' Ferguson told him.

The President glanced at Blake. 'What were those Vietnam statistics again?'

'At its worst, four hundred dead a week and four times as many wounded,' Blake told him.

'Two thousand casualties a week.' Miller shook his head. 'It wasn't sustainable.'

'Which was why we got out,' the President said. 'But what the hell do we do now? We have a large international army, excellent military personnel, backed up by air support and missiles. It should be no contest, and yet . . .'

Harry Miller put in, 'There's precedent, Mr President. During the Eighteen-forties, at the height of its Empire, Britain sent an army of sixteen and a half thousand into Afghanistan to take Kabul. Only one man returned with his life, a regimental doctor. I've always believed the Afghans were sending a message by allowing him to live.'

'My God,' the President said softly. 'I never heard that story.'

'To Afghans, family comes first, and then the tribe,' Miller told him. 'But they will always fight together to defend Afghanistan itself against an invader.'

'And that's us,' Dillon put in. 'And they don't like it. And now even young men of Afghan extraction who were born in Britain end up joining the fight.'

The President turned to Ferguson. 'That's what was in your report. Tell me more.'

Ferguson said, 'Are you familiar with Major Giles Roper, a member of my staff in London?'

'We haven't met, but I know of him. Once a great bomb-disposal expert, until an explosion put him in a wheelchair.'

'Yes. Well, he's since become the king of cyberspace. There's nothing he can't make his computers do – and sometimes that means he can listen in to battlefield chat in Afghanistan. The people flying with the Taliban come from such a wide number of countries that English has sometimes become the language of communication.'

Miller said, 'It's interesting to hear the voices. Yorkshire accents, many from Birmingham, Welsh, Scots.'

'That's incredible,' the President said.

'But true. Young British-born Muslims are being recruited by doctrinaire preachers who not only encourage them to go, but also offer plane tickets and a training camp, all courtesy of Al Qaeda, who then introduce them to the Taliban,' Miller added. 'It's an awfully big adventure when you're eighteen or so.'

'Just like joining the army,' Dillon murmured.

Ferguson glanced at him, but the President carried on. 'You know, there are many good people who advocate we withdraw and continue this as a long-range war.'

'Air strikes, cruise missiles, drones,' Blake said.

Ferguson replied, 'With respect, too often that can result in an indiscriminate attack on civilian targets. Terrorism can only be countered by a resolute anti-terrorism campaign that pulls no punches.'

'I take your point.' The President nodded. 'But let's ask an expert.' He turned to Dillon. 'I've been informed of your past, Mr Dillon. You must have an opinion. Share it with us.'

'General Ferguson is right. The successful revolutionary blends with the people. Which is why, with these British Muslim imports, American and British forces in Afghanistan can't be certain who *is* the enemy.'

'Which we counter by joining with Afghan Army units ourselves,' Ferguson said. 'But there's another aspect that concerns me more.'

'And that is?' the President asked.

'There's an incredible new sophistication by the Taliban concerning improvised explosive devices. Not only in the bombmaking itself, but their usage. They are becoming far too good. The only conclusion must be that they are being coached by experts.'

The President frowned. 'What are you implying? The Cubans or the Russians, something like that?'

'Good God, no,' Ferguson said. 'Those days are long gone for the Cubans, and the Russians wouldn't touch Afghanistan if it was the last place on earth. They couldn't crack that nut with an army of a hundred thousand men.'

Dillon moved in. 'Bombs aren't just bombs, they are tactical weapons, used to achieve maximum results. You must make sure that an ambush is not just an ambush, but a total disaster for the enemy. And to achieve that, you need instruction from an expert.'

'What are you saying?'

'Let me tell you a story,' Ferguson said. 'It's from thirty years ago, when I was a Major in the Grenadier Guards, on my third tour in Ulster, seconded to staff at headquarters in Belfast. I'm not wasting your time, believe me.'

'Then proceed, General,' the President told him, and Ferguson began.

'*August the twenty-seventh, Nineteen seventy-nine.*' Ferguson took a deep breath, as if pulling himself together. 'I'll never forget that date because it was one of the worst days in my life. I was in the Incident Room at the Grand Central in Belfast when we received some truly dreadful news.'

'Which was?' the President enquired.

'The Queen's cousin, Lord Louis Mountbatten, liked to enjoy his family holidays in Ireland, despite the obvious security risks. That year, a radio-controlled bomb blew his thirty-foot fishing boat apart, killing Mountbatten, his grandson, his daughter's mother-in-law and a young boat boy.'

'Dear God,' the President said. 'I remember reading about it.'

'God had nothing to do with it, but the Provisional IRA did. The media went berserk. At the Incident Room, we were besieged, calls from all over the world. Then later that same day, just when I thought it was beginning to calm down, it got worse. Warrenpoint. Two trucks loaded with paratroopers were on their way to a market town called Newry when a huge road-side bomb hidden in a farm trailer was activated by a radio signal. Six paratroopers were killed and others wounded. The survivors took refuge in the ruins of a lodge at a place called Narrow Water. They radioed in for help and came under sniper fire. A Wessex helicopter carrying soldiers from the Queen's Own Highlanders landed close by. As they disembarked, another large bomb exploded, killing twelve soldiers, including their commanding officer and wounding others.'

The President's horror was plain. 'That's appalling.'

'I use it in my lectures at Sandhurst as an example of a classic guerrilla ambush brilliantly executed,' Miller told him.

Ferguson said, 'It was probably the worst incident in terms of casualties in the whole of the Troubles. Eighteen men dead and more than twenty wounded.'

'So where are you going with this?' the President asked.

Miller took a map from his briefcase and unfolded it. 'Afghanistan, Helmand province. See the road running up to the mountains in the north, the small village of Mirbat and the deep lake beside it? The village is in ruins, the people have moved on. A convoy loaded with technicians and electronic equipment needed to get through to the dam at the head of the valley to repair the hydroelectric system that the Taliban had damaged. Two six-wheel Mastiff armoured patrol vehicles led the way. Besides the drivers, there were twelve Rangers. When they got to Mirbat they found it deserted, got out to explore, and a massive roadside bomb killed six of them instantly and wounded others.'

The President said, 'What next?'

'The remaining Rangers came under sniper fire from across the lake. A Chinook helicopter with an instant response medical team happened to be close by, Brits as a matter of fact. They reached Mirbat in fifteen minutes and landed. As the medics jumped out, a second roadside bomb was activated and the helicopter fire-balled.' Miller shrugged. 'The firing stopped, the Taliban cleared off. In all, there were twenty personnel involved. The entire Chinook team were slaughtered, and ten Rangers. Two Rangers survived, along with the driver.'

'Sixteen dead,' the President said grimly.

Ferguson said, 'Shocking, isn't it? Even more so to listen to.'

'Listen to? You mean, this is one of the things your Major Roper picked up? With the British voices?'

'Yes. Voices calling to each other in the fog of battle, the death of men, the triumph of the victor,' Ferguson told him. 'The Taliban force could have been as many as thirty. The experts estimate about fifteen were British.' He removed a cassette from his pocket.

The President took it and said, 'Clancy, would you put this on? We might as well hear the worst.'

The material had been enhanced and edited. Some of the voices were speaking Pushtu and there was an occasional call in Arabic, but English prevailed and the different regional accents were clear. For a while, there was a lot of crosstalk, and then someone cut in with real authority.

'Shamrock here. Cut all this stupid chatter and assume your positions. Mastiffs are on the way. The soldiers in them are American Rangers. They're good, so wait for the bomb to explode before firing. Anyone who jumps the gun gets a bullet through the kneecap from me afterwards.'

There was a certain amount of wild laughter, and then an American voice cut in. 'Calling convoy. Ranger One. Coming into Mirbat now. Looks pretty quiet to me, but we'll see.'

Shortly afterwards, the first explosion was followed by gunfire, voices calling excitedly, screams, the sound of AK47s firing. Then a sudden silence.

Miller said, 'Major Roper's cut straight to the Chinook arriving.'

The pause ended; there was the noise of the Chinook coming in and then the second explosion, deafening in its intensity, followed by further gunfire and then the voice again, loud and clear.

'Shamrock here. Cease firing. You've done well, you bastards. What a spectacular. Warrenpoint all over again and it worked big time. Osama will be delighted. Now let's get out of here before the heavy brigade arrives. You can rest in peace now, Sean. Night bless.'

There was suddenly only the machine whirring. Clancy said, 'Is that it?'

'It sure as hell was enough,' the President said, his face sombre. 'Why haven't I heard of this before, Blake?'

'It only happened nine days ago, Mr President. You were in Mexico for two days, then that courtesy call in Panama, and then the Libyan business.'

'That's what I'm elected for. This is bad.'

'Yes, but Major General Ferguson thought you should hear this personally. This has been the first opportunity.'

'You're right, of course.' The President took a deep breath. 'We're grateful to you, General. Now this leader of the pack, this Shamrock. What do you know about him?'

Ferguson said, 'Our voice experts say he's educated, likely the product of a top public school.'

'And a trained soldier?'

'I'd say so,' Ferguson said.

'Which means the British Army,' Dillon said, 'and he has Irish roots of some sort.'

'How can you be certain?' the President asked.

'The code name he's chosen, Shamrock. What could be more Irish than that? Then there was his joy over the success of the Mirbat ambush, and his comparing it to the Warrenpoint spectacular of so many years ago. Also, his threat to shoot anyone who misbehaved through the kneecap – that's a ritual punishment in the IRA since time immemorial. Finally, this rest-in-peace prayer to someone called Sean.'

'Surely that's a common enough name in Ireland?'

'It certainly is,' Dillon smiled. 'A good Irish name which in Northern Ireland would label you as a Catholic instantly.'

'I'll have to take your word for it, Mr Dillon. Most enlightening.' The President stood up. 'Gentlemen, I'm very grateful, and you've given me a lot to think about. General, I know the White House has owed you and your people a debt on many previous occasions. Keep

Blake informed of your progress and let me know if there is anything I can do.'

'We're grateful for you finding a moment to see us,' Ferguson told him. 'We live in trying times, but we'll pull through, I'm sure of it.'

'God willing.' The President shook hands with the three of them, Dillon last, and said, 'You really believe you can hunt this man, this Shamrock, down, don't you, Mr Dillon?'

'Absolutely, Mr President.'

The President smiled. 'You are a remarkable man, my friend. Don't let me down.'

'My oath on it, sir.' He held the President's hand a moment longer, then turned and followed the others as Blake ushered them out.

Late the next morning, Ferguson's Gulfstream, his regular RAF pilots, Lacey and Parry, at the controls, rose to thirty thousand feet, climbing high over the Atlantic. After a while, Parry looked into the cabin.

'There's some problematic weather in the mid-Atlantic. A question of how heavy the winds are.'

'I'd have said perfectly acceptable if they're flying up your backside,' Dillon told him.

'Right as usual, Dillon, which means our flight time will be cut to about six hours if we're lucky. Anyone like anything to eat or drink?'

'Thank you, no, Flight Lieutenant,' Ferguson told him, and Parry withdrew.

Miller said, 'You certainly impressed the President, Sean.'

'I only told the man what I thought he'd want to hear.'

'Rash promises as usual,' Ferguson put in. 'Shamrock could be anybody.'

'There's no such thing,' Dillon told him. 'Everyone is a somebody, and I intend to find him, one way or another. In fact, I'm so certain, I'll have a drink on it.'

'Not me,' Ferguson told him, and unfolded the quilt beside his seat. 'I'm going to take a nap. I'll have to see the Prime Minister tomorrow. If you want to make yourself useful, Harry, call in to Roper and tell him what happened.'

He switched off his light and pulled up the quilt.

At the Holland Park safe house in London, Major Giles Roper sat in a track suit in his wheelchair, his shoulder-length hair tied with a ribbon, pulling it back from his bomb-ravaged face, as he listened to Harry Miller describe the visit to the White House. Roper lit a cigarette and poured a whiskey as he listened.

'Good old Sean. No one could ever accuse him of lacking confidence.'

'Have you come up with anything else?' Miller asked.

'I can't say that I have, and I've gone over the audio tapes again and again. What you all listened to is still what I've got.'

'So what happens now?'

'I'm not sure. The rumours of British-born Muslims fighting for the Taliban are now confirmed. What the government can do about it is another matter.'

'Not very much, I imagine. The government is wary about stirring things up with the Muslim population.'

'So we'll all go to hell in a handcart together,' Harry Miller told him. 'But first, what do we do about Shamrock?'

'That's a different matter,' Dillon put in from the plane, 'and quite simple. We find him quickly, shoot him, and pass him over to the disposal men.'

'Ah, if only life were that easy,' Roper said.

'We know a lot about him already. The clues are there,' Dillon said. 'He obviously has military experience.'

'So what are you going to do? Go to the army list and pore over thousands of names going back ten, twenty or even thirty years? What would you be looking for?'

'You're right, but I won't be doing that. I've a strong feeling that going back to the scene of the crime might be the way.'

'To Mirbat?' Roper was aghast. 'Don't be a bloody fool, Sean. If the Taliban got you, they'd feed you to the dogs.'

'I'm sure they would, but I was thinking of Warrenpoint.

I have a feeling that there might be some answer for me there. I was born in County Down myself, you know, at Collyban, no more than a dozen miles from the area.'

Ferguson's voice was muffled by the quilt as he said, 'You are not going anywhere near County Down, and that's an order, so shut up and stop disturbing me.'

'I hear and obey, oh great one.' Dillon switched off the telephone. 'Sorry, Harry.'

Ferguson said, 'Call Roper back and tell him to contact Daniel Holley in Algiers or wherever he is. Get him to share all our information with Holley. I'd value his opinion on the matter.'

Dillon was astounded. 'You mean the Daniel Holley who tried to put us all out of business permanently? Who nearly succeeded in blowing you up in your limousine and arranged for hit men to have a try at Harry and Blake Johnson, whose shoulder still aches on a rainy day from the bullet he took?'

'Yes, well, he didn't succeed . . .'

'He came bloody close.'

'He also saved your good friend Monica Starling from certain death. Don't forget that, Sean. And as far as both the Americans and ourselves are concerned, he's clean now. He's too useful not to be. Especially since he's become full partner with Hamid Malik in that shipping company. They're respected throughout the Mediterranean, you know.'

'They're also arms dealers,' Dillon said.

'Not any more,' Ferguson told him. 'Well, only occasionally. In any case, Holley's been given Algerian nationality and a diplomatic passport by their Foreign Minister. He can come and go anywhere these days. It's the way the world turns, Dillon.'

'Next thing you know, he'll be staying at the Dorchester, having tea and scones.'

'I had a drink with him there two months ago,' Ferguson said wearily. 'In his suite. With Roper. I don't tell you everything, Dillon.'

He retreated under the quilt and Dillon, feeling strangely helpless, turned to Miller. 'Did you know anything about this?'

'Not a thing,' the Major said. 'But, really, Sean, I don't care. As you know, Protestant terrorists raped and murdered his young cousin, so he executed all four of them and took refuge from the law by joining the IRA. I don't hold it against him – any more than I hold your past against you.'

'Okay,' Dillon said. 'You don't have to make a production out of it. I was just getting adjusted to the idea. Go to sleep.'

He picked up the telephone and made the call to Roper, who had just brought up the County Down border on one of his screens. When Dillon called, Roper took it on speaker.

'Sean, me boy, I expected to hear from you. Your "hear and obey" to Ferguson didn't fool me for a minute, so I was just about to look at things again to see if I'd missed anything.'

'Forget about me. The situation has changed dramatically.'

'Okay, tell me the worst.' Dillon did, and when he was finished, Roper laughed. 'My God, Sean, you almost sound indignant.'

'You've got to admit that Holley could have finished us all off.'

'Well, he didn't, and he saved Monica from a certain and unpleasant death. The love of your life, Sean – at least that's the impression we all get.'

Dillon said, 'Damn you for being right. I guess I just felt left out of things.'

'That's understandable. Where Holley is concerned, though, Ferguson wanted to handle everything with care. With that diplomatic passport from the Algerian Foreign Minister, the whole wide world's opened up for him again. Ferguson wants to take advantage of that.'

'It makes sense,' Dillon said, grudgingly.

'And you'll never feel lonely again, as far as we are concerned. After all, he's IRA, just like you.'

'You have a way with the words, Roper.'

'It's a hell of a world we live in these days,' Roper said. 'Not so easy to see the difference between the good guys and bad any more.'

'Oh, I think I can manage to do that well enough,' Dillon said. 'But I'll leave you to hunt Daniel Holley down.'

It was quiet then, as Roper sat there in the computer room on his own, just the glow of the screens around him. He sat in his state-of-the-art wheelchair, suddenly feeling tired and weary and badly damaged – which he was, past everything there ever was. But that would never do. He poured himself another whiskey, reached for his Codex mobile and went in search of Daniel Holley.

PARIS

ALGIERS

2

Daniel Holley was running alongside the Seine, darkness beginning to take over, the heat of the day lingering ominously as if a storm was brewing. He'd purchased a furnished barge a few months earlier, convenient for business trips for both him and his partner, Hamid Malik. He wore a black track suit, looked younger than forty-nine, his hair still brown. Of medium height, fit and well, he had the permanent slight smile of a man who found life a little absurd most of the time. The Irish in him, as his mother used to say. The other half was from the city of his birth, Leeds, which meant pure Yorkshire. His mobile sounded and he took it out. It was a Codex of advanced design, only available to Ferguson's people, which his previous masters at Russian Military Intelligence, the GRU, had stolen.

'Hello, Roper,' he said, 'what a surprise. What can

I do for you?' He paused, leaning on a convenient wall.

'Tell me where you are, for a start.'

'Paris, and running beside the Seine. It's been a lovely day, but rain threatens. But you didn't call for a weather report.'

'No. To be brief, Ferguson, Dillon and Harry Miller have just been meeting with the President in Washington. They were discussing the Taliban's use of British-born Muslims in their army – and there seems to be an Irish dimension emerging.'

'Is there, by God?' Holley's voice was serious, the Yorkshire accent more pronounced.

'The General would like your opinion. After all, you were trained at one of those camps yourself in the middle of the Algerian desert. All those years ago, and paid for by Colonel Gaddafi.'

'So was Sean Dillon.'

'A good point. You've got extra credentials, though. You're joint owner of one of the biggest shipping firms out of Algiers, with Algerian nationality, and – thanks to that diplomatic passport from their Foreign Minister – you get waved through security at airports all over the world.'

'It's even better when I fly privately,' Holley told him. 'I get diplomatic immunity.'

'I'm so happy for you,' Roper teased. 'So Ferguson has asked me to send you the full details of the meeting at the Oval Office. I think you'll find it pretty grim. Will you look?'

'Of course I will, you daft bastard; I wouldn't miss it. You've got my email address from when we met at the Dorchester. Do the others know about that yet, by the way?'

'They've just been told on the Gulfstream at thirty-five thousand feet over the Atlantic. Miller was completely pragmatic about it; Dillon was mortified, more than anything else. He doesn't like being kept in the dark.'

'Well, that's just too bloody bad. Send that material and I'll read it when I get back to the barge. I must go now. I've got a business transaction waiting.'

'Straightforward, I hope?'

'When I say Albanian, what would you think?'

'God help you, my friend. Watch your back.'

Holley put his Codex in his pocket, thoroughly stimulated by the entire conversation. Heady stuff. As it started to rain, he ran through the gathering darkness towards Notre Dame, floodlit, incomparably beautiful in the night, and came to Quai de Montebello, illuminated by lamps, where barges were moored together. He boarded his own by a roped gangplank and went below.

The barge's previous owner had been a well-known fashion designer and it was extremely comfortable:

panelled state room with comfortable sofas, shelves of books, a television, a long table in the centre. A small alcove at one end held the computer. The kitchen was opposite, small, but with everything he needed. The sleeping quarters and shower room were at the end of a passage in the bow of the barge.

The computer-linked phone system was flashing, so he took a half-full bottle of champagne from the fridge, poured a glass, pressed a replay button and quickly found himself talking to Hamid Malik at the villa in Algiers.

'I was worried,' Malik said. 'What's happening?'

'Not much. The meeting with Ali Kupu is on. Eleven o'clock, about fifteen minutes from here.'

'So late?' Malik sighed. 'I don't know, Daniel. Do we really have to deal with people like Ali Kupu still? These Albanians are pigs. Bastards of the first order. Completely untrustworthy. Most of them would sell their sisters on the streets.'

'A great many do,' Holley said. 'Since we spoke, I had another message from him. He wanted to change our meeting to Havar. Can you believe that?'

'But that's in Kosovo, close to the Bulgarian border. You couldn't even consider it!'

'Of course not, especially when you remember what happened the last time I did business there.' Holley had been betrayed to the Russians and ended up with a life sentence at the Lubyanka Prison. It was only by luck that Vladimir Putin, searching for someone to make mischief against General Ferguson and his people in

London, had heard about him and pulled him out of his cell.

'But in the end, everything's turned out for the best, my friend,' Malik said. 'Business couldn't be better; your rather violent past is no longer held against you. You are not only a millionaire businessman, but a respected diplomat. Don't spoil it. This Ali Kupu is scum. The arms deal he wants is maybe two hundred thousand dollars. Petty cash. Who needs it?'

'It's an easy one,' Holley told him. 'Trust me.'

'A gangster,' Malik said. 'He deals in drugs, violent prostitution. Pah!'

'But this has nothing to do with any of that. He's told me the material is for Muslim village defence forces in Kosovo. They aren't being protected by the central government any longer – and that's a known fact. AK47s, RPGs plus ammunition – we can meet the order at the Marseilles warehouse, ship it out by air this week, and we're done.'

'On condition he pays in advance.'

'Absolutely. Cash on the nail or he doesn't get the goods. Don't worry.'

'But I do. You're like a son to me. Finish it quickly and get out of there. You have the Falcon there, don't you? Thank God I agreed when you suggested we buy it for the firm.'

'It's parked at Charles de Gaulle Airport waiting for me. I'll leave tonight, but I might call in at London before I return home.'

'Any particular reason?'

Holley hesitated, but decided not to mention the other business. 'Oh, I fancy a couple of days at the Dorchester after meeting with someone like the Albanian. Maybe I'll walk up to Shepherd Market, visit your cousin, Selim.'

'I envy you. I'd enjoy that myself.'

'I could send the Falcon.'

'Nonsense. So expensive.'

'We're making millions.'

'Leave me to mind the store. Allah be with you.'

The connection went silent. It was just past nine o'clock, still time to have a quick look at the computer to see if Roper had sent the material. He poured another glass of champagne, sat down and scanned the first page.

It took him twenty minutes to go right through it all, very briefly and far too quickly, but it was enough. 'My God,' he said softly. 'What have we got here and what in the hell is to be done about it?'

And then a strange thing happened. He was aware of an energy; a cold, hard excitement he hadn't known in years. He called Roper and got him at once.

'Did you get the material?' Roper asked.

'You can tell Ferguson I want to be part of whatever operation you're putting together. I'll be in London tomorrow,' he said, and hung up.

* * *

At Holland Park, Roper sat there in silence. 'Good God,' he said softly. 'What a turn-up for the books.'

He debated whether to put the news directly through to the Gulfstream, but decided against it. Such good news could keep. He brought Warrenpoint up on the screen and started to go through everything again.

Holley had a quick shower, thinking of what lay ahead. Kupu was a dangerously violent man who had killed many times, but he was not stupid. Business was business, and he needed what Holley could provide. It wasn't logical that he would do anything but behave himself.

But nothing in this life was certain, and Holley slipped on a nylon-and-titanium bulletproof vest next to his skin. It was guaranteed to stop a .44 round at point-blank range, and had done so on several occasions in his violent career.

He dressed in a fresh track suit and sneakers. There was no point in wearing an ankle-holster. Kupu's goon, Abu, would certainly check on that. A Walther in his pocket, so easy to discover, would keep him happy. For his personal safety, he could rely on an old reliable, and he took it out of the wardrobe. A crumpled Burberry rain hat. Inside, a spring clip held a snub-nosed Colt .25 and its cartridges were hollow point. One of those in the right place was all it took. So, he found a light raincoat, slipped the Walther in a pocket, carefully arranged the hat on his head, found an umbrella and left.

The unexpected and heavy rain had emptied the pavements, especially at the side of the Seine. Around him were quiet buildings, dark at that time of night, narrow streets leading down to the river, the faint sounds of traffic in the distance. Holley hurried on, without meeting a soul, and eventually reached his destination. In the gloom, there was something sinister about it, dark and threatening. There were two old street lamps on the jetty itself, another in the yard at the end, where there was a huge warehouse door. In the door was the usual small access entrance for workmen, and he opened it and stepped inside, the door banging.

He saw several rows of old workbenches, some machinery, a couple of vans at the far end, and a wide exit door, open, lights above it so the heavy rain glistened like silver as it fell. To the left was an office, partly glassed in, so you could see inside. Ali Kupu was sitting behind a cluttered desk and appeared to be fondling a young woman who was standing obediently beside him.

'Ah, it is you, Mr Holley. Enter, my friend.'

His English was surprisingly good, but then, as a youth, Kupu had worked in Soho for two years until he'd finally been expelled as an illegal immigrant.

He was an overweight, unshaven, coarse animal with a shaven head.

'Come in, come in.'

Holley moved forward, passed the first van, and was not in the least surprised when the rear door opened and Abu scrambled out behind him. He was enormous, with a face like stone, hair down to his shoulders. He wore a black suit.

'You know what to do,' he said.

Holley obliged, leaned on the van, and the Walther was discovered. 'My, but you are getting to be a big boy,' Holley said as he straightened, 'You should enter the Mr Universe competition this year. Muscles gleaming under all that oil. You'd like that, wouldn't you?'

'No, Mr Holley, what I'd really like is to tear off your head – and I will do exactly that, the first chance I get.'

He moved into the office ahead of Holley and put the Walther on the table, then stood at the back of the room. Kupu was very drunk and yet reached for an open bottle of vodka and swallowed deeply from it.

'You shouldn't anger Abu like that. He's a very violent man when he gets angry and does terrible things, doesn't he?' he said to the woman, who looked terrified. She wore a raincoat over a light black dress and clutched a handbag.

'I'm sure he does.' Holley walked to a chair at one side of the door, sat down, took off his Burberry rain hat and put it on his lap.

33

'This is Liri.' Kupu encircled her waist. 'One of my best girls. Empty your handbag and let's see how well you've done tonight.'

'The rain,' she said as she fumbled. 'Business wasn't good.' She emptied the handbag of not very much.

Kupu glanced at it, then took a Gladstone bag from under the desk, opened it and swept in Liri's earnings.

'Excuses, Mr Holley, it's all I get.' He slapped her face, then said to Abu, 'Search her next door. See if she's hiding anything.'

'No, please,' she begged Kupu, as Abu grabbed her arm, opened the far door and shoved her through.

'Stupid bitch, they are all the same. I give them employment, look after their interests and how do they repay me?' He swallowed more vodka. 'But to business. You can supply what I need? I'm a serious man. I desire only to help my Muslim brothers who are being butchered every day in Kosovo.'

'Very commendable.'

'And I have good references.' He patted the side of his nose drunkenly. 'AQ, eh?'

'Is that a fact?' Holley said.

There were muffled cries from the next room, but Kupu ignored them. 'You don't believe me, do you?' He reached for the vodka bottle, swallowing again. 'My father's brother, my Uncle Mahmud, is an art dealer based in Tirana. He specializes in rare holy books and manuscripts. He travels all over Europe, knows people at the highest level. I act as his contact man in Paris. He tells me everything. For example, what if I told you that Prime Minister Putin intends to make a visit to Chechnya this weekend? All very hush-hush. The sort of thing you only hear about afterwards.'

Holley said, 'And why would he be doing that?'

'A meeting requested by a very high-level Muslim holy man. A famous Mullah, now in his nineties, Ibrahim somebody.' He leaned forward. 'But here's the thing, my friend. This holy man, this Ibrahim? He intends to become a martyr this weekend. He will be carrying religious scrolls, which of course security men would not dare to search. A profound insult. And inside the scrolls – Semtex. You wouldn't need much to do the job at close quarters. The Prime Minister would be blown to hell.'

'With everyone around him.'

'What a moment,' Kupu roared, and the door to the other room opened and Liri staggered out, trying to cover her torn dress with the raincoat and still clutching her handbag. She stood there, crying bitterly.

'Look at you,' Kupu said. 'Disgusting. Who in the hell would want you? Go on, get out.'

'But I've no money for a cab,' she wailed.

'Then you can walk in the rain. Better than a shower. Wash the stink off you.'

At which point Holley, having had enough, said, 'No need for that, Liri. I'm leaving myself. I'll be going by cab and I'll drop you off.'

Suddenly Kupu didn't seem as drunk as he had been. 'What is this about you leaving?'

'I don't like the way you do business.'

'Really? Then obviously you need to pay a visit to the next room, where Abu will indicate what is expected of you. I don't think it will take long for you to get the point.'

As Holley stood up, he produced the Colt .25, extended his arm and shot Ali Kupu twice in the heart, knocking him back over the chair. Liri gave a strangled cry, then leaned over to look. Abu seemed stunned and uncertain what to do.

Liri recovered a little and turned to Holley. 'He's dead.'

'That's what I meant him to be. Can you drive?'

'Yes.'

'Take one of the vans and get out of here, and you can also take the Gladstone bag with you as far as I'm concerned. Will you be okay?'

'Fine. I've got a passport. I'll be out of Paris first thing in the morning. God bless you. I'll never forget you.'

'I'd rather you did.'

He picked up the Walther, put the Colt in his pocket and pulled on his rain hat. Liri was already disappearing into the night at the wheel of a van. Abu said, 'What happens now?'

'You pick up the body, carry him out to the jetty like a good boy, and we dump him into the Seine.'

'And if I refuse?'

'For starters, I'll have to shoot you in the right
kneecap.' He produced the Colt from his pocket.
'Hollow point cartridges, Abu. You'll never be able to
stand up on the podium again.'

'You bastard,' Abu told him, went round the desk,
picked up Ali Kupu as if he were a rag doll and walked
towards the other end of the warehouse. Holley
followed.

It was raining harder than ever and Abu paused,
looking down through the lights to the Seine, Notre
Dame floating in the dark way up to the right.

'Now what?'

'Straight to the end of the jetty and drop him in. Go
on, get on with it.'

The big man walked through the lights, holding the
body in both hands, paused at the end for a long
moment, then dropped the corpse in. It surfaced for a
moment, then drifted away into the darkness.

Abu turned and faced Holley. 'She won't get away
with it, that bitch, or you. The Albanian Mafia will
hunt you both down.'

'Thanks for reminding me. Since you are the only
witness, it leaves me with little choice.'

There was sudden alarm on Abu's face and he put a
hand out. 'No, let's discuss this.'

But Holley's hand was already swinging up. The
silenced Colt coughed once, the bullet hitting Abu
between the eyes, and he lurched back over the end of

the jetty into the water. Holley returned to the warehouse, opened the small door by which he'd entered and retrieved the umbrella he'd left there. He started to walk back to the barge, thinking about it. The Albanian Mafia was the bane of Paris. The deaths of Abu and Ali Kupu wouldn't disturb the Paris police in the slightest. He would have to take a chance that Liri would forget all about him, but then she would value her own anonymity. Always with him, a woman in trouble was one thing he could never turn away from. In a way, he'd been a fool, but there it was.

But what Kupu had said about AQ – Al Qaeda. Was it just the idle boast of a drunkard or was there genuinely something to it? Whatever – if there really was a plot to assassinate Vladimir Putin, it would create chaos, and that was bad for everybody. It left him with only one choice, and he quickened his pace and hurried back to the barge.

Colonel Josef Lermov of the GRU had been appointed London's Head of Station by Putin himself and was the man who'd taken Daniel Holley out of the Lubyanka Prison and told him to deal with Ferguson and his people once and for all, a business which had not really worked out as intended.

He answered the phone in London, astonished at who was calling him.

'Good God, Daniel. I can't believe it.'

'Where are you, Josef?'

'London. Putin made me Head of Station here.'

'So he forgave you for your failure?'

'Your failure, too, Daniel, but yes, I am forgiven, and I think you are also. I've followed your success with a certain pride. The Algerians regard you highly. Malik is truly proud of you, as if you were his son.'

So he's been talking to Malik, and Malik hasn't told me. Holley stored the information away. 'That's nice.'

'So what can I do for you?'

'Certain information has come my way concerning a possible attempt on Vladimir Putin's life.'

'Are you serious?'

'I can only put the facts before you and you must judge for yourself.'

When he was finished, there was total silence, as if Lermov was taking it all in, so Holley said, 'Okay, the ravings of a drunken lunatic, I know—'

Lermov cut in, his voice hoarse, 'The Prime Minister visits Chechnya tomorrow afternoon, and a meeting like the one you describe has been arranged between him and a Mullah named Ibrahim Nadim. The security on it has been massive.'

'Not massive enough, it seems,' Holley said.

'I'll call the Prime Minister immediately. But, Daniel, I'm curious. You're leaping to his defence. Why?'

'Actually, I admire many things about him, even if

39

we don't always see eye to eye. He's taken the Russian Federation by the scruff of the neck and made it feel proud again – he's a genuine patriot. But mostly . . . I simply don't think it's a good idea to assassinate him.'

'Neither do I. Thank you, Daniel. I'm going now.'

Sitting there, nursing a drink, Holley had a sudden urge to call Roper, and he did so, finding him wide awake.

'How did your business appointment turn out?' Roper asked.

'What the hell, why shouldn't I tell you?' Holley said. 'The ramifications, in a way, touch the world. I may just have saved Vladimir Putin from assassination.'

Roper took it surprisingly calmly. 'Tell me more.'

Which Daniel did.

The first thing Roper said was: 'What am I going to do with you? You're getting worse than Dillon. You've been shooting people again.'

'If ever two people deserved it, those two did, but isn't it incredible that the apparent boastings of a drunken fool turned out to be true?'

'Because somebody talked, somebody at the very heart of Russian intelligence, told the wrong person. Everyone in the business over there will be working flat out to find out who. Of course, there is the mention Kupu made about his uncle in Tirana.'

'They'll hunt him down like a dog,' Holley said.

'I wouldn't like to think what they're going to do to him to make him talk.'

'But the source of the leak is the thing. It's got to be at the highest level,' Holley persisted. 'And yet someone willing to deal with Al Qaeda.'

'And someone interested in getting rid of Putin,' Roper said. 'A palace revolution.'

'God help whoever it is, with Putin on their case. Now, to other matters, the Afghan business. There's talk of training camps in Northern Pakistan, but traditionally most of the good ones are in Libya and Algeria. Both Dillon and I were trained in the same place, though at different times: Shabwa, deep in the Algerian desert. Check up on it for me.'

'I'll get right on it,' Roper told him.

'I'll be there mid-morning.'

'Looking forward to it.'

Which only left Hamid Malik, who would undoubtedly be sitting in his villa with its magical views of the great harbour of Algiers, biting his nails about the outcome of the Kupu business. Better to get it over with.

'Praise be to Allah to hear your voice,' Malik told him. 'I've been genuinely worried about this business, Daniel; it didn't sit right with me.'

'You were right about Kupu. A bastard of the first order. He even had connections with Al Qaeda.'

'No, surely this cannot be?' There was a wariness in his voice now, a touch of fear, but then that was a common reaction of many Arabs when a mention of Al Qaeda was made.

'Don't worry, Ali Kupu is now feeding what fish there are in the Seine, accompanied by his revolting muscle man, one Abu.'

'Allah preserve me,' Malik was truly shocked. 'You did this?'

'Who else? They were going to do worse to me.'

'Tell me what happened. I need to know in case of repercussions.'

'There won't be any. Two members of the Albanian Mafia turn up in the Seine – it happens all the time. The Paris police will say "good riddance" and move on.'

'But . . . Al Qaeda. What has that got to do with anything?'

'A great deal, as it happens.'

He told Malik everything and, when he was finished, the Algerian said, 'You never do things by halves, Daniel. Where will it all end?'

'This time with Lermov and his people rooting out those assassins. Did you know he's GRU Station Head in London now? He told me Putin has forgiven him. Me, too!'

'Fine words, but after this you'll deserve a medal.'

'I'll settle for never having to eat at the Lubyanka again. Are you happy now?'

Malik shrugged. 'I should be, I suppose, but even the

slightest hint of anything to do with Al Qaeda freezes the heart.'

'Yes, the very name frightens the hell out of people,' Holley agreed. 'Do you think they might be recruiting for Afghanistan?'

Malik said quickly, 'I wouldn't have thought so. The Taliban are perfectly capable of recruiting for themselves.'

'I'm talking about something different. There are many British-born Muslims fighting out there.'

Malik laughed. 'Daniel, one hears stories, but this is nonsense, pure myth.'

'I'm afraid not, old friend. I've seen the evidence, heard recordings of radio communications in the heat of battle, working-class accents from many of the great cities in the UK.'

'I don't believe it.'

'I've heard it, Malik. In fact, Ferguson, Dillon and Miller have just had a meeting with the President in Washington to work out what to do about it.'

Malik was stunned. 'All right, supposing it is true, what can anyone do to prevent it? If young British Muslims decide to take a holiday in Pakistan to visit the old folk, then end up in a training camp in Waziristan, who can stop them? It's impossible.'

'Well, Ferguson and his people are at least going to make an effort, and I've offered to help.'

Malik was truly shocked. 'But why you, Daniel? This is not your business. You could be asking for big trouble.'

'I have a grasp of the Muslim world that few Christians do. I speak Arabic and, as a young volunteer in the IRA, I was trained in terrorism at Shabwa. I wonder if Shabwa is still in business. And Omar Hamza, the camp commander? What a bastard he was.'

'He would be seventy or more if he is still alive. Shabwa closed down some years ago, though. The IRA no longer used it and, as things changed for the German groups and ETA and the like, there was little need for the facility,' Malik said. 'The thought of young British Muslims using it, though . . . Why on earth would they want to come to Algeria for their training?'

'You could have said that about the young Irishmen too,' Holley told him. 'Anyway, I'm out of here, off to London.'

'Are you going to see Ferguson?'

'Yes, I want to hear what he intends to do. I feel very strongly about this matter. If there is anything I can do, I will.'

Malik gave in. 'So be it. The blessing of Allah go with you. Do take care, Daniel.'

'Don't I always?'

It was very quiet sitting there in the darkness, the long white curtains ballooning like sails at the window, and Malik went out to find a full moon and the terrace flooded with light. The vista in the night of the harbour below was astonishingly beautiful. He loved this city, always had, just as he loved Daniel Holley, but trouble and Daniel seemed to belong together naturally, and Malik was filled with a grim foreboding.

'What now?' he asked softly, leaning on the balustrade. 'What next?'

LONDON

—

NORTHERN IRELAND

3

The Gulfstream landed at Farley Field late that night. Ferguson's Daimler was waiting, as well as the Mercedes provided by the Cabinet Office for Miller.

'We'll get together later,' Ferguson said. 'I've got to get cracking and prepare that report for the Prime Minister.'

His Daimler moved away and Miller said, 'We'll take you to Holland Park, Sean.' His driver, Arthur Fox, was behind the wheel.

'Care to join me for a late dinner there?'

'No, I need to get to Dover Street and sort this sack of mail that Arthur has brought me. Ferguson's not the only one with problems. I've got the Cabinet Office on my back.' Mentioning his sister, he added, 'I had a text from Monica while you were asleep. She's enjoying being Visiting Professor at Harvard so much, she's agreed to an extension.'

'She didn't tell me.'

'Maybe she's going off you, you mad Irish bogtrotter.'

'And pigs might fly,' Dillon told him. 'Tell her congratulations and I'll be in touch. Now we've got an hour before we get to London, so start on your mail and let me sleep.'

Two hours later, the Malik Shipping plane landed at London City Airport and taxied to the private facility – Daniel Holley had decided to leave Paris earlier than he had planned. His diplomatic passport sped him through and, forty-five minutes later, he was at the Dorchester, where he found Concetto Marietta, the guest liaison manager, waiting to escort him to one of the Park Suites.

He slept for a few hours and then he called Roper. 'When can we meet? I'd love to see what your famous Holland Park safe house looks like from the inside.'

'Ferguson's seeing the Prime Minister this morning, and Miller probably feels he should show his face in the House, but I'm here. So's Dillon, who's upstairs asleep. Come along whenever you want; we'll have lunch.'

'I might just do that. I want to stop off and see a friend first, but then I'll come over.'

'I'll see you when I see you.'

*   *   *

Holley walked up to Shepherd Market, past the restaurants and the shops, then paused at a door with the name 'Selim Malik' painted in gold above it, admired the Egyptian hand-painted temple effigies displayed on either side of the frame, then pressed a button.

The door opened and Selim was there, exactly the same as the last time Daniel had seen him: small and happy, with dark curling hair turning silver, olive face, fringe beard and good humour in his eyes. He wore a ruffled shirt, velvet jacket and trousers, as always.

He was crying as he embraced Daniel. 'It's so good to see you. My cousin Hamid phoned me to say I might expect you, but still I am overcome. This is a champagne moment!'

Selim Malik produced a bottle of Krug and poured each of them a glass, saying, 'It's so wonderful the way everything has turned out. You've outfoxed them all, even the great Putin. Hamid has told me of how you sorted those Albanian bastards out, and the Al Qaeda plot on Putin.' He gripped Holley's arm. 'He will be your friend for life now.'

'I didn't do it for gain,' Daniel told him. 'I did it because what they were planning was wrong.'

'You are a saint.' Selim got up. 'But you must take great care. People who say bin Laden is dead are stupid. What he is, what he stands for, will never die. This doesn't mean I admire him. I fear him, but what I have said is true.'

'I'm afraid you have a point,' Daniel agreed.

Selim went into the other room and returned with a Gladstone bag. 'I've been keeping this in my strong room. It's exactly what you had last time.'

There was an ankle-holster, a silenced Colt .25 and a couple of boxes of hollow-point cartridges, a silenced Walther, ammunition, a razor-sharp flick knife and a bulletproof vest.

'This is wonderful,' Daniel said. 'But hang on to the knife and the vest. I brought my own.'

'You must be prepared for any eventuality,' Selim said. 'If word of your involvement ever got out, Al Qaeda would put you on its international hit list. The blessings of Allah would be on any man who disposed of you.'

'Well, let's hope they don't hear. I've something else to ask you. What do you know about British-born Muslims fighting for the Taliban in Afghanistan?'

Selim frowned. 'Where have you heard this? Some newspaper story, I suppose.'

'Not at all. Selim, you're my friend. Last time we met, we had to face bad men and great danger and you were brilliant, so believe me when I say I know for a fact that many young British Muslims are fighting in Afghanistan. The evidence has been presented to me. Let me tell you about it.'

When Holley was done, Selim was distressed. 'What can I say? I must believe what you tell me is true. But a mystery man known only as Shamrock leading Taliban recruits in a successful battle with Allied troops? It still sounds incredible.'

'Have you heard anything that would confirm it? Even a hint?'

'I don't know. I have been to North Pakistan and the border areas as an art dealer, and of course there are many Brits in that area, contractors dealing with the Pakistan Army, others offering their services as security experts, many of them obviously ex-soldiers. I am sure there is a lot of illegal arms-dealing with the Taliban, too. But these are just guys out to make a buck. This other business, this Shamrock . . .' He sighed wearily. 'It's so nonsensical that it must be true. I shall ask around.'

Holley got up and picked up the Gladstone bag. 'I'd appreciate it. I'm at the Dorchester. I'll see myself out.'

Selim sat there thinking about it, then reached for his mobile and started to ring round, choosing a few old friends only, people he'd known in the art world for years; people he felt he could trust.

Military rule was the accepted way in Algiers, certainly to men such as Hamid Malik. Law and order was an essential requirement to the development of good business, and this benefited the poor as well as the rich. But even for a wealthy man, it was sensible to cultivate people in the right places. The man he was enjoying coffee with was certainly that: Colonel Ali Hakim, a no-nonsense military policeman. He and Malik had been close friends over years of political upset and violence, the kind that had made military rule so necessary in Algiers in the first place.

What Malik didn't realize, however, was that Hakim had orders from the Foreign Ministry to cultivate him, with the aim of keeping an eye on Daniel Holley's activities. Holley's access to the international scene was undoubtedly of advantage to the government, but his past argued the need for a certain control as well. Which was where Hakim came in.

Malik poured the Colonel another coffee and Hakim said, 'And how is Daniel? I was told he went to Paris on your company plane.' He smiled gently. 'Forgive me, but air traffic control passes such information to my office on a regular basis.'

'Of course,' Malik said. 'And I understand.' He was tense and his hand shook as he poured another coffee.

Hakim said, 'You seem out of sorts. Is something worrying you?'

Malik said, 'How long have we been friends?'

'I would say thirty years. What's brought this on?'

'Through years of unrest, bloodshed, revolution, fundamentalist terror, one government after another – and yet here we are, still just as much friends as when we were dodging bullets together back at the university. If I can't trust you, I can't trust anyone. Would you agree?' Malik asked.

Hakim said, 'Of course.' He put down his cup. 'What is this, old friend?'

So Malik told him everything. The Albanians and the business with Putin, Afghanistan and Shamrock.

When he was finished, he said, 'What do you think?'

He had made the worst mistake of his life, but Colonel Ali Hakim, delighted at such a treasure trove of information, managed to look alarmed and worried at the same time.

'This is grave news indeed. We must proceed very carefully. Daniel will be seeing your cousin, Selim, in London?'

'That's right. He said he would value his opinion.'

'And this General Charles Ferguson? I know of him, of course. He is a major player in the world of anti-terrorism and covert operations. So Daniel intends to offer his services in this affair?'

'So he says, but what do you think about British Muslims operating with the Taliban?'

'My friend, thirty years in my line of work means that nothing surprises me any longer. The Muslim population of Britain is substantial these days. That a few misguided young men would be tempted to join in the battle for the prospect of glory would not surprise me. But only a few, I think.' He reached for his cap and swagger stick and got up. 'I must go now. Try not to worry. I'll keep a close eye on things, I promise you. If anything of interest turns up, I'll report it to you. It would be useful if you could do the same.'

He went down the outside steps and walked away through the garden. Malik watched him go, suddenly feeling very much better.

Like many Arabs, Ali Hakim had grown tired of the uncertainty of Arab politics, the power usurped by one general after another, and the autocracy of the men with their oil billions to back them up. And then Osama bin Laden had appeared like an avenging angel, instantly embraced by Muslims all over the world, Colonel Ali Hakim among them. In spite of NATO and Britain and America, Hakim still believed in what to him was the nobility of bin Laden's message. He had served Al Qaeda ever since.

He sat in his police Land Rover on a bluff looking out to sea, an encrypted mobile in his left hand. It had a tape device as well, and he switched on to record and dictated everything Malik had said. He felt no guilt. This was too important. He ended by punching his personal recognition button and hitting 'Send'.

Hakim dealt with a man known as the Preacher, the individual responsible for all London-based operations, who had been placed in charge by Osama bin Laden himself. Thanks to modern technology, the Preacher remained anonymous and untraceable, though he knew the identity of everyone with whom he dealt.

But this did not apply to Ali Hakim. Uncomfortable with entrusting a mystery man with his life, Hakim had sought expert help from Wali Sofit, a computer expert of genius who, unfortunately for him, was serving fifteen years' imprisonment for transferring many thousands of dollars to various bank accounts in Algiers. Presented with Hakim's special problem and even more special mobile phone, plus the promise of future leniency, Sofit had gone to work. Hakim had told him he believed the Preacher to be a major criminal of some sort. Sofit had been somewhat surprised to come up with the name of a Professor Hassan Shah, based in London, but was delighted to be transferred to a soft job in the prison administration offices as a reward for his skill.

Ali Hakim waited in the Land Rover until a reply came back. *Your information of crucial importance. It will be dealt with as a matter of the highest priority.*

Hakim switched off. So that was that. He felt sorry for his old friend Malik, and he'd always liked Holley, but the cause he served was more important than individuals. He switched on his engine and drove down into the city towards the police headquarters.

The man known as the Preacher, Hassan Shah, continued to sit on the bench outside the London School of Economics, where he had taken Hakim's call. A pleasant-looking man of medium height, he was wearing a khaki summer suit, a faded denim shirt and tinted Ray-Ban sunglasses with steel rims. His black hair was too long.

Forty years of age, an academic and a working

barrister when he wished it, with no wife or girlfriend (which made some people talk), he lived alone in the pleasant Edwardian villa where he'd been born in Bell Street, West Hampstead. His parents had departed for Pakistan years ago, his father having retired as a surgeon.

He was thinking of them now because of Hakim's recording, thinking of Pakistan and the visit he had made on a holiday when he was sixteen, when he'd been taken to a youth camp and Osama bin Laden himself had appeared. The speech he had made had shaped Shah's life.

Shah was a practising Muslim, but in a quiet way, nothing flamboyant. His rapid rise both as an academic and a barrister had, to a certain extent, been because he was a Muslim. The Foreign Office had sent him to Bosnia to investigate war crimes and then, pleased with his work, had sent him again and again, to Iraq many times and Kosovo. He'd been noticed, no question of that, and his success in court on a few difficult cases had led to the position he held now: Professor in International Law at the London School of Economics.

But he'd been noticed elsewhere also, the approaches cleverly disguised: simple requests for legal opinions relating to Islamic matters. Eventually, he discovered that, in effect, he'd been working for Al Qaeda without knowing it – and then he'd realized he didn't mind; in fact that he welcomed the idea. Really, an opportunity to serve the cause was what he'd been looking for all his life. His own experience of the law, the courts, the legal system, the behaviours of the kind of people involved – they'd all taught him a great deal about human nature. He knew what made people tick, how to handle them, and most important of all, what made people afraid.

To run the London operation for Al Qaeda required brains and organizing ability. When it came to necessary violence, he only had to make a call to bring in whoever was best for the job. An inner circle of twenty stood ready to act.

The beauty of it was that not one of them knew Hassan – they connected by encrypted mobiles only. Shah remained just a voice on the phone: the Preacher.

Yes, it all worked extremely well.

'Let's see what we can do about this,' he murmured softly, and he made a call.

Selim Lancy was the result of a mixed marriage. His father, a sailor, had insisted he be baptized Samuel, then gone back to sea, never to return. So his mother had made it Selim, the Muslim equivalent, and raised him in the faith. He never tried to pretend he wasn't Muslim, and was particularly handy with his fists when he joined the army, 3 Para, where he endured three hard years in Iraq and Afghanistan, rising to the rank of Corporal. His service ended with one bullet through his left side and another in the right thigh.

He passed through the rehabilitation centre, where

doctors put him together very nicely, but the army decided that enough was enough and he was discharged.

He returned home, and moved in with his mother, who was still fit and well at first, then started to attend the mosque again. He was surprised at the respect everyone gave him, and then realized why – when overtures were made suggesting that, as a good Muslim, he could serve Al Qaeda well. The idea appealed to him, just for the hell of it; for the truth was, he was anything but a good Muslim.

He made a living as a hired driver now. Sitting behind the wheel of a silver Mercedes, handsome enough in a dark blue suit and regimental tie, he was eating a chicken sandwich when his special mobile sounded.

'Where are you?' Shah asked.

'Oh, it's you, boss. I'm at the back of Harrods, waiting for a customer. I'm sitting behind the wheel of my new car – a second-hand Mercedes. My compensation money from the army finally came through.'

'Well, that's nice for you,' Shah told him.

'I haven't heard from you for a while. Is this a business call?'

'You could say that. I want you to check on a man called Selim Malik. He's an art dealer with a place in Shepherd Market.'

'What's he done?'

'He could be showing an unhealthy interest in rumours of British Muslims serving with the Taliban in Afghanistan.'

'They're not bleeding rumours, they're facts, boss. I should know. I probably killed a few of them over there.'

'That isn't the point. I want to know if he's actively investigating these stories. Check with other Muslims in the market; see what you can find out. No rough stuff. He's precious cargo.'

'Why's that, boss?'

'He knows things and he's got a friend named Daniel Holley, who's a killer of the first order. He may look Malik up. If he does, you must let me know at once. I've found a security photo of Holley. You'll find it on line now.'

Lancy thumbed away at his mobile and Holley appeared. 'He doesn't look much to me, boss.'

'Don't go by looks, idiot. Holley's a nihilist. That's someone who believes nothing has any value and so he kills without a second of regret. That includes you.'

'I'll bear it in mind. When do you want this?'

'A couple of days. Do what you can.'

Shah hung up. Now, he thought, what to do about Shamrock. He'd been shocked to hear the name from Hakim. He checked his watch. The stupid bastard was still up there at thirty thousand feet for at least another couple of hours. Better to wait and try to contact him at the Talbot office. He got up from the bench and walked quickly across the campus towards the university buildings.

*   *   *

At that same moment, Shamrock was sitting in the first-class compartment of a British Airways jumbo-jet flight from Cairo. His name was Justin Talbot. He was forty-five and looked younger, favoured dark cropped hair and a slight stubble to the chin, the fashion of the moment. He wore jeans, a light open-necked khaki shirt and a dark blue linen jacket. His face was heavily tanned, as if he'd been out in the sun a lot, which he had, and had an aristocratic look to it.

Members of the cabin crew had earlier noted that his English had a public school edge to it, and he spoke with a cynical good humour that they'd found as intriguing as the fact that he was described on the passenger list as Major Talbot.

One of the girls approached and said, 'It always gets boring with so few passengers. Not much to do.'

'Nobody's got any money at the moment. You're lucky to have any passengers.'

She smiled. 'I suppose you're right. We'll be landing in an hour or so. You'll be glad to stretch your legs, I bet. It's a long trip, Cairo to London.'

'Actually, I started in Peshawar yesterday. Stopped off in Cairo on business, then joined you.'

'Pakistan! I hear it's bad on the North-West Frontier these days. Are you in the army, Major?'

'Not any more. Twenty-odd years was enough. Grenadier Guards. I did a certain amount in Northern Ireland, both Gulf wars, Bosnia and Kosovo, then two tours in Afghanistan. I was lucky to get out of that in one piece. When I was shot in the right shoulder,' he smiled, 'I decided that was it and took my papers.'

He didn't mention the Military Cross he'd earned in Afghanistan, and the years with the SAS and the Army Air Corps. The young woman nodded seriously. 'You've done your bit, if you ask me. What do you do now?'

'I work for the family firm, Talbot International. We sell trucks to the Pakistan Army, Jeeps, second-hand armoured cars and helicopters.' He smiled. 'Have I disappointed you?'

She shook her head. 'The other side of war.' She hesitated. 'Do you miss it? The dark side, I mean?'

'Let's say there's nothing quite like it. There's no drug that could possibly match the force, the energy, of the killing time in which you're immersing yourself. War itself is the ultimate drug.'

She looked a bit shocked. 'Well . . . business must be booming, with the war spilling over from Afghanistan. Can I get you a drink?'

'Large vodka would be good, with iced tonic water and a twist of lemon.'

She was back in three minutes and handed it to him. 'Enjoy.'

He drank half of the drink straightaway and sat there, suddenly yawning. Since Lahore yesterday morning, he'd only had four hours' sleep. He finished the drink, put the glass down, tilted his seat back. A hell of a trip, and Afghanistan had been particularly rough, but bloody marvellous. The buzz of action never failed to thrill him. It was what he'd missed when he left the army.

You could make millions out of the sale of second-hand military equipment in Northern Pakistan – but there was a lot more money to be made from dealing in illegal arms. Even respectable firms were at it, and nobody was more respectable than Talbot International. Its Chairman, General Sir Hedley Chase, presented the face of integrity itself at the small but elegant office in Curzon Street. The real business took place in Islamabad, where dozens of firms jostled one another for advantage.

It had been only a step from selling illegal arms to providing training in their use. He'd enjoyed every moment of that in the mountains over the border in Afghanistan, and then it had been only logical to take the next step – from training the Taliban to leading them in battle. He'd immediately been seized by the old thrill, and he felt no guilt at all.

The surprise had been when Al Qaeda had discovered what he was up to, and not only approved, but insisted he continue. The strange thing was that there had been a thrill to that, too. It wasn't as if he needed the money. It was all part of a wonderful, lunatic madness. Anyway, right now he needed rest and recreation. It would be nice to see his mother again. He hadn't kept in touch much this time. It was better to use mobile and satellite phones sparingly these days, unless they were totally encrypted and encoded.

Too many people failed to realize that every conversation you made was out there somewhere and capable of being retrieved.

He wondered if his mother had made one of her rare visits to the family estate, Talbot Place, in County Down. Her own mother, Mary Ellen, had died the previous year, but his grandfather, 'Colonel Henry' to the servants, was still alive at ninety-five.

Soldier, lawyer, politician, Member of Parliament at Stormont, and a Grand Master in the Orange Lodge, Colonel Henry was a resolute defender of the Protestant cause who had loathed Roman Catholics – Fenians, as he called them – all his life. Now in his dotage, he was surrounded by workers and house servants who were mainly Catholic, thanks to Mary Ellen, a Protestant herself, who had employed them for years. Justin Talbot's mother despised the man.

Talbot yawned again and decided that if his mother had gone to Ulster, he would fly across himself, possibly in one of the firm's planes. He could use a break. He closed his eyes and drifted off.

At that moment, his mother, Jean Talbot, was crossing a hillside high above Carlingford Lough, the Irish Sea way beyond. A seventy-one-year-old woman, slim and fit and young for her age, in both looks and energy, as the Irish saying went, was wearing an Australian drover's coat, heavy boots, a cap of Donegal tweed and carrying a walking stick. The house dog, Nell, a black flat-coat retriever, was about her business, running hither and thither. Jean reached her destination, a stone bothy with a bench outside. She sat down, took out a packet of cigarettes, and lit one.

The sun shone, the sky was blue and the morning wind had dropped to a dead calm. This was an amazing place with an incredible backdrop, the Mourne Mountains. Far down below was the village of Kilmartin, and Talbot Place, the splendid old Georgian house that had been the family home for two hundred and fifty years, the house in which she had been born.

She stubbed out her cigarette carefully, stood up, whistled to Nell and turned. It was good to be back and yet, as always, she already felt restless and ill at ease; as usual, her father was the problem. During the Second World War, with him away and her mother in charge, she had been educated at a local Catholic boarding school run by nuns who accepted day-girls and didn't mind a Protestant or two. She had never known her father and was terrified of the arrogant, anti-Catholic bully who returned after the war and was outraged to find his daughter in the hands of nuns, and 'bloody Fenians' all over the estate.

Mary Ellen's quiet firmness defeated him, as did the good humour of his tenants, who smiled and touched their caps to Colonel Henry, convinced, as Jean Talbot realized as she grew up, that he was a raving lunatic. The nuns succeeded with her so well that she was accepted by St Hugh's College, Oxford, to study fine art.

To her father, busy with the law and politics at Stormont, it was all a waste of time, but she had enough talent to then be accepted by the Slade School of Fine Art, University College, London, after Oxford. Mary Ellen hugged her in delight, but her father said it was time she settled down and gave him an heir.

Her answer was to get pregnant by a sculptor named Justin Monk, a Roman Catholic separated from his wife who'd refused him a divorce on religious grounds. Shortly after the birth, he'd been badly injured in a motorcycle accident. Jean was able to visit him once and show him the baby and promised to name it after him. He died soon afterwards.

When Henry Talbot and Mary Ellen came to visit her in her London lodgings, he had looked at Justin in his cot and destroyed any hope his daughter might have had left for a future relationship with her father.

'A bastard, is that the best you can do? At least he's a Protestant; I suppose that's something. I've got things to do. I'm meeting people at Westminster. I'll leave you to your mother.'

After he had gone, Mary Ellen said, '*Is* he a Protestant?'

'Justin begged me to have him baptized in the faith. What could I do? He was dying. Do you hate me for it?'

'My darling, I love you for it. It was the decent thing

to do.' She embraced the baby. 'But I'd make it our secret, if I were you. If they had even a hint of it on the estate, it would be all over Kilmartin.'

'All over County Down,' Jean had said. 'And what about my son?'

'Don't tell him, either. It's a burden to tell a child and expect him to hold it secret. One day in the future, when you think it's right, you can tell him. So what will you do now?'

'I intend to continue my work. At the Slade they feel that I have a gift for portraiture, and I intend to concentrate on that.'

'Excellent, but you'll need a home. I'll stay a bit in London and we'll find you a house. In Mayfair, I think, and we'll need a housekeeper and a nanny.'

'But what will he say?'

'He's left everything to me. We can afford it, dear. I don't think you've ever appreciated how wealthy you and Justin will be one of these days, whether you like it or not. Talbot money is old money – and you'd be surprised how much property we own in the West End of London. In fact, now that I think of it, there's a superb Regency house on Marley Court off Curzon Street, very convenient for Park Lane and Hyde Park. Let's take a look.'

Marley Court it was, and her beloved son had grown up there, and gone to school as a day-boy at St Paul's – she couldn't bear the thought of sending him away. His visits to Talbot Place were frequent, of course, particularly during the long summers, for his grand-mother adored him and his grandfather grudgingly admitted he was a fine rider.

He was also popular with the estate workers and the locals, but their respect for Mary Ellen ensured that anyway. Through the long, hard, brutal days of the Troubles, Talbot Place had remained inviolate because of her. It was remarkable when you considered that most Catholics in the area were Nationalists, and the Provisional IRA was so powerful that the countryside from Warrenpoint as far as Crossmaglen in County Armagh was designated bandit country by the British Army.

Talbot Place could have been burnt to the ground, not a stick nor stone left standing, and certain extreme elements would have done exactly that, but local opinion stayed their hand. Half the village was employed on the estate, and Mary Ellen and the boy were inviolate – which also meant that Colonel Henry's life was spared as well; though it wasn't deserved, many people would say.

There had been a problem in August 1979, when her son was fifteen, when the British Army had suffered its worst defeat in the Troubles, that terrible ambush only a few miles away at Narrow Water, near Warrenpoint. That many of the local men were IRA did not surprise her. It meant that some of her workers would be, too. But she had been shocked to hear that a nineteen-year-old stable boy named Sean Kelly, son of Jack Kelly, publican of the Kilmartin Arms and a great friend of her son's, had been killed in an exchange of fire with wounded soldiers at Narrow Water.

Justin had been at Talbot Place for the summer holidays and she had joined him for a couple of weeks before returning to London for the start of the autumn term at school. He had been terribly upset at the death of his friend. There was no question of them attending the funeral; even Mary Ellen admitted that. The deaths of all those Highlanders made it impossible, and yet Justin had gone of his own accord, had stood at Sean Kelly's graveside, had been hugged and thanked by all the Kellys, and admitted to the clan. The priest, Father Michael Cassidy, had also blessed him for it.

The confrontation at Talbot Place had been terrible, such was Colonel Henry's rage. He'd slapped Justin across the face, called him a damn traitor, and Jean had pulled her father off and called him a bully and a bigot. Justin had shouted at him, called him a Prod bastard, and said he would join the IRA if he only could. Every servant in the house had heard it. Jean Talbot and her son left for London within the hour. There was a long break for a while. Eventually, Mary Ellen smoothed things over, but Jean visited rarely after that. Her gradual success with her painting, the fact that she'd been commissioned to do a portrait of the Queen Mother, meant nothing to her father.

With Justin, it was different. He was, after all, the heir, and when he chose Sandhurst Royal Military

Academy instead of university, and embarked on an army career, the Colonel had been delighted.

Justin made one thing clear, though. After finishing at Sandhurst and joining the Grenadier Guards, he'd visited the Kilmartin Arms and given his oath to Jack Kelly that he would never fight against them in Ulster.

In any event, there was enough happening elsewhere to keep him occupied. Jean knew that he'd flown for the Army Air Corps, helicopters and light aircraft all over the world. She also knew that he'd served with the SAS, but only because – many years earlier when he'd been spending a week's leave with her in Mayfair – a dispatch rider had delivered an envelope. A recall to duty at once, Justin had told her, and had gone off to pack leaving the letter on the desk in the study. She'd read it, of course, and discovered for the first time that he was serving with 22 SAS. She hadn't mentioned it; there was no point as he hadn't told her.

Not that it mattered now. All that was over. Afghanistan had seen to it, and he had survived, covered with glory, wounded and decorated and alive, which was something to be thankful for these days. The business trips to Pakistan and the North-West Frontier were only something to do. He needed action of some sort, it was his nature, and she'd long since come to terms with the fact that women were something he could never take seriously.

So here she was back at the Place again because of a call from Hannah Kelly, the housekeeper, to tell her Colonel Henry'd had another bad turn, and that was something you couldn't ignore where a ninety-five-year-old man was concerned. She'd flown over at once, seen him with Dr Larry Ryan, and there was little comfort from him. One of these days, the bad turn would carry Colonel Henry off, and perhaps that would be in his own best interests, but not this time. So, she faced the prospect of a miserable day or so with a half-mad old man in his dotage, shouting one insult after another at the servants, in language out of the gutter, sitting in his wheelchair in that conservatory that was like a miniature jungle, a decanter of Cognac and a glass on the cane table beside him.

She looked at her watch and saw with a start that she'd been sitting there a long time. She rose, dreading the return to the house, and then like a miracle, her mobile sounded as she started down the track to the house, and Nell barked frantically. 'It's me,' Justin told her. 'I've just got off the plane at Heathrow, tried you in London and got your message. How is he?'

'Still with us and even more dreadful than usual. How was your trip?'

'Wonderful. There's so much going on up there on the border; loads of companies vying with one another. The war inflates everything; it's like a bad movie. You're lucky to get a hotel bed. I've got to call in at the office, meet with Sir Hedley and inform him how things went.'

She was disappointed. 'I was so hoping to see you.'

'So you shall. I'll drive out to Frensham. We've got four planes parked there. I think I'll use the Beech Baron.'

'I haven't flown in that,' she said.

'A new acquisition. Twin engine, can carry six, and it takes off and lands on grass, so I'll be able to land at Drumgoole Aero Club. No need to feel down, Mum. I'll be with you later in the afternoon.'

'All I can say is, thank God, darling.'

'See you soon.' He switched off, leaving her there on the track, suddenly unbelievably happy.

4

After dropping Dillon off at Holland Park, Miller had continued on to Dover Street and got some sleep. Since his wife's murder the previous year, in a bomb attack aimed at Miller himself, he had lived alone, managing with just a daily housekeeper, a Jamaican widow named Lily Pond, who saw Miller as a tragic figure who needed mothering.

Miller was in his study, working on the stack of mail, when his Codex sounded and Ferguson said, 'The Prime Minister's decided he wants you with me.'

'Can I ask why?'

'I don't know, Harry. I suppose he wants your opinion as well as mine. You *are* known in the House as the Prime Minister's Rottweiler. So, get your arse down here double-quick.'

'Twenty minutes,' Miller said, and called Arthur to get the car.

* * *

75

He found Ferguson sitting outside the PM's study in conversation with Cabinet Secretary Henry Frankel, a good friend to Miller in bad times.

'You're looking fit, Harry.' He shook hands. 'So you've been visiting the great man himself in Washington?'

'If you say so, Henry,' Miller answered.

'I know the General thinks I'm a terrible gossip, but it's not true, love. Let's face it, all the world's secrets flow through here.'

'Yes, well, save them for your memoirs,' Ferguson told him. 'Do we go in now?'

'Of course, now that Harry's arrived.' Frankel crossed the corridor and opened the door.

'I've examined all the material your Major Roper has put together,' the PM said, 'and I'm not surprised the President was so disturbed.'

'We all are, Prime Minister,' Ferguson told him. 'I believe it to be one of the gravest matters I've put before you for some time.'

The Prime Minister was obviously concerned, and turned to Miller. 'What do you think?'

'I'd say it's a small number of people we're talking about, British Muslims in Afghanistan. But it's a pattern all over the world, isn't it, Islamic extremism? There is a Muslim saying: Beauty is like a flag in the city.'

The PM nodded. 'The green flag of Islam flying over Downing Street?'

'Flying over a damn sight more than that,' Ferguson said. 'I'd say we've got to do something about it.'

'I agree.' The PM nodded. 'But individual young Muslim men buying a plane ticket to Pakistan is one thing, a system that facilitates this is quite another. Does such an organization exist? That's what we need to find out. The man who calls himself Shamrock could be the key here. Find him and we may be able to discover the rest.'

'Of course, Prime Minister.' Ferguson got up, as did Miller. 'We'll get on with it.'

The door opened and they left, passing Henry Frankel, who stood to one side and winked at Miller. Both their limousines were waiting outside.

Miller said, 'Where do we start then?'

Ferguson glanced at his watch. It was noon exactly. 'I could use a drink. Tell Fox to deliver you to the Garrick Club.'

'The Garrick?' Miller was surprised. 'I thought you were a member of the Cavalry Club.'

'Of course, but everybody likes the Garrick; all those actors and writers and so on. It makes a difference from matters military. I'll see you in the bar.'

Justin Talbot went straight to his mother's house at Marley Court to unpack and get a change of clothes. He had just come out of the shower when his mobile sounded. He answered and found himself speaking to the Preacher.

'Good to hear from you,' Talbot said. 'I had an excellent trip.'

'You had a disastrous trip, you stupid fool,' Hassan told him.

Talbot said, 'What the hell? I don't have to put up with you talking to me like that.'

'Listen to the tape I received, Talbot. Then you'll see why I'm angry.'

Talbot did, and with some horror. When it was finished, he called the Preacher back and Shah answered at once.

'What have you got to say?'

'It was in the heat of battle, so I shot my mouth off. Regrettable, and I apologize, but I don't see how it hurts us.'

'You think not? This General Charles Ferguson is a legend in the counter-terrorism field. He has been an absolute thorn in the flesh of Al Qaeda, and so are the people who work for him. Dillon, Holley, Miller; they'll all start nosing around. If Holley hadn't kept his business partner, Hamid Malik, informed of all his doings, and Malik hadn't confided in Hakim, we'd never have known.'

'So what's the problem?' Talbot asked. 'If this Holley guy tells his business partner about everything, then we should be able to find out about what happens next, shouldn't we?'

'You just don't get it, do you? All Charles Ferguson

and this Major Roper had to go on was a muddled tape, and then in you came with that absurdly dramatic code name, Shamrock, announcing to the world: *What a spectacular. Warrenpoint all over again and it worked big time. Osama will be delighted.*'

Talbot had made a mistake there, and he knew it. 'So I got a bit overenthusiastic.'

'And what was your touching dedication supposed to mean? *You can rest in peace now, Sean. Night bless?*'

Talbot said, 'That's got nothing to do with you.'

'Everything has something to do with me. Answer me.'

'Sean Kelly was my friend, a stable boy at Talbot Place. He was only nineteen, but he was a Provo like all his family. Some of those wounded Highlanders managed to fight back, and Sean took a bullet.'

'How heart-warming. When you joined the Army, the Troubles must have given you a problem, didn't it, knowing which side you were on?'

'I was never in Ulster with the Grenadier Guards.'

'But you certainly were with Twenty-Two SAS. More than twenty covert operations, wasn't it? One in County Tyrone where your unit ambushed and killed eight members of the PIRA. I wonder how your friends in Kilmartin would react if they knew?'

'You bastard,' Justin Talbot said.

'Action and passion, that's what you like, a bloody good scrap; and you don't care who the opponent is. Of course, you've never been certain which side you were on, Fenian or Prod. If only your mother had told you that you were Catholic years ago, you might have turned out different.'

Justin Talbot struggled to control his rage. 'That is nonsense. What the hell are you saying?'

'Your father was a Catholic.'

'Of course he was. Everyone knew that. But I'm a Protestant. My grandfather is a Presbyterian Unionist who loathes Catholics beyond anything else on this earth. He enjoyed telling me throughout my childhood that I was a bastard, but at least a Protestant one.'

'And he was wrong. You were baptized into the Roman Catholic faith on the fifth of August, Nineteen sixty-four, two weeks after your birth, by Father Alan Winkler of St Mary the Virgin Church, Dun Street, Mayfair.'

Talbot tried deep breathing to steady himself. 'What are you saying? Is this true? Did anybody know?'

'I believe your grandmother did. She was a remarkable woman to put up with your grandfather all those years, and your mother takes after her. You're hardly a fool. You must have been aware that I'm a careful man. I do my research, Justin.'

'All right,' Talbot said wearily. 'Where is all this leading?'

'Everything stays as it is. Since the Peace Process, many old IRA hands have sought employment in London.'

'What about them?'

'I'm sure your IRA connections in Kilmartin would be able to contact such people if necessary.'

'What for?'

'Ferguson and his people are formidable foes. It pays to be just as formidable an opposition.'

'What the hell are you talking about: open warfare in the London streets?'

'No, I'm saying we must be prepared. The opposition knows your code name is Shamrock. They surmise you might be Irish. Your leadership of the ambush seems to indicate you are a soldier of experience, and because of the name Warrenpoint, it reinforces their opinion that you could be a military man. We must stay vigilant, that's what I'm saying. If we receive the slightest hint, from Hakim or anyone else, that they're getting close to your identity, then we'll have to deal with them.' Shah took a breath. 'All right. That's enough for now. What are your plans?'

'My mother is at Talbot Place. I'm going to fly myself over to join her this afternoon. The old man is poorly again.'

'I'm amazed he hasn't managed to fall downstairs by now. Perhaps he needs a nudge?'

'Don't think I haven't thought of it.'

He dressed quickly in clothes suitable for flying, jeans and an old jacket. He had plenty of clothes at Talbot Place, and so took only a flight bag with a few things in it. Before leaving, though, he phoned Sir Hedley Chase at his house in Kensington to tell him he intended to call. Chase's job as Chairman of Talbot International might be a well-paid sinecure, but the old boy was sharp and took things seriously.

'I'm just going out for lunch,' the General said. 'At the Garrick Club. Got a taxi waiting. Why don't you join me?'

Justin Talbot hesitated, for he wanted to be on his way, but there was that military thing that bound soldiers together and had done so since time immemorial. A general was a general, and you didn't say no. A couple of hours wouldn't make any difference.

'I'll be with you as soon as I can, Sir Hedley,' he said, and was driving out of the garage in his mother's Mini Cooper five minutes later.

At the club, Sir Hedley Chase was greeted warmly by the porters on duty, and he told them who his guest was going to be. Then, helped by his stick, he negotiated the stairs, and went into the bar. It wasn't particularly busy. Two men were sitting comfortably at a corner table drinking brandy and ginger ale, and Sir Hedley realized with pleasure that he knew one of them.

'What a perfectly splendid idea, Charles, a Horse's Neck. I'll have one, too. How long has it been. A year? Two?' he asked.

'Three,' Ferguson told him, and said to his guest, 'General Sir Hedley Chase, Grenadier Guards. A Captain when I was a Subaltern. Very 'ard on me, he was.'

'Made a man of you,' Sir Hedley told him.

'And this,' said Ferguson, 'is Major Harry Miller, Intelligence Corps, Member of Parliament and Under-Secretary of State.'

'For what?' Sir Hedley enquired.

'For the Prime Minister, sir.' Miller shook hands.

'Oh, one of those, are you? I'll have to be careful. The Queen, gentlemen.' He toasted them. 'What are you up to, Charles? Still a security wallah?'

'I'm at the PM's bidding. What about you?'

'Bit of a sinecure, really. I'm Chairman of Talbot International. We're in the Middle East and Pakistan, supply the army there with trucks, helicopters, armoured cars, that sort of thing.'

'The Gulf War and Afghanistan must have boosted business,' Miller said.

'Certainly has. We've made millions.'

'And weaponry?' Ferguson asked.

'We decided as a matter of policy not to bother. There's lots of old-fashioned communist rubbish available, masses of AK47s, RPGs, Stingers. On the North-West Frontier, weapons like that are flogged in the bazaars like sweeties. It's dirty business. Lots of people do it, even some respectable firms, but we don't. Talbot International is family-owned, the ex-Chairman an old comrade of mine. Colonel Henry Talbot. Old Ulster family, Protestant to the bone. Henry was an MP at Stormont and they made him a Grand Master in the Orange Lodge. I always said he was to the right of Ian Paisley.'

'And now?'

'Retired. The grandson's the Managing Director – he's the one who really runs things. Major Justin Talbot – Grenadier Guards, you'll be pleased to know – got shot up on his last tour in Afghanistan and felt it was time to go. He goes where I can't. I managed to make it to Islamabad last year for discussions with the Pakistan government, but that was it. I'm too old for that kind of thing. It's bloody rough these days. All sorts of illegal arms traffic passing over the Afghan border.'

'Arms for the Taliban?' Ferguson asked.

'Who else?' Sir Hedley frowned. 'Have you got a particular interest in this?'

Miller answered. 'The Prime Minister is concerned about reports that British Muslims are serving with Taliban forces.'

Sir Hedley nodded. 'I've seen the odd newspaper reports to that effect, but I can't believe it's in any great numbers. I know one thing. It would be treason.' He turned to Miller. 'Wouldn't you agree?'

'Yes, I would, but in the brave new world we live in, it'd be a nightmare for the government to prosecute.' He smiled crookedly. 'But we'll have to cross that bridge when we come to it. Would you like another drink, sir?'

'I think I would,' Sir Hedley said, and added, 'Here's Justin, just coming in the door.'

Justin Talbot had left his flight bag with the porter and had put on a tie. He stood there, smiling, a slightly incongruous figure with the tie and the old flying jacket.

'Come in, Justin, and join us. I've just run into an old comrade, Major General Charles Ferguson and his friend, Major Harry Miller.'

Justin Talbot was thunderstruck. Of all the people to meet – the two men he'd been most warned about. The voice in his brain said: *Don't panic. Smile. Your background is impeccable. You're Managing Director of a firm worth hundreds of millions of pounds; you're a war hero.*

So he produced that easy charm and said to Ferguson, 'Quite an honour, General. You're a legend in the regiment.'

It had the desired effect, for Ferguson was only human, but Miller was not taken with him and wondered why. The deliberate stroking of Ferguson, perhaps, or the wonder-boy appearance. Certainly the air of cynical good humour was used for effect, and most people probably fell for it, especially women.

'You'll have a drink with us?' Sir Hedley asked.

'No can do. I'm back from Lahore and found out my mother has gone over to County Down to see to her father, who's apparently not too well. I'm flying myself over, so no alcohol for me.'

'Indeed, but well-met, anyway. Our friend, Major Miller here, is apparently an Under-Secretary of State, although we're not allowed to know what ministry.'

'Sounds intriguing,' Talbot said.

'We've been having an interesting debate about the suggested presence of British Muslims fighting for the Taliban,' said Sir Hedley.

'I see,' Talbot said.

Ferguson said, 'There's a concern in government circles. Have you any opinion on the matter?'

Which was exactly the question Talbot had been hoping for. 'I certainly have. It's not a "suggested" presence: it's very real. I have excellent connections with the Pakistan Army and they tell me many of the voices on the radio are definitely English.'

'Have you heard them yourself?' Miller asked.

'Yes, on a few occasions when I was up near Peshawar and very close to the Afghan border. Sometimes you can pick up the sounds of battle on the other side.'

'In Afghanistan itself? Can I ask what you were doing there?' Miller went on.

'We sell trucks used for army transportation and driven by civilian personnel. Part of our sales package guarantees maintenance.'

'A big operation,' Ferguson told him.

'Yes, it is. If the government is concerned about anything up there, I suppose they could always send somebody to take a look.'

Sir Hedley broke in. 'We'd be happy to assist in any

way. Maybe you and Miller could go and have a look-see, Charles?'

'It's certainly a thought,' Ferguson said. 'Would you be there?' he asked Talbot.

'Not if I can help it. It's the pits, and I've had enough of Afghanistan to last me a long time. But I have excellent staff, and I'd be happy to put them at your disposal. Just let me know.'

'I will indeed. Come on, Harry, we'd better move.' Ferguson got up. 'Take care of yourself, Hedley, old son. Let's not leave it so long. Nice to meet you, Major.' He shook Talbot's hand. 'My regards to your grandfather. I had some dealings with him when I was in Belfast at the height of the Troubles. Frankly, he was a bit of a bastard.'

Talbot held on to his hand for a moment. 'You're wrong, General. He was *the* bastard.'

Ferguson and Miller went downstairs and called in their limousines. 'What did you think?' asked Ferguson.

'Of Talbot? I can't say I warmed to him.'

'Perfectly understandable, Harry. He's too good-looking, he's heir to a family fortune of eight-hundred million pounds, he's a war hero. Shall I carry on?'

'I'd rather you didn't,' Miller said. 'What now?'

'Time for a council of war. I'll see you at Holland Park.' Ferguson got in his Daimler and was driven away.

* * *

An hour later, they met in the computer room, Ferguson presiding, with Miller, Holley, Roper, and their occasional colleagues Harry and Billy Salter.

Ferguson said, 'I'm pleased to say that Daniel Holley has agreed to join us and offer his special services to the matter in hand.'

Harry Salter glared at Holley, then said, 'This is completely out of order. This geezer arranged for someone to try and burn down my pub.'

'Which is still standing,' Ferguson told him. 'We're all in one piece, including Lady Monica Starling, whose life he saved. It's like war, Harry – yesterday's enemies are today's allies. All sins are forgiven. Daniel has even passed on to our old friend Colonel Josef Lermov information about a possible Al Qaeda assassination attempt on Vladimir Putin.'

'Christ,' Harry Salter said, 'whose side are you on, Holley? You certainly spread yourself around.' He turned to Ferguson. 'Okay then, what's it all about?'

Roper said, 'I've got quite a show for you. Listen and learn.'

When it was over, Harry Salter said, 'What a bastard, that Shamrock guy. Calls himself British. He should have his balls chopped off.'

'Rather drastic, but you have a point,' Ferguson said. 'Anyone else?'

Billy Salter said, 'The business about these young

Muslims turning up in battle with the Taliban. Yes, it's diabolical, but I've got a feeling there probably *is* no organization as such behind this. They've all got relatives in Pakistan, they were born here, they've got a passport, they can travel there any time they want. So maybe some Mullah at the local mosque who's a Jihadist has given them an address. That's probably the extent of it.'

'I agree with him,' Dillon put in. 'I think the important thing here is for us to find out who Shamrock is.'

'You're right, Sean,' Miller told him. 'But we can't exactly go hunting for him in the depths of Helmand province. He isn't out there leading a life of daily hardship. He's staging a "spectacular", as he calls it, and then getting out of there. Who knows where he is?'

'I still say Ireland's the place to go,' Dillon said. 'Visit the scene of the original crime.'

Ferguson opened his briefcase, took out a book and put it on the table next to Roper, who picked it up and examined it. 'From Waterstone's. A history of the IRA, with a detailed account of the Warrenpoint ambush of Nineteen seventy-nine. Anybody can read about it, Sean – it doesn't have to be somebody who was there.'

'And as I've already mentioned,' Miller said, 'I've used the Warrenpoint disaster in my lectures at Sandhurst for ten years. Hundreds and hundreds of officer cadets have heard that lecture.'

'Let's move on,' Ferguson said. 'By chance, Major Miller and I bumped into an old comrade of mine today,

General Sir Hedley Chase, Chairman of Talbot International. He was with his Managing Director, Major Justin Talbot, who was just back from Pakistan. I presume you know the firm, Daniel?'

'Of course I do. It's one of the biggest in the business. Family-owned – the Chairman for years, Colonel Henry Talbot, was involved in Ulster politics.'

'And that's a polite way of putting it,' Dillon said. 'The kind of old-fashioned Protestant politician who'd have welcomed another potato famine just to reduce the Catholic population to manageable proportions.'

'You appear to feel strongly on the matter, Sean,' Ferguson said.

'And why wouldn't I, living only a few miles up the road at Collyban for some years in my youth? It was with my uncle on my mother's side, Mickeen Oge Flynn – good man; still has a garage there. And I can assure you, Colonel Henry Talbot was one of the most hated men in County Down. The grand house he had where he lorded it over the Catholic "scum of Kilmartin", as he described them. The only thing that kept someone from shooting him was his wife, Mary Ellen. Mickeen Oge used to say, if ever a saint walked this earth, it was her, even if she was a Protestant.'

'He certainly sounds a real old bastard,' Harry Salter said.

'Warrenpoint must have been a bitter pill for him to swallow,' Ferguson said. 'Only a few miles away.'

Dillon said coldly, 'Enough of the ould sod, and back

to our problem. We know there are British Muslims in the Taliban ranks: we have recordings of them. I'm with Billy in thinking that most of them simply make their own way to Pakistan and join up there. I shouldn't imagine there is any organization as such. Information about where to join is probably available at any local mosque.'

'So what is your point?' Ferguson demanded.

'That the job comes down to one thing: find Shamrock. The President asked me if I thought we could, and I said yes. He said, don't let me down and, with all due respect to you, General, I don't intend to.'

Ferguson turned to Holley. 'For twenty-five years, behind the respectable front of Malik Shipping, you've sold arms to anyone who could pay. You must be one of the most experienced dealers in the business. Who would we get in touch with? In our discussion with Talbot and Sir Hedley, we kept it general, made no mention of Shamrock. They both felt that if the government was concerned about the situation, they should send someone to take a look. Talbot said he had an excellent staff who would be willing to help.'

'They wouldn't be much help for what you're looking for,' Holley said. 'They're far too respectable. I could provide two or three names, the kind of people who have their hands in everything. But you really have to do it face-to-face: it's the only way. Peshawar International may not be the biggest airport in the world, but it'll handle an RAF Gulfstream, I should think.'

91

Harry Miller said to him, 'What a splendid idea.'

Ferguson turned to Miller, 'By heavens, I could go with you. I've excellent contacts with Pakistan Intelligence.'

'That's up to you,' said Holley, 'but be careful what you say. Pakistan Intelligence is riddled with corruption and Taliban sympathizers. As for Shamrock, I'd keep that for the lowlifes whose names I'll give you.'

'Thanks for the warning, Daniel. Give Roper the names of the dealers you suggest we meet in Peshawar, if you would.'

'I can do more than that. They all have laptops, I'll give you their email addresses. Just remember: these are ruthless men, all out to make a buck. They don't know what a scruple is. I'd go armed at all times.'

'Give me the names of this unsavoury lot,' Roper said.

'Dak Khan, José Fernandez and Jemal Hamid. I'll give you their emails later.'

Billy Salter said, 'So while you and Harry are over in Pakistan, what do we do?'

'Try to behave yourselves,' Ferguson told him. 'And watch Dillon for me. We won't be away long.'

Holley's Codex sounded. He answered it and found Josef Lermov. Holley waved frantically at Roper and mouthed 'speaker'. Roper turned it on and Lermov's voice boomed a little.

'I thought I'd let you know that there's been a terrible accident in Chechnya. Mullah Ibrahim Nadim met a bad end on a country road outside some small town with an unpronounceable name. A car bomb killed him, two bodyguards and his driver.'

Holley felt no remorse for the part he had played in the affair. 'Well, he wanted paradise, so at least he got that. *Inshallah*. It was his time.'

'You know,' Lermov said, 'during the Battle of Algiers, Muslim girls threw away their traditional clothes, cut their hair and wore make-up and pretty frocks to fool French paratroopers into believing they were Europeans. That way, they were able to visit coffee shops and leave bombs under the seats.'

'Yes, I know that. Very ingenious,' Holley said. 'What's the point?'

'The point, my dear Daniel, is that Chechnyan Muslim women appear to have adopted the same idea. An unfortunate Colonel in the GRU's Planning Cabinet apparently made the mistake of enjoying the charms of such a woman.'

'And how is he?'

'Dead. He shot her and then shot himself.'

'Well, there you are, that's the way it goes,' Holley told him.

'Prime Minister Putin has asked me to tell you he owes you one, Daniel.'

Holley laughed. 'Now that really does frighten me, Josef. Thank him for the kind thought, but I think I'll still lock my door at nights.'

Lermov hung up. Harry Salter said, a kind of

admiration in his voice, 'What a cool bastard you are, my old son. I'll have to keep my eye on you.'

'Well, that will keep me safe, if nothing else,' Holley told him. 'What happens now?'

'Luncheon,' Ferguson said. 'Is that all right with everybody?'

'Not me,' Roper said, 'you've given me the rush job of all time. I've got a million things to do. You lot just get on with it.'

'So where shall we eat?' Ferguson asked.

'What about the Al Bustan in Shepherd Market?' Holley said. 'Great Lebanese food.'

'Let's go,' Ferguson said.

Selim Lancy had been keeping an eye on his namesake at his shop, which was easy enough to do in the congested and narrow streets of the market. There were also numerous cafés with tables outside, and he was sitting at one, observing the shop, when the party from Holland Park arrived at the Al Bustan, which was just on the corner. It was a surfeit of riches, for the Preacher had followed up his photo of Holley with further ones covering Ferguson's most important people. And now here they were, just dropped into his lap.

The waiters pushed tables close so they could sit together under an awning outside the restaurant, and wine was ordered. It was all very good-humoured.

Lancy sat down at a small table on the edge of things,

but not too close. He didn't need to be close, for the hearing enhancer he slipped into his right ear enabled him to eavesdrop. He ordered wine himself and began reading his newspaper.

It was Ferguson who gave it away by asking Holley, 'How long since you were last in Peshawar, Daniel?'

'Five months ago,' Holley said. 'Flying visit. I was only there three days. Long enough to complete business, then get out. You wouldn't want to linger, and you shouldn't, General.'

A moment later, Ferguson had to answer his Codex. He listened for a few moments, then said, 'Excellent.'

He said to the others, 'That was Roper. The Pakistan Embassy has agreed to our visit. A Military Police Colonel named Ahmed Atep will be our contact, Major. Parry and Lacey have been alerted and are already on their way to Farley to get the Gulfstream ready.'

'And what about the dealers I suggested you meet?' Holley asked.

'Roper's emailed them and said it was your personal request that they co-operate.'

'Has he had replies?'

'Yes, from this Dak Khan and José Fernandez, who both indicated that they would help in any way possible.' Ferguson shrugged. 'They probably think there might be money in it.'

'And Jemal Hamid?'

'Apparently killed in a roadside ambush of a convoy close to the border some weeks ago.'

'On the Pakistan side?'

'It would appear so.'

Holley shrugged. 'That's the way it goes. It's a thoroughly dangerous adventure, General. When do you go?'

Ferguson glanced at his watch. 'As soon as we're done with lunch. So let's order, gentlemen.'

Lancy asked for his bill, paid the waiter and walked away, not only satisfied, but excited. His Mercedes was parked in a nearby mews and he went and sat behind the wheel and reported in to the Preacher. Professor Hassan Shah was in the garden of his house, sitting at a table on the terrace, marking a student's thesis.

'Excellent,' he said when Lancy was finished. 'You've done brilliantly. Is there anything to report on Malik?'

'I've had a word with a few of the Brotherhood with shops in the area.' He was speaking of the Army of God, on the face of it a Muslim charity. 'He seems harmless enough.'

'Then you can forget him from now on. I want you to drive out to this airfield and confirm their departure.'

'You've got it, boss. Ferguson said they'd be leaving in three hours, so I'll wait till nearer the time. I don't want to stand out or anything.'

'Just get it right.'

* * *

After lunch, Holley stopped for a moment at the Dorchester to collect a couple of things before going on with Ferguson and Miller to the airfield. Just as he was going back out through the door, Malik phoned him from Algiers. 'How are you? I was speaking to Cousin Selim and he's worried about you.'

'No need,' Holley said. 'I'm taking it easy for the time being. It's Ferguson and Major Miller who are putting themselves in harm's way. They're going on a flying visit to Peshawar to nose around.'

'But why?'

'Just to get a feel for the situation. I gave them names of people who might be able to help. Dak Khan, José Fernandez and Jemal Hamid.'

'And have they agreed to help?'

'It seems that Jemal Hamid was killed in a convoy ambush the other week, but the other two have. Ferguson and Miller will be looked after by a Colonel Ahmed Atep – does he mean anything to you?'

'No, he's not familiar to me, though it's years since I was there. Wasn't he there when you visited five months ago?'

'No, he must be new.'

'So what happens now?' Malik asked.

'I haven't the slightest idea. I just had a meeting with all of Ferguson's people. I was able to put a face to everybody, something I couldn't do before. Roper, Ferguson, Miller, Dillon, and the two gangsters, the Salters.'

'Gangsters?' Malik said.

'Well, that's what they used to be. Young Billy is MI5 now and his uncle has millions in developments by the Thames. It pays better than robbing banks.'

'Everything is a joke to you, Daniel.'

'It's the only thing that got me through five years in the Lubyanka Prison, my friend. Take care, Malik, I'll be in touch.' He hung up.

Malik sighed, deeply troubled by the direction in which the whole affair was going. There was a step on the terrace and he turned to find Colonel Ali Hakim there.

'Forgive the intrusion; your gatekeeper let me into the garden. I was passing and wondered how you are.'

'Not good at all,' Malik said. 'I worry so much about Daniel. I just can't help it.'

Hakim managed a look of concern. 'My dear old friend, what's he been up to now?'

Farley Field belonged to the Ministry of Defence and was restricted, but the public car park next to it was not, and was popular with plane-spotters due to the increase in military traffic. Lancy had out his binoculars along with the rest of them and found the Gulfstream, waiting to go, the steps down, two RAF officers beside it.

He could recognize Ferguson, Dillon and Daniel Holley standing together by a Daimler limousine, and then a Mercedes appeared. The man who got out was Miller. It was five-thirty. He waited. Finally, the Gulfstream started across the runway and rose into the air.

He got back into the Mercedes and called the Preacher. 'They've just left.'

'Excellent,' Shah said. 'Let's hope they enjoy themselves.'

'You're going to do the business on them, aren't you, Boss?'

'I would think Peshawar dangerous enough without my help,' Shah told him.

Lancy said, 'What do I do now?'

'Go back to making a living, Selim. I'm sure the ladies adore your manly good looks. You'll find, by the way, that your bank account has been inflated by five thousand pounds. I know your mother's cancer treatment means she can't work. Give her my blessing, but remember you belong to Osama.'

To which there could be no answer, and Selim Lancy switched off, shaking his head. What kind of geezer was he, the Preacher? One minute he was the lord of life and death, and the next he was the soul of kindness and charity. Lancy had punished people for him, wounding to keep Muslim wrongdoers in line, and he'd shot dead two Muslim men from Kosovo involved in a prostitution ring importing young girls. Death was all they deserved, the Preacher had said, and Lancy had obliged, dumping the bodies in the Thames.

It didn't bother him. After all, it was small beer after Afghanistan. On the other hand, the business with his mother was a debt that should be repaid. He sat there behind the wheel of the Mercedes, thinking about the situation. Ferguson and Miller were out of the way, which left Dillon, Holley and the Salters. He smiled. Thanks to the information the Preacher had supplied, he knew all about the Salters, and their history intrigued him. East End gangsters who'd made good, millionaires up there with the toffs. He admired that and felt no animosity. They were on the wrong side, that was all.

There was a restaurant called Harry's Place and a pub, the Dark Man, in Wapping. It was where Salter had started out, his favourite place, and he had a boat there called the *Linda Jones* tied up at the end of the jetty outside. That's where any aggravation would hurt him most. Lancy smiled and took out his mobile.

Like many young and unemployed Muslim men, Kalid Hasim made a bare living on the fringes of the drug trade as a delivery boy. It was a great risk for a small return, but Hasim considered it only temporary. For him, boxing was the way out, and he was punching the bag in his gym in Camden when his mobile sounded; he'd put it with his towel on a bench.

'It's me, number one man,' Lancy said.

They had never met. Lancy was a voice on the phone since the first call, when he'd suggested that Hasim and a couple of his friends might like to smash up a shop selling anti-Muslim literature, promising five hundred pounds in the post. Hasim had taken a chance and had been delighted with the outcome. He'd repeated the exercise on many occasions.

'So what have you got?'

'Just listen.' He explained the situation. 'Just aggravation is what I'm after. Smash up a few motors in the car park . . . and there's a boat tied up at the jetty. Sinking that would be good.'

'When do you want it done?'

'Tonight, but I've got to warn you. The Salters are real hard men, so don't hang about. In and out before they know what's going on. There's a grand in it for you.'

'Consider it done.'

'Good lad,' Lancy told him. 'But remember that right hand. You're leaving yourself wide open when you punch.'

'Fuck off,' Hasim told him.

'Not nice, a decent young Muslim talking like that,' and then he surprised Hasim by speaking in Arabic for the first time. 'Allah is great and Osama is his prophet.'

He switched off and drove away.

Meanwhile, the Preacher was contacting his most important Al Qaeda asset in Peshawar. He got an instant response.

101

'The day of wrath must come,' Shah said, establishing his credentials.

'Then only the believers will survive. It is good to hear you, Preacher. How can I help?' his asset answered.

'Not me, but the cause of Al Qaeda. You are to have two visitors. They have just left London by Gulfstream. They are important because they are on British government business, but they are a problem for us.'

'Who are they?'

'A General Charles Ferguson and Major Harry Miller. They are there on a fact-finding mission. There is alarm in London over reports of young British Muslims fighting for the Taliban.'

'Which is true.'

'Yes, but there is more to their trip. There is evidence of a mercenary commander operating with the Taliban who uses the code name Shamrock. Have you heard anything of such a man?'

'Not a whisper. Are you sure about this? Perhaps it's only rumour?'

'No. Shamrock is one of Al Qaeda's most important assets. His identity must be protected at all costs. As far as you are concerned, he doesn't exist. My information is that Ferguson and Miller have been promised the assistance of two men in Peshawar. Their names are Dak Khan and José Fernandez.'

'I know these men well. Illegal arms dealers, amongst other things. I can put my hand on them at any time.

As regards the visitors from London, do I frighten them or kill them?'

'Both Ferguson and Miller have done great harm to Al Qaeda in the past. I think it is time that their debts were paid.'

'No problem. Leave it with me.'

'Osama's blessing on you.'

Shah hung up, and the man at his desk at Military Police Headquarters in Peshawar, Colonel Ahmed Atep, lit a cigarette and sat back, smiling. So, life could get interesting. The prospect pleased him very much.

NORTHERN IRELAND

————

LONDON

5

Earlier in the day, Justin Talbot's flight had taken him over North Wales and Anglesey, and now he was sweeping in towards the Mourne Mountains, a wonderful sight on a perfect day.

It had been an excellent flight, but he hadn't enjoyed it as much as usual. His dealings with the Preacher had been deeply disturbing. It wasn't just the shock of discovering that his mother'd had him baptized a Catholic as a baby. It was more that the Preacher knew about his exploits with the SAS, which were supposedly top secret. Where in the hell had all that come from? The power of these Al Qaeda people was frightening, and he cursed the day he'd ever got involved.

He wondered for a moment if he could buy his way out. On his grandfather's death, he would become fabulously rich, and he was cynical enough by nature to believe that most people in life had their price, particularly when you were talking in the millions. But on the other hand, Islamists like Al Qaeda, men who could kill and execute without a second's hesitation, had rigid moral and theological codes that Westerners found it difficult to understand. In the end, money meant little to them.

He doubted that was his escape.

He turned parallel to the Mourne Mountains as they swept down to the sea, and dropped on to the long grass runway of the Aero Club just outside the village of Drumgoole. There were three hangars, five small aircraft parked on the grass, a small terminal building with a café and a stub of a control tower above it. In front of the terminal was a maroon Shogun, his mother leaning against it, wearing sunglasses because of the glare, watching as an overalled mechanic waved him in to park in the right place. The club's chief pilot, Phil Regan, was standing with her, and they came towards him as he got out of the Beech Baron.

'Wonderful to see you, darling.' She flung her arms round him and hugged him fiercely. 'My God, but you're brown.'

'Good to see you, Justin.' Regan shook hands. 'If you wore the right clothes, people could mistake you for a Pathan.'

'It's fierce sun up there on the North-West Frontier,' Talbot said. 'I've never experienced anything like it. The plane did well, Phil. I hope I'm staying for a few days, but give it a full engine check, full everything, so that it's ready to go at a moment's notice.'

'We'll see to that, never fear.' Regan turned to consult the mechanic.

Jean said, 'Do you want to drive?'

'I've just clocked three hundred miles or more flying that plane, so I think I'll take a rain check.'

'Fine by me.'

They got in and she drove away, following the coast road. 'I was worried when I didn't hear from you on this trip. I always thought that's what mobiles were for.'

'Service can be difficult if you're in the wrong terrain. It's a hard, unforgiving landscape out there. It's defeated everybody who invaded that bloody country, even Alexander the Great.'

'But that's Afghanistan. I thought you never went over the Pakistan border.'

He'd made a mistake and struggled to make it right.

'Borders meant nothing to Alexander.'

'Of course, silly of me.' She concentrated on the road, but, glancing sideways at her face, he knew that she didn't believe him, just as she hadn't believed so much of his army life over the years. Secrets, always secrets between them, but also a love that was so deep it was never mentioned.

'How is he?' he asked, referring to his grandfather.

'Pretty bloody awful. Dr Ryan said he really did think he might go this time. That's why he phoned me to come. Dad insists sometimes on getting up with two sticks and lurching around and striking out at any servant within range. This time, he lost his balance and fell over, and that's what brought on the attack. We've got a local man with him now named Tod Murphy; he spent years at the Musgrave Park Hospital in Belfast. He's sixty, a hard man, and deaf as a post, so your grandfather's rantings pass right over him. He'll just sit reading in the conservatory, ignoring him, until Dad needs feeding or toileting or putting to bed. And, of course, there's Hannah Kelly,' mentioning the housekeeper. 'Couldn't manage without her, so I pay her a damn good salary, and thanks to her I don't have to be over here on a regular basis.' She shook her head. 'What's the solution? It drives me mad thinking about it.'

'He dies, I suppose,' Talbot said. 'He could stumble and fall at any time and break his bloody neck and do us all a favour.'

'You really hate him that much?' she asked.

He shrugged. 'I was his Protestant bastard for years, so what did that make you? How could you ever forgive him for that?'

'I know, love,' she said. 'Such behaviour goes beyond any hope of forgiveness.'

'Mind you, what would life have been like if I'd been a Catholic bastard? Imagine, Colonel Henry Talbot's grandson! What would the Orange Lodge have made of that?'

Because of the special bond that had always been between them, she could tell he wasn't quite ready to face the house, so she swerved to the side of the road by the sea wall, switched off and got out. She leaned on the wall, took out her cigarettes and lit one, and he joined her.

A narrow road dropped down to a hamlet called Lorn: seven small cottages if you counted them. Several fishing boats were drawn up on the narrow beach and there was a boathouse and jetty that belonged to the Talbot estate. A sport fisherman was tied up there, gleaming white with a blue stripe. It was called *Mary Ellen*.

Justin said, 'Have you taken the boat out since you've been back or been flying with Phil Regan? I thought you'd be airborne all the time after you got your licence.'

Instead of replying to his question she said, 'You know, don't you?'

'August the fifth, Nineteen sixty-odd, Father Alan Winkler, St Mary the Virgin Church, Dun Street, Mayfair. A good address.'

'He was a nice old man. Very understanding. He held my hand and prayed for me and you and your father, and said that, in the circumstances, it was God's will that you should be baptized.'

'The persuasion of the truly good,' Talbot said. 'How could you resist that?' He kissed her gently on the forehead. 'What a wonderful person you are. I expect that's why I can't take girls seriously, and never have. They're lucky if they can get a week out of me.'

'But you aren't going to tell me how you suddenly know? Oh, the secrets between us, darling.'

'I've an idea that Mary Ellen knew, am I right?'

'I had to tell her because I told her everything and she blessed me, for it was your father's dying wish. As far as telling you . . . she felt it should be left to the right moment.'

'I'm forty-five, Mum, if you remember. A long time waiting.'

'We all have our secrets, even from our loved ones.'

'And you think that applies to me?'

'More years ago than I care to remember, you were spending a week's leave at Marley Court when a dispatch rider delivered an order. You read it, told me you'd been recalled for some special operation, went upstairs to pack and left the order on the study table. I know I shouldn't have, but I read it and discovered my son was serving in Twenty-second SAS.'

'So you knew, all those years, and never told me?'

'I couldn't. It was a betrayal, you see, and I couldn't live with you knowing that. My punishment was that I've had to imagine supremely dangerous things happening to you every day. So, yes, my darling boy, I knew then, every time, just as I know now.' She stubbed out her cigarette. 'I've tried to give up these things, but I'm damned if I can. Let's move on. You must be famished.'

'I'd like to call in and see Jack Kelly before we go up to the house,' he said. 'If you don't mind, that is.'

She glanced at her watch. 'A little early for the pub. It's only four-thirty.'

'I'm sorry, Mum.' He laughed, looking like a young boy again for a fleeting moment. 'I suppose I am putting off seeing Colonel Henry for as long as possible. And I do have letters for Jack from his extended family, relatives we have working out there in Pakistan.'

'Of course, love. I'll drop you off and get on up to the house and see how Hannah Kelly is coping.'

They continued in silence for a while and finally he said, 'I've been thinking about our secrets. If it leaked out that I'd operated in the SAS during my army service, I think it would finish me here.'

'I agree, but they'll never know from me. Answer me one question as your mother, though. Did you actually take part in SAS operations in Ulster during the Troubles?'

He had so much to lie about, particularly his present activities. Perhaps he could more easily avoid that by admitting a sort of truth.

'Yes, I did, and on many occasions.'

She kept on driving calmly. 'In view of the personal difficulties in your background, our situation in Kilmartin, couldn't you have avoided it? I understood that the Ministry of Defence allowed choice.'

'It was still left to the individual to make a personal decision.' He was getting into real trouble here. 'It's difficult when the regiment's going to war, for an individual to opt out.'

'I could see that with the Grenadier Guards,' Jean said. 'But you volunteered to join the SAS, am I right?'

'Yes, that's true.'

'So you knew what you were getting into. Covert operations, subterfuge, killing by stealth, action by night. You must have known that your enemy would be the IRA.' She shook her head. 'Why did you do it?'

He broke then. 'Because I loved it: every glorious moment of it. Couldn't get enough. Some psychiatrists might say I was seeking death, but if I was, it was only to beat him at his own game. I lived more in a day . . .' He broke off, shaking his head. 'Nothing can describe it; it was so real, so damned exciting. It was impossible to take ordinary life seriously ever again.'

'But Afghanistan got you in the end.'

'I think not. Death looked down, took one look and said: Oh, it's you again. Not today, thank you.'

She managed a laugh. 'You fool. Anything else?'

'I don't think announcing to all and sundry that I'm a Catholic is a sound thought. The news that the heir to Talbot Place is a Fenian would have some people dancing a jig for joy – and many who wouldn't.'

'It's your decision, not mine,' Jean Talbot said. 'I'll go along with anything you want and we'll keep our fingers crossed, but remember, Justin, this is Ireland, where a secret is only a secret when one person knows it.'

'Then God help us.' They had passed down the main street, a few parked cars, not many people about, and there was the Kilmartin Arms and the Church of the Holy Name to one side of it, a low stone wall surrounding a well-filled cemetery, the church standing some distance back. There was an old-fashioned lych-gate, a roofed entrance to the churchyard.

'Let me out here,' Talbot said, and his mother braked to a halt. He got out, taking his flight bag with him, and examined the notice board. 'Church of the Holy Name, Father Michael Cassidy. My God, the old devil goes on forever. How old is he?'

'Seventy-eight. He could have had preferment years ago, but he loves this place. You've got the times for Mass and the Confessional.'

'Don't tempt me, but I will have a word with him, and in friendship only. The fact of my new religion stays out of it.'

'I'll get moving then.'

'I shan't be long.'

He walked through the lych-gate as she drove off, and threaded his way through the gravestones to a horse-shoe of cypress trees. There was a monument there, which bore the names on a bronze plaque of local men who had died while serving in the IRA. He didn't bother with that, but walked through to a well-kept grave with a black granite headstone. The inscription was in gold and read: Killed in Action, Volunteer Sean Kelly, Age 19. August 27, 1979. It said other things, too, about a just cause and the IRA love of country, but Justin Talbot ignored them. Only the name and the age of someone

115

he had truly loved meant anything to him. He turned away, close to weeping, and found Jack Kelly standing some little distance away, lighting his briar pipe.

He carried his sixty-nine years well, dark hair streaked with silver now, a face that had weathered intelligence there, also a quiet good humour. He wore a tweed suit and an open-neck shirt and there were good shoulders to him, a man who could handle himself, which wasn't surprising in someone whose life had been devoted to the IRA.

'Good to see you back, boy,' Kelly said. 'Tim keeps in touch on his mobile. I heard from him you'd been disappearing over the border again to Afghanistan.'

Tim Molloy was his nephew, one of many men in the Kilmartin district who had eagerly accepted the recruitment to Talbot International at good salaries. Tim, for example, was contract manager to the vehicle maintenance side of the business based in Islamabad, servicing civilian convoys to Peshawar and beyond, to the Khyber Pass itself. It was an important and hazardous job.

The truth was that Molloy and the Kilmartin group used their privileged position to off-load arms close to the border to dealers who took them over. Honed by years of experience with the IRA, Molloy's group of ten men, all mainly in their middle years, formed a tightly knit crew that kept themselves to themselves. No one at Talbot International headquarters had the slightest idea of what was going on, except Justin Talbot.

'Tim's a good man, even on the worst of days,' Talbot said. 'But he hates me changing my clothes and slipping off over the border to have a look around and visit.'

They had moved to a bench close to Sean's grave and were sitting. Kelly's pipe had gone out and he lit it again. 'He thinks you're a lunatic going over for a stroll in a place like that – and disguised as a Pathan. He's convinced that, sooner or later, someone's going to take a pot shot at you.'

'God bless Tim, but then he doesn't know what we do,' Talbot said.

'And a burden it is sometimes.' Kelly looked sombre. Jack Kelly was the nearest thing to a father Justin Talbot had known, that was the truth of it, and Justin was well aware that in many ways he had stood in for Sean, and not only in Jack's eyes, but in those of his wife, Hannah, also. The word from Molloy about Talbot's trips had worried the Kellys, and Jack had raised the matter almost a year before.

It had been at a bad time or a good time, depending how you looked at it, but it was not long after Al Qaeda and the Preacher had invaded Talbot's life. So, sitting in the study of Talbot Place with Kelly, just the two of them, with whiskey taken, Talbot had unburdened himself.

Kelly had been shocked and angry. 'What the hell were you playing at? Surely you must have seen that once you put your foot on such a road, there could be no turning back?'

'I got tired of big business. I missed what I had in the army – excitement, action, passion; put it any way you like. It started simple, then it got out of hand.'

'And Shamrock? Whose bright idea was that?'

'Mine.' Talbot shrugged. 'Okay, a bit stupid, but I certainly wasn't going to say Major Talbot here, are you receiving me?'

'You bloody fool,' Kelly had said.

'That helps a lot. The thing is, how do I get out of it? You're the experts, you've had thirty-five years of fighting the British Army.'

'You don't,' Kelly said, a certain despair on his face. 'This is Al Qaeda we're talking about. You're too valuable to let go. Even if you could find this anonymous man, the Preacher, and managed to kill him, it wouldn't make the slightest difference. You belong to them. They'll never let you stop. Your mother knows nothing of this, I hope?'

'Certainly not.'

'Thank God. She'd never be able to cope.'

'So I just keep going?'

'I don't see what else you can do.'

But all that had been almost a year before, and a lot had happened since then. Sitting there on the bench, Talbot brooded for a while, at a loss for words. It had certainly been a day for disclosure, but of things it would not be a good idea to reveal to anyone else. His service with the SAS and his new Catholic self were matters best left alone.

Kelly said, 'You've got something else on your mind, haven't you? You might as well spill it.'

Talbot said, 'Okay, I will. It will take a while to cover everything, but bear with me. You thought I was in a mess, but with the things I've done over there – now it's infinitely worse.'

It took a long time in the telling, almost an hour, because he told Kelly everything right up to Ferguson and Miller flying to Pakistan.

'So there it is,' Talbot said. 'I don't think I've missed anything. What do you think?'

'That you're probably a lunatic. You must be to dig yourself in so deep.'

'Do any of the names mean anything to you?'

'They certainly do. General Charles Ferguson was in and out of Ulster throughout the Troubles, a thorn in our side.'

'And these two IRA men? Are they genuine?'

'You can bet your life on it. Sean Dillon's a Down man who became a top enforcer and then ended up in a Serb prison some years ago. Ferguson saved him from a firing squad and the payment was that Dillon had to join him.'

'And Holley?'

'Half-English. His mother was a Coogan from Crossmaglen. He's highly regarded by that family. His cousin, Rosaleen, was raped and murdered by four

Protestant scumbags. He shot the lot of them.' He shook his head. 'He and Dillon are serious business.'

'Yes, but they don't know who I am; I'm just a name.'

'Not to the Taliban who fight with you, and don't tell me you wear a turban and pull your robes about and wrap a scarf around your face. Some of those men will have seen you.'

'No Taliban I know would sell me out,' Talbot told him. 'If anyone did, they'd hunt him down and feed him to the dogs.' He shrugged. 'I don't know. It's a bugger.'

'One of your own making,' Kelly said.

'I suppose so. Maybe I have a death wish. Anyway, I suppose I'd better get up to the Place and see what's what. I mustn't forget your mail, though.'

He opened his flight bag and took out a stack of letters held together by a rubber band. Kelly took it and said, 'The ladies will welcome them. They can all call up Peshawar on their mobiles, but everyone loves a letter. The money is just pouring in for them. Some of them don't know what to do with it.'

'I'm sure they'll think of something. How's Hannah? My mother tells me that the old bastard is worse than he ever was.'

'We all do our best. I'm sorry for your mother, Justin.'

'Aren't we all . . . ? But I'd better be off.'

'I'll give you a lift.'

'No, thanks. I could do with the walk. My legs are a bit stiff after the flight.' He smiled cheerfully, as if he didn't have a care in the world. 'I'll see you later,' and he picked up his flight bag and walked away.

He had not gone very far, was climbing over a stile, when his mobile sounded. It was the Preacher. 'Have you arrived?'

'Yes, I'm just walking up to the house. What is it?'

'Just keeping you informed. I thought you'd like to know that Ferguson and Miller are now on their way to Peshawar. But don't worry. I have a very reliable asset in Peshawar. He can be trusted to handle the matter.'

'Anybody I know?'

'None of your business. All you need to know is: they may be going there, but I doubt they'll be coming back. Have a good holiday. You need the rest.'

He switched off and Talbot stood there, thinking for a moment, then continued walking briskly through the estate, past the prized herd of Jersey cows and a particularly fine herd of sheep. He approached the rear courtyard, came to the stables and looked in. It was well-kept, neat and tidy, the stalls swept. He didn't see a horse. Then there was a clatter of hooves outside and his mother appeared by the open door on a black gelding and dismounted. She was wearing jeans and a sweater.

'There you are,' she said. 'Is everything all right?'

'Oh, fine, I saw Jack and delivered the mail.'

She started on the saddle and Andy, the stable boy, came out of the kitchen and hurried across. 'I'll do that for you, missus, I was just having my tea.'

'Good man,' Talbot told him. 'Give him a rubdown.' He followed his mother across the yard.

The kitchen was huge and suitably old-fashioned. Hannah Kelly, sorting vegetables by the sink, wiped her hands and came to kiss him.

'God save us, Justin, you look like an Arab.'

'I'd rather not,' he told her. 'It's only tan. With the Ulster rain five times a week, it will soon wear off.'

A young girl named Jane was peeling the potatoes and Emily, the cook, was busy at the stove. 'Hello to everybody,' he said cheerfully. 'Why does it always smell so good in here?' He put an arm around his mother's waist. 'Come on, let's get it over with.'

They went out into the panelled dining room and through to what was called the Great Hall, where an old-fashioned lift stood to one side of a huge staircase rising to a railed gallery above. There was a study, a library, a drawing room, and then, in the centre, a Victorian glass doorway misting over with the heat. Jean Talbot opened it and Justin followed her in.

It was a Victorian jungle, and quite delightful if you liked that sort of thing. Green vines and bushes and exotic flowers everywhere, medium-sized palm trees, the sound of water from a white-and-black tiled fountain;

it ended in a circular area with a statue of Venus on a plinth.

Colonel Henry Talbot sat in his wheelchair, wearing a robe, a white towel around his neck. His grey hair was so sparse that, with the sweat, one could imagine he was bald. A brandy decanter was on the ironwork table beside him and a glass that was a quarter full.

Sitting at a cane table on the other side of the circle was Murphy, the nurse. His head was shaven and he resembled a Buddha in a way; the face very calm, very relaxed, as he sat there in a white coat and read a book.

The heat was incredible and Justin said, 'How can anybody stand this?'

Murphy stood up. 'Is there anything I can do, Madam?'

'How is he?' she raised her voice so that he could hear.

He came forward. 'A little calmer, I think.'

Colonel Henry turned his head and examined her. 'Who the fuck are you?' he demanded, and glanced at Justin. 'And who's this?'

'It's your grandson, Father,' she said.

The man resembled nothing so much as a ghoul with his hollow cheeks and rheumy eyes, as he glared at Justin, his right hand clutching a blackthorn walking stick. Then something sparked in the eyes.

'The bastard,' he cackled. 'The Protestant bastard.'

'Please, Father,' she started to say, and he tried to strike out at her with the blackthorn. She managed to jump out of the way, and Murphy blocked the blow with his right arm.

'That's it,' Justin said. 'I'm out of here. I'm going to have a shower and change into something comfortable. I sincerely hope that I'm not expected to eat with him, because I won't, I'll have it in the kitchen.' He turned and walked out.

Nine-thirty on a weekday night wasn't the busiest time in most London pubs, and the Dark Man on Cable Wharf by the Thames at Wapping was no exception. Harry Salter still had a weakness for the place, for it was where he had started out all those years ago, when he'd realized that more money could be made in business than crime, and you didn't have to constantly run the chance of going down the steps at the Old Bailey for twenty years.

He'd invited everybody round for drinks and supper, Dora's hotpot if they were lucky, and that included Roper. Dillon would be bringing him in the back of the people carrier from Holland Park. Holley got a cab from the Dorchester and arrived just after they did, paid the driver off, then walked to the edge of the wharf and looked across the Thames as a riverboat passed by, ablaze with lights.

He was standing in a place of dark shadows beyond the lights from the pub, and was turning to go, when he saw three young men in track suits jog down from the direction of Wapping High Street. They moved apart, one of them turning into the car park, two of them running along the jetty to where Salter's boat, the *Linda Jones*, was tied up. A few moments later, the one from the car park emerged and went to join the others as they ran back to join him.

Holley regarded them for a moment and then dismissed them, and went into the Dark Man. The Salters sat in their usual corner booth, with Dillon and Harry's two minders, Joe Baxter and Sam Hall, lounging at the bar. Roper sat facing them in his state-of-the-art wheelchair in his favourite reefer coat, his long hair framing the bomb-scarred face.

'Here he is,' Harry said. 'The guy who planned to have us burned down.'

'Well, it didn't work, did it?' Holley said.

'I won't mention it again, old son. Bygones are bygones as far as I'm concerned. What will it be?'

'My Yorkshire half says beer and my Irish half says a Bushmills Whiskey.'

'Good man. I'll join you in that,' Dillon said.

Outside, Kalid Hasim was discussing the situation with his friends, Omar and Sajid. He said, 'The boat's locked up tight. No way of going below. That's where they have things called seacocks. If you open them, water rushes in and the boat will sink.'

'So what do we do?' Omar asked.

'We'll cut the ropes holding it close to the jetty. I've got a good knife. We'll shove it so that the current takes it out into the river. Then a quick run-through the car park, smashing every headlight and car window you can and just keep on running.' He took out a baseball bat that Holley had missed in the dark. The others did likewise.

'Sounds good to me,' Sajid said.

It was then that Hasim made a bad mistake. He said, 'First let's go inside. I want to see how many customers there are, so we know what we're up against.'

'What about the bats?' Omar asked.

'We'll just leave them over there in the corner where that flower trellis is. Nobody will see.'

Holley noticed them as they entered the pub, surveyed the room for a few minutes, then left again. He said, 'Something strange about those three.'

'What would that be?' Roper said.

'I noticed them when I arrived, jogging down from the main road.'

Harry frowned. 'What were they doing?'

'One ran through the car park, the other two went along the jetty to the boat. I couldn't see what they were up to there. The other one joined them for a chat, and I came in.'

'I don't like the sound of that,' Harry Salter said. 'Billy?' Billy was on his feet in an instant and called to Baxter and Hall, 'Let's get moving.' He ran out of the door. Hasim had already sliced through the stern line of the *Linda Jones*, and the stern itself was starting to swing out in the current. Omar had switched on the desk light under the awning, which automatically put on two lights on the prow, something Hasim had not expected.

'What the hell do you bleeders think you're doing?' Billy Salter called, and Baxter and Hall started to run. Billy produced his Walther and fired in the air.

The three young men turned in alarm, and Sajid cried, 'Let's get out of here!'

But there was nowhere to run. The jetty extended for perhaps fifty feet beyond the *Linda Jones*, then stopped abruptly.

'I'm nearly done here,' Hasim told his friends. 'Get on board, Sajid, and we'll shove off.'

But this line was a hawser and much thicker, and Billy fired again, the dull thud of the silenced Walther sounding. 'I'll put you on sticks.'

He took careful aim and Hasim paused, picked up his baseball bat and backed away. 'Come on then, let's be having you.'

It was a brave but futile gesture. Omar jumped into the water and started to swim into the darkness, and Sajid ran at Baxter and Hall, flailing out at them with the baseball bat, catching Baxter on the shoulder. Hall blocked the blow aimed at him and wrenched the baseball bat from Sajid's hand.

Behind them, Harry Salter was approaching, and Dillon and Holley stood in the doorway of the pub. Dillon said, 'I think this could get nasty.'

He half ran across to the jetty and approached the

men. Baxter and Hall had Sajid between them and Baxter was holding the baseball bat in the other hand.

'Give it here,' Harry said. 'I could do with one of those. You okay, Joe?'

'It could be worse. The young bastard didn't break anything.'

'Well, we'll soon fix that. Hold out his left arm.' Sajid tried to struggle, but it was no good. Baxter held him from behind, Hall extended the arm and the baseball bat descended.

Sajid cried out in agony and Harry said, 'Now I think you'll find that's broken. Wapping High Street's where you want to be, St Luke's Hospital. They've got an excellent casualty department. Now get out of my sight.'

Dillon came up behind and Sajid stumbled past him, sobbing. Billy stood confronting Hasim, Walther extended. It made for a dramatic tableau, the deck lights from the *Linda Jones*, the darkness all around, some vessel passing in the distance, the river sounds.

Dillon said, 'Do you think the other one will make it to the other side?'

'I doubt it. I was the original river rat as a kid,' Harry said. 'I know the Thames backwards. Big tide tonight, four-knot current at least. Of course, he could also get run down by a boat out there.' He grinned. 'But I'm not concerned about him. Young punks getting up to a bit of aggravation is one thing, but my nose tells me there's more to this than meets the eye.'

He moved up beside Billy and confronted Hasim,

who crouched defiantly, the baseball bat ready to swing, 'What's your game?'

'Go fuck yourself,' Hasim snarled.

'Don't waste my time. I'm Harry Salter; everybody knows that. I own half of Wapping and you, you maggot, come along here and have a go at a boat I've spent thousands restoring. That isn't your usual petty vandalism; it was a personal attack on me. So who put you up to it?'

'I've told you what you can do.'

'We're wasting time here,' Billy said. 'Let me put a shot in his right kneecap. That should jog his memory.'

Hasim suddenly looked uncertain, but lengthened his double-handed grip on the baseball bat. Dillon pulled out his own Walther and shot the bat out of Hasim's hand, who jumped back in alarm as it bounced on the cobbles of the jetty, rolling towards Harry, who picked it up, examined the splintered end and stood there, holding it.

'Take him,' he said.

Hasim made a sudden move as if to attempt to run past, Baxter tripped him, and he and Hall pulled him up between them. Billy and Dillon put their Walthers away and stood watching.

Harry said, 'Somebody put you up to this, and I want to know who.' Hasim spat at him, Harry took his handkerchief from his breast pocket and wiped his face. 'Very nice that, isn't it? I've had enough. Just hold out his right arm.'

Hasim went crazy, struggling in the grip of the two men. They punched him several times to bring him under control and stretched out his arm.

'Not that,' he screamed, as the bat was raised. 'I'm a boxer.'

Salter was astonished for a moment, then smiled. 'Well, that's good news, because if you don't tell me what I want to hear, I'll break *both* your arms.'

Half sobbing, Hasim couldn't get it out quick enough; he told them everything about his dealings with Lancy.

When he was finished, Harry Salter said, 'And you expect me to believe that's the way this geezer operates: a voice on the phone and payment by mail?'

'I swear it's true,' Hasim said. 'I can't tell you anything else about him. On my mother's life.'

'What does he sound like?' Dillon put in.

'Cockney, no doubt about that, but I think he's Muslim. When he gave me this job, he spoke in Arabic for the first time. It was when he was saying goodbye.'

'And what did he say?' Dillon asked.

'He said Allah is great and Osama is his prophet.'

'Are you sure about that?' Dillon added. 'It should be Mohammed is his prophet.'

'He said Osama.'

Dillon and Billy exchanged glances. Harry tossed the baseball bat into the river. Hasim said, 'What happens now?'

Harry took out his wallet and extracted a fifty-pound note and gave it to him. 'Take that and run after your mate. He won't have got far. Give him a hand to the hospital. It's a good thing for you I'm in a friendly mood. If I see you round here again, I'll kill you.'

Hasim took to his heels, and ran into the darkness, and the others returned to the Dark Man and joined Roper and Holley in the corner booth. Selim Lancy, who had observed everything from his Mercedes parked nearby, got out, put his hearing enhancer in his right ear, and followed. He saw the others settling themselves back in the corner booth. Selim got a pint, went and sat in the next booth, which was unoccupied, and opened an *Evening Standard* he'd been carrying.

'So what happened out there?' Roper demanded.

It was Billy who answered, and it didn't take long. The end of the story was what mattered most. 'Allah is great and Osama is his prophet, that's what he said.'

'Could that mean Al Qaeda's behind it?' Harry asked.

'I'd say definitely. I think we all have to be on our guard from now on.'

'I'm frightened to death, and I'm also starving,' Harry Salter said, and called to Dora, 'What about our supper, love? Bring on the hotpots!'

Lancy left shortly afterwards and called Hasim from the car. When he answered, he said, 'I was there, sitting in a car outside the Dark Man. I saw everything. Where are you now?'

'I just delivered Sajid to St Luke's Hospital. His arm's so badly broken they've admitted him.'

'And your other pal decided to go for a swim?' Lancy shook his head. 'Why didn't Salter break your arm?'

'How the hell would I know?'

'I think you blabbed, my old son. In fact, I was listening to what they were saying in the pub, and I know you did. They know it was Al Qaeda.'

'That isn't true!' Hasim was suddenly desperate. 'I didn't say a word to Salter!'

'You're a dead man, sunshine,' Lancy told him. 'I know you, but you don't know me. Think about it.'

He switched off his mobile and drove away.

At Talbot Place, dinner had been late because Jean had insisted on Jack and Hannah Kelly joining them. 'We'll make an occasion of it,' she told Justin.

She did just that herself, wearing her hair up and finding an attractive dress in green silk by Versace that she hadn't worn for some time. With high-heeled shoes, she looked quietly attractive as she descended the stairs. Justin, who had just gone down himself, greeted her with a glass of Krug, holding one for himself.

'You know what they say.' He smiled. 'If you're tired of champagne, you're tired of life.' He raised his glass. 'To you, Mum, you look absolutely smashing.'

'You don't look too bad yourself.'

He wore a black single-breasted suit, white shirt and

Guards tie, his dark hair cropped. He still had slight stubble on his chin.

She touched it. 'What's this? Did you run out of razor blades?'

'It's the fashion at the moment. I think it's meant to make you look as if you've done things and been places.'

'But you've done both, you idiot.' She shook her head. 'Honestly, men are the end sometimes. Has Jack arrived?'

'He's in the kitchen, where Hannah is running around like a dervish. Young Jane has produced her waitress outfit, black dress and white apron. She looks quite charming.'

'And your grandfather, have you seen him?'

'Must I?' He immediately regretted it. 'I'm so sorry. Callous of me when I think of how much you've put up with.'

Jack Kelly appeared from the dining room, looking slightly old-fashioned in a tweed country suit, soft-collared shirt and knitted tie. 'You look grand, girl,' he told Jean, and kissed her on the cheek.

'An evening for compliments.' She smiled. 'Get him a drink and I'll see how things are coming along in the kitchen.'

Talbot found Kelly a Bushmills Whiskey in the study bar. 'Here's to you, Jack. What you and Hannah have done to support my mother is beyond price.'

'How is he?'

'We'll take a look.'

'Quietly is my advice,' Kelly told him. 'One minute he's sitting there like a living dead man and then, and often for some unknown reason, he explodes into one of his worst moments, screaming obscenities, slashing out with the blackthorn stick. God save us, but he could kill somebody with one of his blows.'

'So I believe.'

In the conservatory, they walked softly along the path. Murphy saw them coming and nodded slightly. Colonel Henry seemed somnolent; his head had fallen to one side and it was shaking slightly.

'Is that enough for you?' Kelly asked.

'What do you think, Jack?' Talbot's face was bleak. 'Let's go and eat.'

The meal was simple but sensational: an onion soup with cheese that wouldn't have disgraced the best of Paris restaurants, lamb chops that were simply superb, cabbage and bacon, Irish-style, and roast potatoes. Young Jane in her waitress outfit acted the part to perfection, serving wine as to the manner born, left hand behind her back.

'I can't remember when I last ate like that,' Justin said as Jane cleared the plates on to a serving trolley.

'Well, it's not over yet,' Hannah told him. 'We've got your special favourite since you were a boy.'

'Emily's apple pie,' Justin said.

At the same moment, there was a disturbance in the

Great Hall, shouting, and then the door burst open. Colonel Henry stood there in his robe, leaning on his stick, looking quite different. He seemed alert, his head up, and his voice was sharp and strong. There was an energy to him.

'So there you are,' he shouted. 'What's all this behind my back?'

Behind him, Murphy moved in. 'Now then, Colonel.' He put a hand on the old man's shoulder. Henry turned and struck out at him with the blackthorn, slashing him across the right arm.

Murphy backed away and Jean moved forward. 'Father, this won't do.' She reached for him, and when she was close enough, he slapped her across the face. 'How dare you touch me, you bitch?' He moved back as Justin took an angry stride towards him.

'And who are you?'

'Your grandson.'

He whirled round with surprising energy, collided with Murphy, knocking him to one side, and crossed the Great Hall, waving his stick and cackling. Justin had moved forward, and Jean and the Kellys followed. The old man got to the stairs, reached for the rail, hauled himself up three steps and paused, turning.

His face was something out of a nightmare, absolutely malevolent as he glared at Justin. 'I know you. You're the Protestant bastard.'

For Justin Talbot, it was enough, and the pain and resentment of a lifetime at the hands of this man erupted in an anguished cry. 'No, Grandfather, I'm the Catholic bastard.'

The words seem to echo around the hall, and Hannah Kelly cried out, 'Oh, God in Heaven.'

Colonel Henry stared at Justin, stood there swaying, his left hand on the banister. 'What did you say?'

Justin spaced each word and said clearly, 'I'm the Catholic bastard.'

Colonel Henry seemed to howl, head back, raised the blackthorn high and struck for Justin's head, at the same time releasing his grip on the banister. Justin stepped to one side and his grandfather fell from the steps to the floor.

Young Emily screamed and everyone seemed to move at once. It was Murphy who reached him first; he dropped to his knees to put him in the recovery position, for there was bleeding from the nose. The eyes weren't closed, but staring rigidly, and it was no surprise when Murphy, feeling for a heartbeat, looked up and shook his head.

'He's gone.'

Jean Talbot, the Kellys and young Jane stood there in a kind of tableau, Jane crying. Justin said, 'That's it, then. We'd better call Dr Ryan. There will be things to do.'

Jean said in a strangely calm voice, 'I'll see to that now.' She took a mobile from her handbag and walked back into the dining room, and Hannah and Jane followed. Murphy had picked up Colonel Henry's shawl and now he covered him with it. He turned to look at Justin.

'He's better out of it, Major Talbot,' he said. 'He was like a man possessed. It wasn't his fault.'

'Really?' Justin said. 'Well, I suppose it's a point of view.' He turned to Kelly. 'Are you all right, Jack?'

'Is it true, Justin?' Kelly asked.

'It was my father's dying wish, so my mother had me baptized a Catholic and kept quiet about it. Only Mary Ellen knew. Certainly not me. I've only discovered it recently. Would you care for a drink?'

'I don't think so. I'll go and see to the ladies.'

'Well, I could.'

He went to the study bar, poured himself three fingers of whiskey, went and sat in a club chair and looked up at the painting of his grandfather as a Grand Master in the Orange Lodge.

'Mad as a hatter,' he said. 'So what does that say about me?' And he swallowed the whiskey straight down.

Doctor Larry Ryan, summoned to view the body, had no hesitation in concluding that Colonel Henry Talbot had died of a heart attack. He had, after all, been the dead man's physician for some twelve years.

In the circumstances, he had consulted the local coroner, who had concluded that there was no need for an inquest, which could only cause distress to what was, after all, the most important family in that part of the county. With the coroner's permission, Ryan phoned a funeral firm in Newry to come and receive the body, which Tod Murphy, with his strength, had carried reverently into the study and placed on the large sofa. Hannah Kelly, Jean behind her, appeared with fresh sheets and covered him. Jack Kelly looked on, accompanied by Father Michael Cassidy who, informed by Kelly, had immediately driven up from the Presbytery.

He stood by the body, murmuring a prayer, and Justin Talbot appeared from the study, a glass of whiskey in his hand. 'Ah, there you are, Father,' he said. 'Bad news or good news, depending on your point of view, spreads quickly.'

'I'm here to offer what solace I can,' the old man said.

'If that means to me personally as a newly discovered member of your flock, you're wasting your time. The whole wide world can know I'm a Catholic, there's no shame in it, and my mother meant well. As far as I'm concerned, nothing's changed. I haven't suddenly discovered God or anything.'

'Justin – please.' His mother was distressed.

'Well, let's face facts,' Justin told her. 'We can hardly bury him in the cemetery at Holy Name with the monument to the Sons of the IRA dominating the scene.'

Alcohol affected him in the strangest of ways, and always had. His version of drunkenness was quite different from other people's. He became ice-cold, hard; not reckless, but calculating, and instant violence

138

was there just beneath the surface if he did not get his way.

'But what is your alternative?' Father Cassidy asked.

Justin turned to Dr Ryan. 'There's a crematorium at Castlerea, isn't there, Larry, with some sort of chapel?'

'Yes, that's true,' Ryan said.

'Can I presume they'll do a Protestant burial service as good as anywhere else?'

'Of course, but the crematorium service is meant to handle relatively few people, just family and close friends.' Ryan hesitated, but went on, 'There would be those who might not consider it appropriate in the case of such a prominent man.'

'You mean we should expect Ulster Unionist MPs from Stormont, and the Orange Lodge marching behind the hearse complete with a drum and pipe band?' Justin shook his head. 'I'm head of the Talbot family now and I want it over and done with. The crematorium it is.' He turned to his mother. 'Does any of this give you a problem?'

Jean Talbot seemed all hollow cheeks and infinite sadness. 'You must do as you see fit, Justin. I'm going upstairs for a while. I suddenly feel rather tired.'

He put an arm round her. 'Leave everything to me. I've phoned Gibson in Belfast, his old campaign manager. He'll notify the party, so Ulster Television will get their hands on it – and the BBC. It will be a circus for a while, but everything passes.'

The front door bell sounded. 'That should be the funeral people,' Jack Kelly said.

'The last people I want to see,' Jean said, and hurried across the Great Hall to head upstairs.

No more than forty minutes or so later it was strangely calm. The funeral people had departed with the body, Dr Ryan had moved on, and Father Cassidy had also left. Justin Talbot was back in the study, pouring another whiskey at the bar when Kelly appeared.

'Do you want that drink now?' Justin asked.

'Why not? Hannah's just finishing in the kitchen. She intends to stay. Your mother will need her. I'll walk back over the estate. It'll give me time to think; there's a full moon.' He accepted his whiskey. 'Big changes, Justin.'

Talbot nodded, looking up at the painting of his grandfather over the fireplace. 'That will have to go, for starters. Maybe the Orange Lodge will find a place for it.'

'Who knows?' Kelly said.

'Let me see you off. It's been a hell of a day, Jack.' And he led him out.

At Holland Park, Roper had dozed off in his wheelchair for a good two hours. He woke to find Sergeant Doyle looking concerned.

'Are you okay, Major?'

'Aches and pains, Tony.' He checked the time. 'No wonder: two o'clock in the morning. Mug of tea, please.'

He lit a forbidden cigarette and checked his screens for the overnight news, and there it was, the death of Colonel Henry Talbot. He hesitated, then called Ferguson on his Codex, who replied at once and sounded perfectly civil.

'Is it something important, Roper? We'll be landing in an hour and a half.'

'Two o'clock in the morning here, General, and a news report's beginning to filter through which I thought might interest you. Colonel Henry Talbot died a few hours ago at Talbot Place in County Down.'

'Did he, by Jove?'

'What do you think will happen now?'

'My dear old chum, General Sir Hadley Chase will bow out gracefully as Chairman of the company and Justin Talbot will become an extremely wealthy man. Eight hundred million, I hear. Thanks for letting me know. We'll talk later, I'm sure.'

'Before you say over and out, there's also been an incident you'll want to know about.'

'Then tell me about it.' Roper told him about what had happened at the Dark Man and, when he was finished, Ferguson said, 'Damn sinister, wouldn't you agree?'

'The hint of Al Qaeda certainly makes one think.'

'More than a hint,' Ferguson said. 'Allah is great and Osama is his Prophet. That would seem a clear indication to me.'

'I agree, General. Though to many Muslims, it would be counted as blasphemy.'

141

'You've got a point. All I can say is, it would be sensible for us to conclude that we are being targeted and act accordingly. We'll talk about it when I return, but I want all of you to take care.'

Doyle brought the tea and Roper sat there, considering the matter. Eight hundred million. It didn't bear thinking about, so he dismissed it and went back to the news.

PAKISTAN

———

NORTH-WEST FRONTIER

PESHAWAR

6

It was eight-thirty in the morning as the Gulfstream descended towards Pakistan. As Holley had said, Peshawar International wasn't the biggest of airports, but it did belong to the modern world. The mountains of Afghanistan and the North-West Frontier made an impressive backdrop and, unusually, a railway crossing stood at the end of the main runway.

'What about that?' Miller said to Ferguson as they peered out.

'Days of the Raj, I suppose.' Ferguson suddenly felt nostalgic.

They landed, and Squadron Leader Laccy, following instructions from the tower, taxied to a corner of the airport where two Chinook helicopters were parked. The ground personnel who waved them in wore air-force overalls.

Ferguson and Miller got out of the Gulfstream, and

Lacey and Parry joined them, passing out the luggage. A few yards away, two army officers were engaged in conversation and turned to greet them. One was a Captain wearing a khaki summer uniform, a line of medal ribbons above his left pocket, carrying a swagger stick. He was a handsome man, possibly Pathan, although he was wearing a cap, not a turban, and the belt at his waist carried a holstered Browning pistol.

'General Ferguson, Major Miller.' He saluted. 'A pleasure to meet you. My name is Abu Salim, Military Police. I'm here to welcome you and take you to see my commanding officer, Colonel Ahmed Atep.'

'Very civil of you, Captain.' Ferguson shook hands.

Salim turned to Lacey and Parry. 'My colleague, Lieutenant Hamid, will see to your needs, gentlemen. There is a guesthouse close by which takes care of visiting pilots.'

Lacey turned to Ferguson. 'We'll get a full engine check and refuel, sir. We'll be ready to move on whenever you like.'

'Very good.' Ferguson turned to Salim. 'Ready when you are, Captain. Customs, immigration, security.

Salim picked up his bag. 'Good God, no.' He smiled. 'Diplomatic privilege. If you could manage your bag, Major Miller.'

He walked across the tarmac to a gate between hangars. The two soldiers waiting patiently were Military Police Sergeants in crisp khaki uniforms, both bearded and wearing scarlet turbans.

'I must say they look perfectly splendid,' Ferguson said. 'They certainly look imposing.'

'Our own version of a British Army redcap,' Salim said. 'It's supposed to intimidate the tribesmen. Colonel Atep insisted on trying it out. Sergeants Said and Nasser.'

The two men saluted, picked up the bags, walked out of the gate into the parking area and approached an armoured vehicle. There were three banks of seats. A canvas roof rolled back to cover the rear two, which was necessary because of the general-purpose machine gun mounted on the front beside the driver. It was painted in a wavy khaki pattern, a sort of desert camouflage.

'What is this?' Ferguson asked.

'A Sultan armoured reconnaissance car.' It was Miller who answered. 'Where did you get it?'

'The Russians left more than a few lying around when they left Afghanistan. We got hold of what we could. The armour is stronger than it looks. It gives some sort of protection against improvised explosive devices. A damn sight more than a Jeep or a Land Rover gets.'

The luggage was stacked at the back, Ferguson and Miller took the rear seat, the Captain the second, half turning towards them so they could talk. Said sat at the gun and Nasser took the wheel and drove away.

'Nothing like I imagined, Peshawar,' Ferguson observed. 'Far bigger.'

'It used to be about five hundred and fifty thousand people,' Salim said, 'but it's more now. Lots of refugees from the tribal areas.'

The congestion in the streets was incredible. Every kind of vehicle – from ageing taxis to motor rickshaws, mopeds and light motorcyles, sometimes with two passengers on the pillion seat, hanging on to each other and the driver – thronged the road. Hundreds of people on bicycles weaved between market stalls, mounting pavements where there was one. The military and police presence was very visible.

Salim said, 'There's a war out there, and not just over the border in Afghanistan, but in the tribal areas. This is a military city now. It has to be. We can't say the barbarians are at the gates, but real trouble waits out there. If you and the Americans lose to the Taliban, God help my country.'

'I think you have a point,' Ferguson said.

The Captain nodded. 'Military Police Headquarters coming up, General.' The Sultan swung in between sentries guarding a wide double gate, drove towards an imposing three-storeyed building with a red-tiled roof and a pillared front door that looked as if it might have been a relic of Empire. Ferguson and Miller got out and stood looking at it.

'I know,' Salim said. 'It used to be quite impressive. This way, gentlemen.'

*　*　*

Colonel Ahmed Atep was sitting behind his desk examining some papers and managing to look busy, when Selim ushered them into the office. He jumped to his feet, came round the table and shook hands.

'General Ferguson, Major Miller. What an honour. Be seated, please. Perhaps you would care for some tea?'

'A kind thought, but after such a long flight, the prospect of a shower and a good hotel have quite a pull,' Ferguson said. 'Especially breakfast.'

'Of course, but sit down for a moment. I shan't keep you long. First, I've allocated Captain Abu Salim to take care of you during your visit. One of my finest young officers. A Sandhurst man.'

Salim managed a modest look and Ferguson said, 'So we have something in common.' He carried on, 'This is only a flying visit, Colonel. A day, two at the most, then we'll carry on to Islamabad.'

Which wasn't true, but Atep appeared to accept it. 'You wish to visit the Afghan border area, I believe?'

'Certainly. In London, we hear all sorts of stories about arms-smuggling, obviously to the benefit of the Taliban.'

'Grossly exaggerated,' Atep said. 'We have had considerable success in stemming that flow.'

'And people?' Miller queried. 'Passing over illegally to offer their services to the Taliban? We have evidence that British Muslims are engaged in the fighting over there.'

'Newspaper stories, rumour. If such individuals exist, they will be very few.'

Ferguson decided to take a chance. 'Does the name "Shamrock" mean anything to you?'

Atep managed to keep a straight face. 'No – should it?' He turned to Salim. 'What about you?'

Salim shook his head and answered, 'No, I've never heard the name before.'

'It seems we can't help,' Atep said. 'But I understand you wish to speak with two men called Dak Khan and José Fernandez?'

'That's right,' Ferguson told him, without elaborating.

Colonel Atep picked up a flimsy. 'Fernandez has been called to Lahore. His mother is a Muslim and is ill. Cancer, I understand.'

Ferguson said, 'And Dak Khan?'

'Captain Salim will see to that for you, just as he will also see you to your hotel. He is yours to command, General. Look on him as your military aide for the duration of your visit.'

'Most kind, Colonel,' Ferguson told him, and turned. Then Salim ushered them out.

They got into the Sultan, and Salim said to Sergeant Nasser, 'The Palace.' As they drove out of the gate, he said, 'An old, old hotel from the days of the Raj. For years it was called the Indian Palace, but as local people always called it just the Palace, it was easy to

150

make it official. The manager is simply known as Ali Hamid to everyone. It is on the edge of town, by the river.'

'It sounds like just the thing,' Ferguson said. 'How long have you been in the army, Captain?'

'I did one year at university, applied for the army at nineteen, and was accepted at Sandhurst. I am twenty-seven.' He half turned to Miller. 'We have met before, Major. Your lectures on counter-terrorism were hugely appreciated by all of us.'

'That is good to know.' Miller shook his hand.

'The matter I raised with Colonel Atep, the question of British Muslims serving with the Taliban? Colonel Atep dismissed it as newspaper stories,' Ferguson said, 'and of little account. I know it's unfair to expect you to contradict your commanding officer.'

'In this case, it's easy,' Salim said. 'No disrespect to the Colonel, but we hear the reports often.'

'And the name Shamrock?' Miller asked. 'You said it meant nothing to you.'

'And it doesn't, apart from the fact that it's the Irish national emblem.'

But at that moment, they arrived at the entrance to a wonderful old Colonial-style building surrounded by a high wall. They turned in through the arched entrance and drove along through an enchanting garden to a wide terrace where a double door stood open. The man standing there waiting to greet them was large and imposing. His iron-grey hair was tied in a ponytail and his beard reached his chest. He wore a black ankle-length cotton kaftan.

They went up the steps and he salaamed, his hand touching his forehead. 'Gentlemen, I am Ali Hamid. Welcome. My house is yours.'

An hour later, after being shown to their rooms, unpacking, showering and changing, Ferguson and Miller went downstairs, and were directed to a back terrace with a fine view over the river, where they found no difficulty in ordering a full English breakfast.

Abu Salim came in as they were eating. 'Are you going to have something?' Ferguson asked.

'I already have, while you were upstairs. I've been talking to the Orderly Sergeant in my office to make sure he can cope while I'm dealing with you gentlemen.' The waiter approached and he ordered tea. 'We were side-tracked after you asked me about Shamrock.'

'So I was.' Ferguson looked at Miller. 'What do you think?'

'He's a Sandhurst man.'

'Of course he is.' Ferguson reached for the marmalade. 'Tell him, Harry.'

Salim took it all in, listening intently, and when Miller was finished, said, 'A fantastic business. But what do you expect to find, here in Peshawar?'

'Not very much, but I prefer to see for myself what a situation looks like instead of just thinking about it. It's eleven miles from here to the Khyber Pass. Over that border, the war is real and earnest, and Shamrock exists.'

'And where does Dak Khan come in?'

'A colleague of mine in London tells me he's a thoroughly unsavoury arms dealer who operates in this area.'

'Oh, I know him well, and he is more than unsavoury. He would sell his sister's favours in a house of pleasure if there was money in it.'

'My friend has discussed our problems with Khan, who's willing to help. We're in your hands.'

'All right, we'll go and see him. May I assume that you are both armed?'

'Absolutely,' Ferguson told him.

'Good.'

Dak Khan's house was a mile further down the river, a rambling old bungalow with a tiled roof. The courtyard was large, with a Jeep and a medium-sized truck parked there. Four men in soiled and dusty clothes, wearing turbans, sat against the wall smoking. They ignored Salim and the others, and when Salim was close enough, he kicked a man with a walleye.

'Get on your feet, you dog,' he said in English. 'Where is your master?'

'No need for that, Captain,' a voice called from inside the open door. 'I shall give him the whipping he deserves. Please come in.'

Dak Khan was of medium height, but squat. He wore a soiled white shirt and a shabby fawn suit with a red cummerbund. His hair was greasy, his face brown, and he had a thick black moustache which somehow looked false.

The room was surprisingly sparse; an empty fireplace with a couch on either side, a couple of coffee tables, several cane chairs, and a desk, where Khan now seated himself.

'Please be seated, gentlemen, and tell me how I may help you.'

'Don't let's beat about the bush,' Ferguson told him. 'My friend, Daniel Holley, tells me that when it comes to what's going on over the border in Afghanistan, you're the expert.'

'True, but what's in it for me?'

'I'll pay well. What's your price?'

'That depends on what it is you want to know.'

'Shamrock,' Ferguson said. 'Who is he and, more to the point, where is he? Do you know these things?'

'Of course I do.'

Ferguson was so surprised that he paused, and it was Miller who said, 'How much?'

'Ten thousand pounds.'

Captain Abu Salim said, 'What a creature you are, Dak Khan. Don't listen to him, General.'

'No, let him speak,' Ferguson said. 'How do I know you would deliver?'

'I would come with you: this I promise.'

'I don't believe you,' Salim said.

'You can accompany them, bring your men.' He shrugged. 'I can only do one more thing to prove myself. As I doubt that you have ten thousand pounds in your wallet, I will accept your word that you will pay me later.'

Ferguson looked at Miller, then Salim. 'What can I say, except let's do it.'

Dak stood up. 'Then let us, as you English say, shake hands on it.' His palm felt limp and sweaty and Ferguson withdrew his hand quickly. 'So what happens now?'

'You come back for me in two hours. I must put my affairs in order. I will go with you then, I promise.'

Ferguson nodded reluctantly, and he and Miller went out. The four men had departed; the Jeep had gone. Dak Khan came to the door, and Abu Salim prodded him with his swagger stick.

'Let us down and I'll put you out of business for good.' He went across to the Sultan, joined the others and was driven away.

Dak Khan spat in the dust and went back inside, where he called Colonel Atep on his mobile. 'They've just visited me.'

'Tell me what happened.'

'Ferguson asked me if I knew Shamrock and I told him I did, which I don't. In fact, I've never heard of him.'

'So what do you intend?'

'I'll take them to a house I know in the back country, where I believe I can guarantee a hostile reception. Let's face it, it happens all the time these days in the border area.'

'This is the most important task I have asked you to perform, given to me by Osama's personal representative in London, the Preacher. So, it is very, very important that you succeed.'

'Of course. I know exactly what I'm doing. There is only one problem. Captain Abu Salim and his two Sergeants will certainly be in the line of fire: is this acceptable?'

'As you say, things happen all the time in the border area. Salim is a nothing. He sees things entirely differently from you and me. With Osama's blessing on you, your success is assured.'

Noon: the sun high in the sky, with a wind that stirred the sand. On leaving the city, they joined a convoy of civilian trucks, many of them garishly decorated, military or police vehicles constantly overtaking each of them on the short stretch up to the Khyber Pass. Some time before they got there, under instructions from Khan, Sergeant Nasser turned off on to a well-worn track.

Salim, seated beside Khan, half turned to Ferguson and Miller. 'Federal law only applies on the main road and ten yards on either side. Elsewhere, tribal laws apply.'

Dak Khan said, 'I call this the wilderness.' They passed a small village of four or five mud houses. Two robed men stood by a well watching them, showing no emotion, staring. 'These people are very poor, they have nothing, so they would kill you if they had the chance.'

'Never mind that,' Salim said. 'Where are we going?'

'About eight miles more.' Dak turned his head and added, 'Our destination is very close to the border.'

It was a barren, undulating plain drifting towards the mountains. Dust rose from the burnt, parched land, and Ferguson, holding a handkerchief to his mouth and coughing, said, 'God in heaven, how can anyone live here?'

Khan was wearing a battered Panama hat and a long cotton scarf around his neck, which he occasionally pulled up to his nose.

'It is the will of Allah, it is all they know, General, and we are here.'

Over to the left, the ground lifted to a hillock on which stood a sizeable two-storeyed house that had been painted white at some time. There was an extended wall of mud bricks around it, and windows with wooden shutters, partially open.

A man in blue-and-white robes stood in the yard beside a well, a bucket in one hand and some goats beside him. He looked, turned quickly, opened the front door and stepped inside. The goats came out on to the hillock, bleating, and two or three rough-looking sheep appeared around the side of the house.

A line of stones on either side marked the track up to the house, and beside the entrance, from what passed as a road, was a thorn tree, burnt black by the sun, a dead monument to a dead world.

As Nasser turned the Sultan into the track, Khan said, 'Stop here by the tree.'

Said stood up at the machine gun and charged it, leaning on the frame, looking up towards the house, and Dak Khan took out his mobile and dialled a number.

He spoke in English. 'It's me. Everything is okay. We want to come up to the house.' He listened and then turned. 'He's afraid of the machine gun; he's not certain of our good faith.' He paused, listening again, then said, 'Okay, if that's the way you want it.'

'What's happening?' Ferguson asked.

'He's suspicious. He wants you to stay here and me to go up to the house to establish my credentials.' He shrugged, 'That's the only way he'll do it, otherwise he says you can go away.'

Ferguson turned to Captain Salim, 'What do you think?'

'Well, as we've come this far, let's humour the man.' He said to Said, 'Swing the machine gun on its pivot to cover the house.' He opened the door and got out, and Khan followed him. 'It's all yours. We'll cover you.'

Dak Khan took off his Panama, wiped his face with

the scarf and managed a smile. 'I'm sure everything will be fine.'

He started up the track, and three of the goats came to meet him. Salim, binoculars around his neck, raised them and scanned the house.

'The inside of the place is very dark. No sign of any movement.' He paused. 'Yes, I think there's someone there.'

Dak Khan had reached the house, paused, and the door was opened. As he stepped inside, there was a brief flash of white, and then the door closed again.

'So now we wait,' Ferguson said, and Miller opened the door on his side to get out.

As he did so, a shot was fired, a sharp and peculiar cracking sound that echoed in the desert heat. It caught Sergeant Said in the side of the head, his scarlet turban flying into the air as he was catapulted over the side of the Sultan. Nasser's reflex action was to open the door at his side and attempt to scramble out. Three very quick shots, all making that same peculiar cracking sound, hit him in his neck and back, driving him down to collapse over the body of his comrade.

There were three more quick shots, two smashing the windscreen, flying glass cascading over Abu Salim as he crouched beneath the machine gun, another deflected by armour plating.

There was blood on his face from several cuts, and Ferguson slipped out of the rear seat and joined Miller, crouching behind the Sultan.

'Do you know what that thing is?' Miller demanded.

'Another relic of the Soviets in Afghanistan. A Dragunov automatic sniper rifle. Absolutely deadly with a competent marksman.'

'What in hell do we do?' Ferguson asked.

'Let's try this.' Crouched right down, Salim reached up to the handle of the machine gun, swung it round in the general direction of the house, and gave it a long burst.

Then he scrambled across and found the others. There was another shot from the Dragunov and, as the echoes died away, Salim flattened himself against the ground and peered cautiously round the Sultan to the house.

Ferguson said, 'What the hell is going on?'

The Dragunov fired again, several times, and was joined by another weapon, a different sound. 'An AK47,' Miller said. 'I'd know that anywhere.'

Salim said, 'Help me drop the back flap. I think you'll find I have a surprise for them.'

There was additional ammunition for the machine gun, and flares of one kind and another, but, most important, half-a-dozen rocket-propelled grenades.

'You're familiar with this weapon, Major?' Salim asked Miller.

'Yes, and I can't wait to try it out.'

They crouched together, aided by the fact that the canvas roof covered the back-seat portion of the Sultan. Salim helped him adjust the tube over his right shoulder, Miller straightened and fired. The grenade exploded to the right of the front door. There were flames, and smoke billowed, but there was also another burst from the Dragunov.

'My turn,' Salim said. Chancing it, he stood up, took careful aim, and the grenade went straight through the front door.

They went up the track cautiously and paused a few yards away. The house was a total wreck, half the roof gone, and parts of it were still burning. The first dead man they came to, lying on his back, was the man with the walleye from Khan's house, and it was obvious that the other three were his companions, although damaged so badly that no one could have recognized them.

The rest of the room had suffered badly but, as they stood there, there was a groaning sound from the very back by a door that led to the rear of the house. Legs were sticking out from under a mass of debris and, when Miller and Salim cleared it, they found Dak Khan.

He was soaked in blood, obviously dying, and yet he still spoke, gasping a little. When Abu Salim knelt to check him, Khan grabbed him by the front of his uniform.

'It's all that bastard Atep's fault.'

Salim knelt on one knee. 'Why do you say that?'

'He's the one. Acting on orders from an Al Qaeda man in London. Someone called the Preacher.'

Ferguson said, 'Does he know what he's saying?'

'It would seem so,' Abu Salim said, and returned to Dak Khan. 'You're certain of this?'

'He pressured me again and again to do his dirty work. Who can say no to Al Qaeda?'

He was weakening, and Salim continued, 'What about Shamrock?'

'He exists. Atep told me. Also said General Ferguson was being too nosy and needed dealing with.' He looked up at Ferguson and Miller. 'He said you'd done a great deal of harm to Al Qaeda.'

'So he definitely wanted us dead,' Miller said.

'Oh, yes, and not only you two.' He glanced at Abu Salim. 'I asked about you and your men getting in the line of fire. He told me there was no problem. He said you were a nothing.' He seemed to swallow and whispered, 'He said with Osama's blessing, success was assured.'

There was no death rattle, he simply closed his eyes and died. Salim stood up and Ferguson said, 'What the hell happens now?'

'Let's go back to the Sultan and talk before we leave,' Salim said. 'We need to get our story straight.'

'Do we?' Charles Ferguson said, glancing at Miller. 'Well, that should be interesting.'

Indeed it was as, back at the Sultan, Salim called Colonel Atep on his mobile and reported in. 'Bad news, sir. That swine Dak Khan sold us out. Took us to a house up country where he insisted Shamrock would be, and we were attacked by four of his men.'

Seated at his desk, Ahmed Atep managed to control himself. 'What happened to General Ferguson and Major Miller?'

'They're fine, Colonel, and – except for being cut up a bit – so am I. I lost my two Sergeants, but we managed to kill Khan and four villains in his employ.'

'And he's definitely dead?'

'I'm afraid so, Colonel, but it does mean we avoid the fuss of a public trial, which means that, considering the importance of our guests, it will be much easier to treat the whole unfortunate matter as if it had never happened.'

With considerable relief, Colonel Atep grasped at the straw. 'Excellent, you've done well, Captain. I'll have a medical Chinook with you in thirty minutes.' The mobile went silent.

'You're a marvel, Captain,' Ferguson said. 'This means we can make our return this evening. You handled the call to Atep brilliantly.'

'Thank you, General. Excuse my presumption, but I had got the impression you wanted to keep this whole Shamrock business as low-key as possible, and so I told the Colonel what I knew he wanted to hear under the circumstances. I'm only sorry your journey has been in vain.'

'But it hasn't,' said Miller. 'We now know about that Al Qaeda man in London known as the Preacher.'

'Which could be useful.' Ferguson smiled and glanced up at the noise of the approaching helicopter. 'How's

that for service? There must have been one in the
vicinity.'

Ahmed Atep had come himself, in the helicopter, all
affability and charm and concern. The ambush by
Taliban, which is what it swiftly became in the retelling,
reflected well on his command, and he accompanied
them to the military hospital, where they were checked
thoroughly, Abu Salim needing twenty stitches, the windscreen having done its worst.

After consultation with Lacey, it was decided that a
suitable time to leave would be ten o'clock. Colonel
Atep insisted on giving them a farewell dinner at the
Palace. The news that they had been attacked in the
border country had leaked, as these things do, and
Hamid had pulled out all the stops to give them the
most extraordinary meal on the terrace.

Ahmed Atep was bonhomie itself, the life and soul
of the party, while Abu Salim, with his scarred face,
was much quieter.

The Colonel patted him on the shoulder. 'Come, my
boy, cheer up. You're quite the hero. They'll be impressed
in Islamabad. Who knows, a promotion could be in the
offing.'

'It's kind of you to say so, Colonel, I was only doing
my duty,' Salim said.

Atep glanced at his watch. 'Ah, you must be on your
way. You'll forgive me for not seeing you off to the

164

airport. I have another appointment. I trust your luggage is being taken care of?'

'I'll see to it,' Salim said. 'Excuse me.'

He got up and went out and the bill was discreetly presented to the Colonel, who waved it away to be put on his account. They all went out to the hall, where Salim waited, and said their goodbyes.

Colonel Atep went down the steps to where his Porsche 911 was parked. He waved, got in and drove away.

'He loves that car above all things,' Salim said. 'It's his virility system. He will drive it from here for exactly thirty minutes to that "appointment" at his favourite house of pleasure.'

'How interesting,' Ferguson said.

'Isn't it?' Abu Salim smiled. 'And now let me see you off.'

It wasn't particularly busy, and they walked through the concourse towards the private departure section for VIPs, where they could see Parry waiting, talking to some security man in uniform.

'There he is,' Ferguson said. 'We'll be on our way before you know it. Have a little champagne when we get on board, Harry, eh? That'll be nice.'

The security man's mobile sounded. He answered it and seemed to go rigid, then turned at once to Salim. 'Terrible news, Captain, that was headquarters. Colonel Ahmed Atep has just been blown up in his car!'

Salim barely managed a frown with his scarred face. 'Tell them I'll be there at once. But first I must see our guests off.'

The security man nodded, then hurried away, speaking into the mobile. Ferguson said to Parry, 'Lead the way.' They passed outside and walked towards the Gulfstream, which waited, steps down. 'Do carry on, Parry. We'll only be a moment.'

He and Miller turned to face Salim, and Ferguson looked at him gravely. 'A terrible business, Captain.'

'Car bombs are one of the curses of our age,' Abu Salim said. 'A block of Semtex, a fifteen-minute timer.' He shrugged. 'No one is safe any more.'

'I suppose not. You're a remarkable young man,' Ferguson told him, and went up the steps.

Miller held out his hand and Salim took it for a moment. 'I've always remembered one thing in particular from your counter-terrorism lectures at Sandhurst, Major.'

'And what would that be?'

'That in the world of today, the only rule is that there are no rules.'

He walked away. Miller turned and went up the steps, the door closed, and a few minutes later the Gulfstream moved away.

LONDON

NORTHERN IRELAND

7

It was ten o'clock in the morning when Dillon and Holley turned up at Holland Park and found Roper in his usual place.

'You're late for breakfast,' Roper said.

'We've already had it,' Dillon said. 'Daniel and I had a night out. First Le Caprice. Wonderful food. Finished in the bar at the Dorchester with far too much champagne, then retired upstairs where my friend, being appallingly rich, has booked one of those Park Suites with two bedrooms.'

'What about the hangovers?'

'We don't indulge in those. I'm Irish and Daniel is half-Irish and his other half is Yorkshire, the biggest beer drinkers in the world.' Dillon grinned and, as Tony Doyle entered, said, 'Any chance of one of your big mugs of tea, Tony?'

'Coming right up, Mr Dillon.'

Daniel Holley had pulled a chair forward, sat down on it and started to scan the computer screens. Something caught his eye, and he said, 'What's this about Talbot International?'

'Colonel Henry Talbot passed on last night,' Roper said. 'It'll mean Justin Talbot will want the Chairman's seat for himself.'

'Which makes sense. The ultimate job for the man who's got everything. If you don't mind, Roper, let's have a look at him.'

Roper turned up a family history, which was considerable, stretching back to the Talbots' first appearance in Northern Ireland from Wales in the late seventeenth century.

'Scroll through,' Dillon said. 'Just show us glamour boy.'

Roper did as he was asked, but said, 'Why do you call him that?'

'Because he's too good to be true.' A photo came up of Talbot receiving his Military Cross from the Queen, a dazzling smile on his face.

'You can't argue with his service record,' Roper pointed out. 'Both Gulf Wars, Bosnia and Kosovo, two tours in Afghanistan, badly wounded and decorated during the second.'

Dillon said, 'No Irish time, what do you make of that?'

'Could be he opted out of service there.'

'But it was still a matter of choice,' Dillon told him.

'Somehow it doesn't fit the hero image. I bet if you started digging online, as only you can, you'd probably turn something up.'

'I'll see what I can do.'

A picture of Jean Talbot and Justin appeared on the screen and Holley said, 'Now there's a nice-looking lady.'

'Jean Talbot, his mother.' Roper's fingers moved. 'Here's her background.'

'Clever lady,' Holley said. 'Oxford and the Slade.'

'And look at the results,' Dillon pointed out. 'She won the Hollyfield Award for her portrait of the Queen Mother. Visiting Professor in Fine Art at London University.' He shook his head. 'I didn't think Colonel Henry had it in him to produce someone like that.'

'I'd say her mother had more effect than he did,' Roper said. 'Ah, here we are. Twenty-first of July, Nineteen sixty-four, delivered of a son named Justin Talbot. No entry for name of father.'

'Her privilege,' Holley said. 'Not to name the father. Could be all sorts of reasons.'

'I wonder how Colonel Henry took it?' Dillon said. 'At least he got an heir bearing his name.'

'Here we go: there's more,' Roper said. 'She bought a house in Marley Court, Mayfair, on the thirteenth of August, that year.' He nodded. 'So she was raising her son in London, not Ulster.'

'Probably didn't want her beloved father anywhere

near the boy,' Dillon said. 'We'll leave you to it and indulge in a workout in the gym, followed by a sauna. Don't forget to turn over Talbot's dubious past.'

Information of the type that Roper sought was impossible for most people to obtain, but Roper wasn't most people. Two hours of patient probing finally produced a result, and it was a treasure trove. He was sitting there when they returned.

'You seem deep in thought,' Dillon said.

'I've a lot to think about.'

'Justin Talbot?'

'I've printed it out. You can read it, but I wonder whether I should put a match to it.'

'As bad as that?' Dillon said.

Roper pressed his buzzer for Doyle. 'A first-rate soldier just doing what they told him to do, I suppose.' Doyle appeared and he said, 'Toilet, Tony, shower, clean everything, shirt and track suit.'

'Right, sir, let's go,' Doyle said.

'It's the jobs he handled on his own that I find astonishing,' Roper said to Dillon. 'A one-man killing machine. But you'll see for yourself.'

He switched on his wheelchair and cruised out, Doyle walking beside him.

* * *

Dillon read it, then poured himself a whiskey while Holley worked through it. 'What do you think?' Dillon asked.

Holley handed the report back. 'You and I have done as much. We're not soldiers of virtue, Sean, we are soldiers of fortune. A bad thing happened to me a long time ago and my response changed me forever, and made me what I am. I don't do it for money, I have money.' He shrugged. 'As long as it's bad people I'm up against, I don't care. I'm certainly not going to condemn Justin Talbot for what he's done. Every IRA member I've known told me he was fighting a war. That's exactly what Talbot was doing, only it was for the other side.'

Dillon smiled reluctantly. 'You're right, damn you.'

An Ulster Television news flash appeared on one of the screens, and a reporter in a dark suit read, 'The death of Colonel Henry Talbot at his home in County Down last night may seem by many to symbolize the end of an era of extreme politics for which there is no longer a place in Northern Ireland.'

'Well, that's telling them,' Dillon said.

The reporter continued, 'The funeral will be for family and friends only and followed by cremation.'

The news moved on and Dillon said, 'No Orange Order, no marching bands?' He shook his head. 'Just like the poet said, Daniel. *This is the way the world ends. Not with a bang but a whimper.*'

'Maybe the family didn't like all that kind of thing in the first place. Maybe Justin's just trying to make a fresh start. You noticed they didn't give a where or when for the funeral.'

'You're right,' Dillon said. 'But I know where I can find out.'

'And where would that be?' Holley asked.

'My uncle on my mother's side, Mickeen Oge Flynn, lives at Collyban. I grew up there after my mother passed on, until my father took me to live in London when I was twelve. Mickeen is close to eighty now, but still runs a small garage with one mechanic who's been with him for years, a man named Paddy O'Rourke.'

'They sound like something out of an old Abbey Theatre play in Dublin.'

'Don't mock. I'm off to the library for some peace and quiet where I can have a word with him.'

Flynn's Garage was on the edge of Collyban, and with its ancient pumps and concourse of cracked cement, it was probably as ancient as Mickeen Oge himself, a small, tough old man in a tweed suit and cap. He was badly needing a shave, but there was nothing new in that. The doors were up and the garage was surprisingly large, with four different old motor cars inside. Mickeen was seated at a desk in his old glass office, trying to sort a few bills, when his phone went.

'I don't know who it is, but I'm on my own at the moment and can't do a thing.'

'Would you listen, you silly old bugger? It's your only nephew.'

'Jesus, Sean, can it be true? Where are you calling from?'

'London.'

'Are you coming to see me?'

'Not at the moment, but I'm hoping you can help me.'

At that moment, the old recovery truck drove in, Paddy O'Rourke at the wheel. Mickeen said, 'A wee minute, Sean.' He called, 'Get on with the new tyres for the front wheels on Father Grady's car.' He returned, 'Sorry, Sean, in what way?'

'Colonel Henry Talbot's just died.'

'I know. Last night it was.'

'Ulster Television has just said that the Talbots are going to have a very private cremation ceremony for the family and friends, but they didn't say where and when.'

'They've been doing that since nine-thirty to get the public used to the idea that the family don't want a fuss. Kilmartin's behind them. The Talbots' housekeeper is wife to Jack Kelly, the old IRA chief. Half the villagers work the estate and they know they're all on a damn good thing.'

'Justin Talbot and the family must be glad of the support, being Protestants.'

'Christ, you know nothing, Sean. Justin Talbot's a good Catholic. It's emerged that his mother had him baptized for his dying father's sake, and kept it from Colonel Henry. The wrong side of the blanket, that one.'

Dillon was astonished. 'I would think that piece of news would have been enough to send old Henry flying into the next world. But you still haven't told me where and when. Do you know?'

'Of course I do. I slipped down to the pub for a quick one half an hour ago. Ould Henry will be into the oven at three-thirty over at Castlerea. Nobody would ever expect it so fast, so it'll be over and done with before they know it.'

'But somebody's leaked it,' Dillon said.

'Only the locals, and nobody's going to go ringing up a newspaper or anything.'

'I'm sure some people will turn up. Would you be thinking of going yourself?'

'Well, now that you mention it, I could take a quick spin that way.'

'Why don't you do just that and let me know what it was like.'

'I'll be in touch, so I will. God bless you, Seaneen. I'd love to come over to London and see you, but I'm too old for the travelling, so there it is.'

He put the old phone back and went to check on how O'Rourke, another old man, was getting on. He had the priest's car jacked up and had already replaced the first tyre.

'Was that Sean you were talking to?' O'Rourke said.

'It was indeed, all the way from London.'

'Is he coming to see you or what?'

'And why would he be coming back to Collyban, the arse end of the world?' Mickeen shrugged. 'Just checking I'm still alive.'

'Well, to get down to business, there's a problem with the exhaust on Father O'Grady's car. Do I take it into Newry and get a replacement?'

'He'll scream blue murder about the price. He's away at the moment, so there's no rush. Leave it up on the jack when you've finished the wheels and I'll have a look at it later. I've decided to go for a wee drive and see what's happening with the Talbot funeral at the Castlerea crematorium.

'I didn't have my lunch,' O'Rourke said.

'So you'll have a late one. They keep the Irish stew simmering all day long down at the Green Man. Just finish the tyres like I tell you while I search the cottage for a tie. You can't go to a funeral without a tie,' and he walked out and left O'Rourke there.

At Talbot Place, Justin waited in the study for his mother to join him. He wore not only a black suit but the tie to go with it, presenting a more sombre picture than he cared for, but this was Ireland and it was expected.

He was about to get himself a drink when the Preacher phoned him. 'I was wondering when I was going to hear from you,' Talbot said as he opened a French window and went out on to the terrace.

'I won't offer my condolences,' Hassan Shah said. 'I doubt they'd be appreciated.'

'A time for rejoicing, as far as I'm concerned,' Talbot told him. 'The future beckons.'

'There are infinite possibilities for us working together,' Shah said.

'There are infinite possibilities for Talbot International to expand in world markets.'

'You have so much,' Shah said, 'and yet you want more.'

'Nothing is enough,' Talbot told him, and switched off.

He swallowed a large vodka, then went out into the Great Hall to find the Kellys and Tod Murphy. His mother, dressed completely in black including a hat, was just coming downstairs. Her make-up was perfect, but her face was an ivory mask. A wake was expected later, and several village girls supervised by Emily were setting up long tables at one end of the hall. Throwing convention to the winds, Justin Talbot had insisted the coffin would be waiting for them at the crematorium, but the funeral company had provided a driver and a black Voltern which could accommodate them comfortably.

Emily said to Jean, 'God bless you, my dear, everything will be ready by the time you return.'

'Thank you,' Jean said. 'Do you think many will come?'

Emily was shocked. 'But of course. They'll abide by your wishes over the funeral, but they'll want to pay their respects afterwards.'

A horn sounded outside. Justin Talbot said, 'I'd say that's for us.' He gave his mother his arm. 'All right, love, let's get this over with.'

Paddy O'Rourke sat at the end of the bar, drinking his Guinness. Except for two old men playing dominoes in the corner, the pub was empty. Martin Curry, the landlord, entered and put a plate of Irish stew in front of him.

'Get your head round that.'

Paddy started, glancing up at the bar clock. 'Two-thirty. Only another hour to go and ould Colonel Henry burns in Hell.'

'Good riddance to him,' Curry said. 'Where's Mickeen? He was in early for a drink, but he hasn't eaten.'

'He decided to take a run over to Castlerea and see the Talbot funeral.'

'Now why would he do that when everyone knows the family don't want a fuss?'

'I'm not sure. He was having a chat on the phone to his nephew Sean in London. From what I heard, they were discussing the funeral and so on.'

Martin Curry said, 'By his nephew, Sean, you're speaking of Sean Dillon?'

'Well, Mickeen's only got the one. Big for the Provos in his day, Sean.'

'And big for the Brits now,' Curry said. 'What were they talking about?' He poured another drink. 'On the house.'

The chapel at Castlerea Crematorium was supposed to be open to any member of the public who wished to enter, but not that afternoon, not with a visible Provisional IRA presence arranged by Kelly, several large and intimidating men in dark suits making it plain to the public that they weren't welcome.

There was a pleasant memorial park surrounding the chapel and other buildings and, here and there, individuals were visiting their loved ones or delivering flowers. Mickeen pretended to be such a person and was at least able to observe the hearse waiting by the chapel door. The Voltern appeared with the party from Talbot Place and everyone got out and waited.

Jack Kelly produced a mobile and answered it for a minute or so, glancing round, then put it in his pocket, moved to the men guarding the door and spoke to one of them. The man turned and was obviously searching the memorial park and Mickeen moved away. One look had been enough to tell him who they were and, for the first time, it occurred to him that he might have been foolish to come.

The service in the chapel, with the well-meaning vicar and the piped music, could not have been over too soon for Justin, who felt a certain release as they went out to find it raining.

Jean and Hannah were talking to the vicar and Kelly pulled Justin over. 'Sean Dillon, the one who works for Ferguson, was born in Collyban. He left for London at twelve, but his uncle, Mickeen Oge Flynn, owns the garage there.'

'So get on with it, Jack. Is there some problem?'

'His garage mechanic says he overheard Mickeen having a telephone conversation from London with Dillon. From what he heard, they were discussing the funeral and the fact that you wanted to keep it private. Mickeen said he knew it was today and that he'd attend.'

'And did he?'

'As you can see, there are a few people in the memorial park.'

The two women had got into the car and sat waiting. Talbot said in a low, dangerous voice, 'Can't you give me a straight answer? Did he come?'

'Yes, one of the men thinks he saw him.'

Talbot produced a silver hip flask, opened it and swallowed vodka. As he closed it, he said, 'Charles Ferguson is a major problem in my life, and Sean Dillon seems to be his top enforcer, so when he phones a relative who lives only seven miles from my own home and the said relative turns up as he has done, I get highly suspicious. Tell my mother and Hannah to carry on. Say we'll see them soon.'

'Then what?' Kelly asked.

'Get one of the men to give you his car and we'll take a quick trip to Collyban, just you and me.'

At the garage, Mickeen found O'Rourke brushing the floor. 'I'll finish Father Grady's car in the morning,' he said. 'How were the service and the cremation?'

'It was like a Provisional IRA convention, with Jack Kelly and a few of his men from Kilmartin discouraging the public from going in the chapel. It didn't seem healthy to stay around, so I came away. Get off with you now and I'll see you later for a drink.'

'I'll do that,' Paddy said and went out.

It was after five, and Mickeen stood there thinking about what had happened. The presence of so many old IRA hands had given him a shock. People like that were still a power to be reckoned with. Paddy had left the priest's car on the jack so, with nothing better to do, he switched on the inspection lamp, eased his old bones down, his back on the trolley, and rolled underneath the car.

He was aware of footsteps approaching and stopped his inspection. 'Can I help you?'

He had turned his head and seen two pairs of shoes and started to roll on the trolley but, as his head appeared from underneath the car, he stopped as a foot stamped beside it.

'Stop right where you are,' Justin Talbot told him. Mickeen stared up at him, suddenly afraid. 'Do you know who I am?'

'Yes, Mr Talbot.'

'And you know me well enough,' Jack Kelly said, and Mickeen nodded.

'Why did you try to come to my grandfather's funeral?' Talbot demanded.

'Sure, and I thought it would be open to anyone.'

'And how did you know that it was happening when it was?'

'Everyone in Collyban knew, Mr Talbot. They were all talking about it in the Green Man. Somebody you thought you could trust must have blabbed.'

And because he knew very well that was the logical explanation, Talbot become even more incensed. 'And what about your nephew, Sean Dillon? I know you've spoken to him earlier. What was that all about?'

'Nothing at all, Mr Talbot.' Mickeen was desperate. 'He's family. He just called me from London to say hello.'

'You're lying,' Talbot shouted. 'There's more to it than that. Tell me, damn you.'

He kicked at Mickeen's face, catching the edge of the trolley, sending him swinging further under the car. He almost fell over himself, grabbed at the raised handle of the hydraulic jack, releasing it, and the car subsided. Mickeen cried out in agony and then there was only silence.

Kelly shoved Talbot out of the way, reached for the handle and quickly raised the car. He crouched, picked up the inspection lamp and leaned in. Mickeen's face was covered in blood, there was torn flesh on the forehead and he detected bone. It was a dreadful sight and he moved back.

'You've done for him.'

'Are you certain?' Talbot said.

'See for yourself. Would you think anyone could survive injuries like that?'

'I've seen men wounded in battle survive some terrible things, and not just when I'm Shamrock. It would be simple to make sure if I had a pistol.' Talbot was strangely calm now. 'Do you have one?'

'No, I don't.'

'I assumed you always carried.'

'Not any more,' Kelly said. 'Only on certain occasions, and today wasn't supposed to be one.' He checked Mickeen again. 'No, I say he's dead.'

He lowered the car again and Talbot said, 'Why are you doing that?'

'So that when they find him, they'll think it was an accident. Now let's get out of here.'

They ran through the rain to the BMW and got in. As Kelly drove away, Talbot said calmly, 'Well, that's taken care of that. Dillon won't be pleased about his uncle, but the stupid old bastard had it coming.' He turned to look at Kelly, that strange cold smile on his face. 'Don't you agree?'

And Jack Kelly, not happy at all, managed a nod. 'Yes, I suppose you're right.'

'Good, then let's get back to the house as soon as possible. They'll be wondering what's happened to us.'

It was Paddy O'Rourke, walking down to the pub, who noticed that there were no lights on in either the house or the garage and went to investigate. What he found when he raised the car again horrified him. Like Kelly, he assumed the worst, but called the county air ambulance service, which served remote country areas.

For some reason, he didn't want to leave his old friend, so didn't go seeking help, just sat there holding Mickeen's cold and apparently lifeless hand. After twenty minutes, he heard the sound of the approaching helicopter. He had switched on all the garage lights and went out and waved frantically, and a Chinook helicopter settled on the forecourt, bringing out all the customers in the Green Man, headed by Martin Curry.

The paramedics wasted no time, examining Mickeen, then pulling a kind of turban over his head, strapping him to a special stretcher and taking him inside the Chinook. As O'Rourke watched, they worked on the old man until he was festooned with tubes and bottles.

One of the paramedics shouted, 'You're the one who found him? Give me your name and phone number. The police will want to speak to you. It's a good thing you found him when you did.'

'I thought he was dead,' O'Rourke shouted.

'Almost.'

'Where are you taking him, Newry?'

'No, the Seaton Hospital in Belfast. They have a great neurological unit. Only forty miles. We'll have him there in no time.'

He scrambled back inside, the Chinook lifted and was away. The crowd moved back to the pub. Curry said, 'What happened?'

'He was working under the car and the jack slipped or something and the car fell on him.'

'Where did they say they were taking him?'

O'Rourke told him, and Curry said, 'That's a great hospital. They'll look after him. Anyway, you've earned a drink this night, Paddy, so join me in the pub.'

The wake was in full swing and half the village seemed to be there, enjoying the spread offered by Emily and her helpers on the well-stocked tables. And drink was taken, of course, as one would expect at an Irish wake.

Jean Talbot was working her way through the tenants and she paused to greet her son. 'Where have you been? I was worried.'

'Something Jack and I needed to sort out, didn't we?'

186

Secrets again. She knew instantly from his heightened colour and his glittering eyes. 'Whatever it is, just calm down. Have a word with Father Cassidy, I really think you should.'

He was exasperated and sounded it. 'If that's what you want.'

Young Jane was passing with a tray of glasses of champagne. He took two. 'Good girl,' he said and, as he turned away, emptied one glass in a quick swallow. He looked around the room, saw no sign of the priest. The study door had been closed for privacy, but he found Cassidy in there, sitting in a wing-backed chair leafing through a book.

'Too noisy for you out there?' Talbot said as he closed the door.

'I'm getting old; the years are overtaking me. How are you bearing up, you and your mother?'

'As if a very great weight has been lifted from our shoulders.' Justin tossed back his champagne.

Cassidy glanced up at the empty wall above the fire-place. 'I see you haven't wasted any time in taking down your grandfather's portrait.'

'They have a weekly bonfire behind the stables. I had considerable pleasure in consigning the portrait to the flames personally.'

There was a certain amount of pain on Cassidy's face. 'The man has passed on, Justin, let go, renounce this continuing hatred.'

'Forgiveness, is that what you're preaching today?

Forget how *I* suffered, Father – the way he treated my mother was abominable.'

'Forgiveness is everything. Christ even forgave Judas when he stepped in through the gate at the Garden of Gethsemane to betray him.'

'Well, as he hanged himself, it didn't do him much good.'

'Because he couldn't forgive himself,' Cassidy said. 'Once he stepped through that gate – the Judas gate, as it has become known – there was no going back. It's the same for all of us when our actions betray our loved ones, we also betray ourselves.'

Talbot took it badly. 'Are you suggesting this applies to me?'

Before Father Cassidy could reply, the door opened and Jack Kelly looked in. 'Ah, there you are, Justin. Could I have a word? It's important.'

Justin was so angry that he didn't even excuse himself, and followed Kelly through the crowd and out of the front door. They stood in the porch, rain falling.

'What's the problem?' Talbot asked.

'I've heard from Curry at Collyban. Mickeen was found by his mechanic, who called in the air ambulance service and the Chinook flew in.'

'So what are you telling me?'

'They found a spark of life.'

Talbot grabbed him by his tie. 'You said he was dead.'

'And well he might be. They're delivering him to the neurological unit at the Seaton Hospital in Belfast. Plenty

188

of people on the staff there are sympathetic to our cause. We'll have no difficulty finding out what's going on.'

'If he gets to open his mouth, I'm finished,' Talbot said.

'Let's cross that bridge when we come to it,' Kelly said. 'In the state he's in, he could die at any minute. For the moment, I want you to carry on as normal. Don't discuss this with anyone, and that certainly means your mother.'

'Did Mickeen have any kin in Collyban?'

'All gone abroad years ago.'

'So Sean Dillon could be his only relative.'

'I'd say so, and I know what you're getting at. He's bound to be informed one way or the other.'

'Then I'll have to be ready for him,' Talbot said.

'With a pistol under your pillow?' Kelly shook his head. 'You'll need more than that with Dillon. Anyway, I'm off to make some calls to Belfast. I'll talk to you later.'

He hurried away through the rain and Talbot turned and went back in. A match flared in the depths of the great porch, revealing Jean Talbot lighting the cigarette she'd come out to enjoy earlier when she'd been interrupted by the arrival of her son and Kelly.

Secrets, always secrets. As she inhaled, the glow of the cigarette illuminated that porcelain face and dark eyes. On the other hand, there was a mystery man named Sean Dillon. Perhaps there were things she could find out about him. She flicked her cigarette out into the rain and returned inside.

189

8

It was six-thirty at Holland Park, evening dark closing in when Dillon and Holley called with the intention of taking Roper down to dinner at the Dorchester. As they were discussing it he got a call from the Gulfstream and put it on speaker.

'We're on our way back,' Ferguson told him. 'We left an hour ago.'

'Farley informed me they'd received a return flight plan. I thought you'd be staying longer. Didn't you like it?'

'No, Roper, it didn't like us, which is why we left as soon as possible, so shut up and listen to what happened.'

As might be expected from an old military hand, the report was brief, but concise and clear, leaving nothing out.

'Holley and Dillon are with me,' Roper said. 'You've really been to war, General.'

'You could say that. We've left seven men dead, one way or another. Have you any comment, Daniel?'

'Colonel Ahmed Atep and Abu Salim weren't there when I last visited. I could believe many things about Dak Khan, but the Al Qaeda connection is something new.'

'It's a good thing Captain Abu Salim was on your side,' Roper told Ferguson.

'He certainly saw Colonel Atep off in spectacular fashion, but that was the Pathan in him. A matter of honour and revenge for his two Sergeants,' Ferguson said.

'So where does this leave us?' Roper asked.

'With further proof that Shamrock exists, and another codename – an important person in London known as the Preacher.'

'Unfortunately if we insert that into the computer and demand an answer, it will give us precisely nothing,' Dillon cut in.

'I wouldn't be too sure about that,' Ferguson answered. 'Not when Roper starts digging. I've every faith in him.'

'Most kind,' Roper said. 'We'll be seeing you in about nine hours or so?'

'That's it. Over and out.'

Roper shook his head. 'What an amazing exploit.'

'Something to celebrate,' Holley told him. 'Are you up for the Dorchester?'

'Try and stop me,' Roper glanced at the clock. 'Let's

192

say about a quarter to eight. I've got a few things to wrap up here.'

At Talbot Place, there were still villagers in the Great Hall, many with drink taken, but people were having such a good time that they didn't want to go. Justin leaned against the wall by the study door, watching his mother holding court at the foot of the stairs; so popular, so loved by the people, he told himself with a kind of envy, but then she was Mary Ellen come back to life.

He was waiting for Kelly and getting impatient. It had been almost an hour since the man had gone to his car to get things moving in Belfast, but suddenly there he was, entering through the front door and hurrying over to him.

'I've got news,' he said. 'Let's go in the study.'

They went in, and Justin closed the door and shot the bolt. 'Tell me.'

'I've been in touch with a friend, Brian Carson, who shared a cell with me in the Maze prison. He's a good man and owns a large construction company, but his silent partners are a Provo syndicate. He only has to lift a phone to contact our sympathizers.'

'So?'

'Mickeen was taken straight into intensive care, where a scan diagnosed a fractured skull and possible brain damage. He hasn't recovered consciousness and is scheduled for emergency neurosurgery.'

'Is that it?'

'No, there's more. Apparently he could die at any moment. There's only a five per cent chance of him surviving the surgery.'

'So we just live with it and hope,' Talbot said.

'That's it, Justin, but our source in the hospital is absolutely sound. Whatever happens, we'll be informed as quickly as anybody.'

Talbot laughed harshly. 'Well, let's hope the old bastard obliges us all by dying quickly. We'll have a drink on it.' He started to move to the bar and his mobile sounded.

It was the Preacher, and Talbot nodded to Kelly, a finger to his mouth, and put his mobile on speaker. 'I presume the funeral passed without incident?' the Preacher said.

'Perfectly, but this is Ireland and people expect a wake,' Talbot told him. 'Half the villagers are still here enjoying themselves.'

'I'm glad someone is happy,' the Preacher said.

'What's happened?' Talbot asked.

'Ferguson and Miller were enticed into a trip to the border area by an illegal gun runner named Dak Khan, on the promise of meeting Shamrock.'

'Where an ambush was waiting, I presume? Did something go wrong?'

'My information is sketchy. Apparently Khan and his people were all disposed of.'

'Could we have it in plain language? Khan and

his people have ended up dead and Ferguson and Miller were responsible?'

'So it would appear.'

'Well, good for Ferguson: there's life in the old dog yet. He is, after all, a Grenadier. All I can say is your asset needs changing. He's obviously hopeless.'

'He's dead, too,' Hassan Shah said. 'A car bomb.'

'Not Ferguson, that one.' Justin Talbot shook his head. 'Not his style. I'm sure your man had plenty of enemies. Well, at least that means you don't have to get rid of him yourself now.'

'Al Qaeda will punish his killers as they deserve, and the same will happen to Ferguson and his people. I wouldn't be so cavalier, Talbot. The fact that they're persisting in the search for Shamrock means that they are your problem, too.'

'Well, I've had other things on my mind. For the moment, you'll have to manage without me.'

He switched off and Kelly said, 'You're not going to share the Mickeen Oge Flynn problem with him then?'

'Am I, hell. Now, let's have the drink.' He went to the bar and poured whiskey.

Kelly took the glass offered. 'I remember in the old days when I was on the Army Council, Charles Ferguson was top of the list of people you didn't get involved with if you could avoid it.'

'Now you know why.' Justin emptied his glass. 'It's been a long day. Let's see if we can ease everyone out.' He pulled back the bolt and led the way into the Great Hall.

There was silence, and then Jean Talbot moved in through the curtains. Seeking her son earlier and finding the study door bolted, curiosity had sent her round to the terrace. She'd halted at the study's French windows, partially covered by a half-drawn curtain, aware of the murmur of voices. The window was never locked. She'd eased the handle and opened it just enough to hear everything that was being said, and none of it made her happy. And she had not the slightest idea what to do about it.

Dillon, Roper and Holley were about to set out to dinner, when Dillon's mobile sounded.

'Switch it off, for Christ's sake,' Roper said.

But it was too late, for Dillon, already answering, heard the unmistakable Ulster tones of a young woman saying, 'Would that be Mr Sean Dillon, of Stable Mews, Mayfair, London?'

He slipped back into the accent of his childhood. 'It is indeed, my love.'

'I'm calling from Belfast, Mr Dillon. I'm Sergeant Eileen Flanagan, Police Service of Northern Ireland.'

'And what can I be doing for you?'

'An old gentleman called Mickeen Oge Flynn has been admitted to Seaton Hospital, and a search in his wallet has discovered a next-of-kin card.'

Dillon was all attention. 'Mickeen is my uncle. I'm his only relative. Has he had a heart attack or something?'

'No, it's nothing like that. I'm not supposed to go into clinical details. If you phone the hospital, they'll be able to answer your questions.'

'For the love of God, girl, can't you tell me more? Is it serious?'

'All right, but don't get me into trouble. He was working under a motor car and it fell on him. He was discovered by his mechanic, one Patrick O'Rourke. The air ambulance service brought him to the Seaton Hospital in Belfast. I understand it doesn't look good, but, really, you'll have to talk to the hospital about that. I have Patrick O'Rourke's mobile phone number, would you like it?'

'Yes, I would.' Dillon went to Roper's desk and found a pen and she dictated the number to him.

'Will you be coming?' she said.

'Definitely. God bless you.'

The others waited expectantly and he told them the worst. He said to Roper, 'If you could get Seaton Hospital online and find me the right person to speak to, I'd appreciate it.'

'I'll get right on to it,' Roper said. 'You do intend to go over there?'

'As fast as I can, so we'll need to check out flights from Heathrow.'

'No, you won't,' Holley said. 'I'll fly you myself.'

'Are you sure?' Dillon said.

'Of course, and I'm coming with you. I was at Queen's University in Belfast more years ago than I care to remember. It will be interesting to go back.'

Dillon said to Roper, 'Make sure we're allowed to land at Belfast City Airport by the docks.'

Holley cut in. 'And book us a suite at the Europa.' He turned to Dillon. 'Let's get going.'

Roper managed to get the flight classified as a Ministry of Defence priority, so everything worked perfectly, including the landing at Belfast. As a result, it was only ten-thirty when they reached the hospital and were directed to the neurological unit. At that time of night, it was fairly quiet, the corridors empty except for the occasional nurse.

The reception area was on the third floor. There were chairs, a vending machine for drinks, magazines, and an ageing woman with grey hair behind the desk. She smiled pleasantly as they approached.

'We don't often get visitors this late, so I suspect you'll be the gentlemen from London for Mr Flynn. We were told you were on your way. Dillon and Holley, isn't it? I've issued you with identity tags. Please put them on. It's regulations.'

'How is my uncle?' Dillon asked.

'I'm not allowed to give out that information. All I can say is that he's had major surgery and that Mr Frank Jordan performed the operation himself. He's a truly wonderful surgeon, so your uncle is in good hands.'

'Can we see him?' Dillon asked, meaning Mickeen.

'The surgeon? Oh, yes, he's come in especially.'

At that moment, the man himself came down the corridor. He seemed about sixty, with a well-used face and a shock of grey hair. He wore the standard white coat, a stethoscope sticking out of one pocket.

Dillon stood and held out his hand. 'Sean Dillon and my friend, Daniel Holley. I'm Mickeen's nephew.'

'Let's sit down and talk.' Jordan turned to the receptionist. 'Tea for three, Molly. Make it using your own kettle behind the desk there. I hate that bloody machine.'

'Certainly, sir,' she said.

'So how bad is it?' Dillon asked as they sat.

'I'm a plain man, Mr Dillon, and I always prefer to tell the truth, or at least as I see it. It's as bad as it could be. His left arm is broken – it was obviously raised as the vehicle collapsed – and there's a flesh wound on the right, but those aren't the problems. It's the head injuries. He has skull fractures of the utmost severity.'

'And brain damage?' Dillon said.

'Yes, lacerations to a certain degree. We've worked on him for four hours, and put in a titanium plate in one area.'

Molly had produced the tea, put the tray on a table beside them and poured. Dillon asked, 'What kind of chance does he have, a man of his age who's drunk a pint of whiskey every day of his life?'

'He could die five minutes from now, but head trauma is a strange business. Patients can hang in there for weeks.' Jordan was drinking his tea.

'Is that normal?' Holley asked.

'There's no such thing as normal in a case like this. I've had many patients over the years who continue to sleep.'

'You mean they don't revive at all?' Dillon asked.

'It's been known to last for months, and when the patient comes to, they've been in dream-time. Usually they've completely lost their memory.'

Dillon nodded. 'Can we see him?'

'Only through the door. Come with me.'

The private room was at the very end of the corridor. There was a square observation window in the door. Mickeen resembled a mummy, with all his bandages. He was festooned with bottles and tubes, electronic machines bleeping away. A man in a white coat sat in the corner reading a book.

'Who's he?' Dillon asked.

'The night nurse. With such a serious matter, Mr Flynn will continue to have one at his side in case of emergencies.'

Holley said, 'There's nothing for you here, Sean. Let's go and book in at the hotel.'

They paused before walking back to reception and Jordan said, 'I understand you're based in London, so seeing him on a regular basis would be difficult. There's not much you could do anyway, though, even if you came in every day.'

Dillon shook hands. 'You're right. But what if I moved him to London?'

Jordan paused. 'I think he'd be all right, but that

would require a private air ambulance; it'd cost many thousands of pounds.'

Holley said, 'We've got that kind of money.'

Jordan frowned. 'Just who are you people?'

Dillon produced his MI5 warrant card. 'You look a decent sort of man, so I'm going to take a chance. We work for a special security outfit on behalf of the Prime Minister, and we have a private hospital called Rosedene in Holland Park, small but superbly equipped. It takes care of people damaged in our line of work. It's run by a Professor Charles Bellamy. He's put me together a few times.'

'But I know him,' Jordan said. 'We were colleagues at Guy's Hospital in London for years.'

'Give me your card and I'll have him contact you and make the arrangements. You are sure Mickeen can be moved?'

'Oh, yes, in an air ambulance, but, as I say, it will cost you.' He produced his card and said, 'My private mobile number. I'm used to being wakened at all hours, so your people can call me any time. All I need is the right authorization. Take care, gentlemen.' Jordan walked away.

'A good man, that one,' Dillon said.

'I agree. Now, if you don't mind me bringing up mundane matters, can I remind you we haven't had any dinner?'

'At this time of night, they'll call it supper,' Dillon said, as they arrived back in reception.

Holley thanked the receptionist for the tea. 'Will you be wanting a taxi?' she asked.

'We have one waiting. Come on, Sean,' and they walked down to the lift.

It was quiet again, not a soul about. Molly took a mobile from her handbag and dialled a number and said to the man who answered, 'Is that you, Mr Carson? It's Molly. We've just had two visitors from London to see Flynn, a Sean Dillon and a Daniel Holley.'

'Did they see Jordan?' Brian Carson asked.

'They've just left after a long chat. I heard everything.'

Which she hadn't, of course, for the conversation concerning the possibility of transferring Mickeen to London in the air ambulance had taken place outside his room at the other end of the corridor.

'So what did the doctor have to say?'

'That they'd operated for four hours and there's brain damage. It's the kind of situation where if he died five minutes from now, no one would be surprised. On the other hand, he's not just unconscious, he's in a coma, and he could stay like that for ages. Nobody knows how long, but Mr Jordan said that when such people do awake, they've often lost their memory.'

'Well, dying would be better, but the situation could be worse. My friends will have to accept how things are.'

'They came in a private jet. They must be big operators.'

'That's an understatement. If I told you they were both Provos in their day, would it surprise you? Hell on wheels, those two.'

'Holy Mother of God,' she said.

'You've done well, Molly, it will be noted. Goodnight to you.'

Justin Talbot was sitting in a wing-backed chair on a dais in his mother's studio. He wore an open-necked black shirt and black velvet cord trousers, his arms folded, hair tousled. He'd been there an hour while his mother worked on a new portrait. She was standing at her easel, only a few feet away in her paint-stained smock, a palette in one hand, a brush in the other.

'For God's sake, how much longer? It's been an hour already.'

'It's difficult, love,' she said. 'I can't get exactly the expression I want.'

His mobile trembled in his breast pocket. He answered it and Kelly said, 'Are you alone?'

'Just a minute.' Justin got up. 'I've got to answer this.'

'Really, Justin.' She was annoyed.

The studio was above the east end of the stable. There was an exit door that opened on to a metal platform and stairs down to the cobbled yard. He closed the door behind him. Jean went to the sink in the corner and pretended to be cleaning brushes as she pushed the window open enough to hear him. Not that she learned much, except that he was angry.

Kelly, having told him everything Carson had to say, said, 'It could be worse.'

'Come on, Jack,' Justin said. 'The little bugger might decide to wake up at any time.'

'So what do you suggest?'

'Couldn't your people get someone to pull the plug on him? That would take care of the whole damn business.'

'Very risky. Let's just wait and see for the moment.'

'All right, but nothing'd better go wrong, you hear me?' He switched off in exasperation.

Jean was back at her portrait in an instant. 'Bad news, darling?'

'No, just a problem with the farm. Look, can't we call it a day? I'm tired.'

He was angry and mutinous. She laughed. 'That's the expression I'm after: it's absolutely perfect. Just another half-hour, darling.'

Dillon called Roper and explained the situation to him.

'I can't believe what I'm hearing,' he said, when Dillon was finished. 'Ferguson will have a fit. He gave you explicit instructions not to go to Ireland at the moment, and that ambulance plane will cost a fortune.'

'It was a bloody emergency,' Dillon said.

Holley boomed in. 'And I've already said I'll pay for the damn thing.'

'So forget Ferguson,' Dillon said. 'Will you kindly take Frank Jordan's mobile number, call and make the arrangements? Next, contact Professor Charles Bellamy at Rosedene. Make everything a matter of extreme urgency, so that by the time Ferguson arrives, it's a done deal.'

'All right, I'll get on to it, but only because I can't wait to see Ferguson's reaction when he finds out. Presumably you're coming back in the morning?'

'We'll see. For the moment, all we're interested in is some supper. Take care, Roper.'

The two-bedroom suite at the Europa Hotel had a dining room, and Dillon and Holley ordered room service – a lobster salad apiece, new potatoes, cabbage with bacon – and drank ice-cold non-vintage Krug champagne. It was touching midnight when the waiter reappeared and cleared.

'What time is Ferguson's Gulfstream getting in?' Holley asked.

'I don't know and I don't care,' Dillon said.

'You've got to go back and face the old man's wrath some time,' Holley told him.

'But not just yet.' Dillon yawned. 'We could stay on for a day or so, since we're here. Roper will take care of everything for moving Mickeen. We could rent a car. Go for a drive.'

'To where?'

'My mother died giving birth to me in Collyban. I lived with Mickeen as a child, while my father was away working, then he returned and took me away with him to London when I was twelve.'

'So you haven't seen much of your uncle over the years?'

'Two or three times by night when I was on the run during the Troubles, and I paid him a flying visit the other year on business for Ferguson. The truth is, the old sod's the only close relative I've got left. I was surprised at the sense of loss I felt looking at him in that hospital bed.'

'So where is this leading?'

'Paddy O'Rourke, his mechanic at the garage, found him. I wouldn't mind going to see him. I could let him know how Mickeen is.'

'You're talking nonsense, Sean, that would only depress him. What's really eating at you?'

'Okay, so I hadn't been in touch with Mickeen since God knows when, and I phoned him on a whim because I thought he'd be able to tell me the time and place of the Talbot funeral.'

'And he could. So what's that got to do with anything?'

'I don't know, except that somehow I feel responsible.'

'I don't see how you could be, but if you feel like that, give O'Rourke a call and we'll drive down and see him. How far?'

'Fifty miles, here or there. I'll get in touch with him in the morning. Are you carrying?'

'One of the advantages of diplomatic privilege.' Holley pulled up his right trouser leg and showed the ankle holster with the Colt .25. 'No well-dressed man should be without one.'

'I couldn't agree more.' Dillon put his foot on a chair and showed an identical Colt. 'Silenced, with hollow points.'

'Why settle for less? That will always do the job. But why are you asking?'

'Collyban was always Republican territory, IRA bandit country. I used to be a hero to people there who'd never even seen me, and then Ferguson came along and somehow I doubt they'd still be feeling the same.'

'Once in, never out – that's been the motto of the IRA since its inception, hasn't it? So screw them, we're still Provos, whether they like it or not,' Daniel told him. 'I'm away to bed.'

At eight o'clock the following morning, they were working their way through breakfast in the café when Roper called Dillon.

'Ferguson got in just after three this morning. He asked me if I had anything special to report.'

'And you said nothing, I presume?'

'Exactly. I just hope I don't regret it. Anyway, your

Mr Frank Jordan doesn't let the grass grow under his feet. Mickeen Oge Flynn will be picked up at nine and taken to Belfast City Airport to board the air ambulance for London. Rosedene is waiting for him.'

'Excellent.'

'In fact, Jordan has decided to go along. He said he'd like to keep an eye on Flynn, and, besides, it's costing so much he might as well get something out of it!'

'Roper, you've done wonders,' Dillon said. 'I'm truly grateful – and hopefully, so will be Mickeen.'

'So what are your plans?'

'We've ordered a car and we're driving down to Collyban.'

Roper was concerned. 'What in the hell are you up to, Sean? I'd have thought it very unwise to visit anywhere in that area. And, dammit, you're only fifteen miles from Crossmaglen where Holley's mother was born, so he's as bad as you are. What's this obsession with living dangerously?'

'Oh, Roper, it'll be just a quiet day out in County Down. What could be nicer? You worry too much.' And he switched off.

'We have to put the cat amongst the pigeons,' Holley said.

'No, that happens when Ferguson wakes up and finds out what happened, but we'll deal with that when the explosion takes place.'

He found the piece of paper with O'Rourke's number

on it, poured himself a second cup of tea and called him. 'Who's that?' O'Rourke's voice was wary.

'Paddy, me ould son,' Dillon told him cheerfully. 'It's Mickeen's only nephew, Sean Dillon.'

O'Rourke gasped, 'Jesus, Sean, where are you?'

'In Belfast, Paddy. I flew in last night thinking Mickeen was going to die on me. Four hours they operated on him. The brain was damaged, you see, and him in a coma.'

'What do you mean?' O'Rourke asked cautiously.

'He's in a deep sleep, and nobody knows if he'll wake up. Anyway, I'm having him transferred to London in an air ambulance. There's a special hospital where I'll be able to keep an eye on him.'

'And when's that?'

'Nine o'clock.'

'Well, that's fantastic. I found him, you know. I don't know how to thank you.'

'Save it till I see you, Paddy.'

'See me?' O'Rourke said.

'I've got a friend with me called Daniel Holley. We've hired a car and we're driving down. You can show me where it happened, and I can discuss what we're going to do with the garage.'

O'Rourke was flabbergasted. 'But you shouldn't come here to Collyban, Sean. There's plenty who wouldn't like it. No knowing what they might do.'

'Not to worry, Paddy, I can look after myself.'

'Well . . . if you're sure. What time would you be coming?'

'We should be there by eleven. If you're not at the garage, we'll look for you in the pub.'

'The Green Man?' O'Rourke was horrified. 'Never in there, Sean. It's IRA to the hilt.'

'And didn't I join as a volunteer at nineteen when my father was shot by Brit paratroopers? Do you say I have no right to go in?'

'Not me, Sean, but others would.'

'Well, enough talk. You know when to expect us.' He switched off and said to Holley, 'Did I stir the hornets' nest enough?'

'That's an understatement,' Holley said. 'Let's get moving.'

Martin Curry was working behind the bar at the Green Man, washing glasses. There was not a soul in the place when Paddy O'Rourke entered through the side door, which was hardly surprising at nine o'clock.

'Jesus, Paddy, isn't it a bit early, even for you?'

'Will you give me a large one, Martin, for pity's sake, and me having the shock of my life.'

'And what would that be?' Curry asked.

'I've just had Sean Dillon on the mobile. He's been to see Mickeen in the hospital in Belfast. He says he's coming down to see me this morning to discuss what's going to happen to the garage.'

Curry was thunderstruck 'He must be mad.' He poured Paddy a double whiskey. 'Drink that down and tell me exactly what he said.'

Jack Kelly was sitting at his desk in the back office of the Kilmartin Arms, doing his accounts, when Curry phoned. He ended by telling Jack, 'I'll have two or three of the boys in. We'll sort the bastard out.'

'Take it easy, Martin. The old days are gone. We have to be careful how we go.'

'Christ, are you going chicken on me after what we've been through together? Sean Dillon is a disgrace to the village where he was born.'

'You're right, Martin. He's a turncoat who's been serving the Brits for years now, taking orders from Charles Ferguson, one of our biggest enemies in the old days – but we've got to go carefully here. I don't want to do anything that would bring in the police. I've got the Talbots to consider. They've only just seen off Colonel Henry, for God's sake.'

'So what do I do if the bastard tries to come in the Green Man?'

'We'll handle it, Martin, and I'll be there to stand with you. Do as I say. Take it as a direct order from your old commander.'

'And the other business he told Paddy about? Having Mickeen flown out to London?'

'Black news that, but there's nothing to be done about it.'

Jean Talbot and Justin enjoyed breakfast together, but her pleas for him to sit for her again fell on deaf ears. He intended to go riding and that was that. She retreated to her studio and got to work. The weather outside was dark and oppressive, and there was a hint of rain. It had become incredibly stuffy in the studio overnight and she opened the exit door before starting work on the portrait again.

An hour went by and then she heard a car arrive. She went to a window and saw Jack Kelly getting out of his old Morris. She was about to go out on the plat-form and speak to him when she saw Justin galloping fast across the meadow, only reining in his mount at the last moment so that it reared up and kicked out before settling. He walked it in to the yard through the archway, and dismounted.

'You're a stupid boy still, but then I've been telling you that for years. You'll kill yourself doing that one of these days, Justin.'

'Is that so? What's got into you this morning? Come into the stable. The boy's gone to the village, so I've got to unsaddle myself. Is there a problem?'

'You could say that. Sean Dillon's coming. Curry told

212

me. He'll be at Collyban at eleven o'clock to discuss
Flynn's garage with him.'

Talbot was stunned. 'So I'll actually get the chance
to meet him.'

'I'm damned if you will. Now get that horse inside.
We need to talk.'

Upstairs, Jean was moving fast, hurrying across the
studio, opening another door, because a few wooden
steps gave access to a landing overlooking the stalls
where Justin was unsaddling.

'Tell me all about it,' he was saying to Kelly.

It had started to rain when Kelly was finished, and
Justin went to the door, peering out and thinking about
it. 'What a mess, Jack, so what's to be done? Do we
shoot the bastard?'

'For Christ's sake, will you listen to me, boy? You
do nothing, because it's got nothing to do with you.
So Dillon works for Ferguson, as does Daniel Holley
these days, apparently. They've no idea you're
Shamrock. As far as I know, they haven't even heard
of the Preacher. Dillon is here to sort out Flynn's
garage with O'Rourke. What would Justin Talbot,
Chairman of Talbot International, have to do with
that?'

'You mean I shouldn't even meet him?'

'Absolutely not, and I want your word on it.'

'If you say so,' Justin said wearily. 'Frankly, it's all

213

getting a bit on top of me. How long can we hope for Mickeen to act the sleeping beauty in London?'

'From what Jordan says, a long, long time. Even if he does wake up, he could well not remember a thing about it.'

'It's not good enough, Jack.' Justin's eyes glittered again, his body crackling with energy. 'I've got to find a solution to all this.' He grinned and slapped Kelly on the back. 'When I do, you'll be the first to know what it is, but I'll leave Dillon and his friend to you.'

Kelly got in his Morris and drove off. The stable boy appeared and took charge of the horse. Justin went up to the studio, but his mother wasn't there. He stood looking at the portrait. She was good, he reflected; too bloody good really, as he had recently told her. She didn't just go for appearance, she got what was inside, too. She got the disturbed wildness in him, which made him feel uncomfortable, and he went back down the iron stairs to the yard.

At that moment, the maroon Shogun emerged from the garage, his mother at the wheel. She waved briefly, but didn't stop. He wondered where she was going – not that it mattered. He had enough on his mind with the whole damn situation. The Preacher, Ferguson, Shamrock. He went through the house to the study to get a drink and think about it.

* * *

Paddy O'Rourke was not happy. If the garage was closed down, it would be a serious inconvenience for the villagers who would have to drive as far as Kilmartin to find another, so Martin Curry's orders were plain. If Dillon made him a job offer, which he probably would, O'Rourke was to take it, then send him on his way, which meant anywhere he liked to go as long as it wasn't the Green Man.

Paddy sat on a stool just inside the garage, the main door open, smoked a cigarette between his finger and thumb, and waited, watched by two hard young men named Dempsey and Farrel from behind a half-drawn window curtain.

'Where the fug are they?' Farrel said, and the silver BMW came down the hill and halted on the forecourt. Paddy stood up and Dillon got out, followed by Holley who had been driving.

'Which one is Dillon, I wonder?' Farrel said.

'Neither of them looks like much to me,' Dempsey nodded. 'Let's see what happens.'

'It's me, Paddy, Sean.' Dillon smiled and grasped a reluctant hand. 'I was twelve years old when I last saw you, so how could you remember me?'

O'Rourke tried to smile. 'It's grand to see you and looking so well.'

'This is my good friend, Daniel Holley. He might sound English, but his mother was from Crossmaglen and that's not too far from here.'

'And that's a fact,' O'Rourke said, but before he could say anything else, the Shogun came down the hill, swung in and parked beside the BMW.

'Christ Jesus,' Dempsey said. 'It's the lady from Talbot Place. What's she doing here?'

'I'd better get Curry on my mobile,' Farrel said, and did so straightaway.

'What are they doing?' Curry demanded.

'She hasn't got out of her car yet.'

'Just keep watching and I'll call you back.' Curry rang off, then called Jack Kelly, who answered at once. 'I've got a problem,' Curry said, and told him.

'What the hell is she playing at?' Kelly demanded. 'Never mind. I'll be straight over.'

Curry called Farrel. 'Stay with it, but let me know the moment they start moving anywhere.' He switched off his mobile and turned to the seven or eight people in the bar. 'Drink up and move on. I want you out of here in five minutes.'

The three men turned to look at Jean and she opened the glove compartment and took out a short-barrelled Smith & Wesson .38 revolver, one of a number of weapons Colonel Henry had kept around the house. She slipped it in her trenchcoat pocket and got out of the Shogun.

'Sorry if I'm intruding,' she said. 'Remember me, Paddy, from Kilmartin? Jean Talbot, Colonel Henry's daughter?' He looked slightly dazed and she took his hand. 'I was so sorry to hear about what happened to Mickeen.'

'That's kind of you.' He seemed to come to life. 'This is Sean Dillon, Mickeen's nephew, over from London on hearing the bad news.'

She turned and didn't offer her hand, simply stood there with hands in her pockets, looking him over. 'Sean Dillon.' She frowned slightly, 'A familiar name. I'm sure I've heard it before.'

'And my friend, Daniel Holley.'

She smiled at Holley. 'So how is Mickeen?'

'What can I say?' Dillon shrugged slightly. 'He's had a massive operation which has left him with a titanium plate in the head, and he's comatose. He's been flown to London by air ambulance.'

'So what happens here?'

'The garage, you mean? That's quite simple. I'm offering Paddy a full partnership to keep things going while we see how Mickeen makes out.'

Suddenly, O'Rourke was smiling. 'By God, that's a fine offer, Sean, and I'll take it.' He spat on the palm of his hand, held it out and Dillon shook it.

Jean said, 'May I suggest we adjourn to the Green Man and seal the bargain with a drink?'

Paddy's face fell. 'Well, now, there could be complications about that.'

'What complications? Don't be silly, Paddy.' She took Dillon's arm. 'Shall we go?'

217

'It's entirely our pleasure, Mrs Talbot.' They walked away, Holley and Paddy following.

Farrel called Curry at once. 'They're on their way to the pub, Mr Curry.'

'Then move your arses and get down here fast. Use the back lane.'

Curry was coldly angry. He reached under the bar and produced a sawn-off shotgun, which he loaded and then replaced under the bar. There was no solution there. The woman was a wild card in this game. She was untouchable.

The door opened and she led the way in, just in front of Dillon, Holley and O'Rourke behind.

'Mr Curry, how nice to see you, it's been a while. You may know Mr Dillon here.'

'He certainly does, we're of an age,' Dillon said. 'We were at the village school together. How goes it, Martin?' His smile was mocking.

Curry was struggling to keep control, but before he could make any kind of reply, the back door crashed open and Dempsey and Farrel entered.

'What's happening?' Farrel demanded.

'We're all having a drink to celebrate Paddy being made partner at the garage,' Jean said. 'Why don't you join us?'

'I'm damned if I'll drink with these shites or you, you Protestant whore,' he said, producing a pistol.

Dillon kicked him under the right kneecap and, as he doubled over, raised his knee into the descending face and sent him back to trip over a chair and bounce off the wall, blood oozing from a broken nose as he slid to the floor, dropping his pistol. Curry reached under the bar, producing the sawn-off shotgun. Holley picked up the glass jug of water on the bar, threw it in his face and yanked the shotgun from him by the barrel. He tossed it into the corner, kicking Dempsey in the face as he leaned down to pick up Farrel's pistol.

Jean Talbot took the Smith & Wesson from her pocket and fired a shot into the ceiling. 'Now can everybody calm down?'

The door opened and Jack Kelly stepped in. He surveyed the scene, Dempsey and Farrel crouched on the floor by the wall, Curry drying his face with a bar towel. O'Rourke looked terrified.

Kelly said to Dillon, 'Have you given Paddy the job?'

'I don't know who you are, but, yes, he's now a partner.'

'Excellent. I'm Jack Kelly, estate manager at Talbot Place.'

'Ah, I mind that name from days when you were doing something else,' Dillon said. 'Do you know my friend Daniel Holley?'

'We have mutual friends in Crossmaglen. If you're finished here, Jean, I'll see you home.'

'That's kind of you.' She turned to Dillon and Holley, 'Shall we go?'

'Certainly,' Dillon turned to Curry. 'It's been a sincere sensation, Martin.' He ducked as Curry threw a glass at him.

Outside, Jean was getting into Kelly's Morris. 'He's just running me up to my car. Nice meeting you, gentlemen. It's good to be able to put a face to the name.'

They walked back up the street. 'I feel bad about leaving Paddy in there,' Dillon said.

'He'll be all right,' Holley grinned. 'They've got to get their petrol from somewhere.'

'Yes, he'll survive, but what a bloody place. Thank God my father got me out of it at twelve. Let's get going.'

As Holley drove, Dillon called Roper. 'What's the situation with Ferguson?'

'He's not stirring yet, so I'm leaving well enough alone. Have you been having fun?'

Dillon told him what had happened, because Roper had a talent approaching genius for making sense out of everything.

'What do you think?'

'Jean Talbot? Quite a lady. I liked the bit with the gun. She probably went along to the garage because she wanted to meet you – but I suspect she was also stirring things up. The Catholic and Protestant thing is what she was raised on all her life. She knew you'd have trouble at the Green Man.'

'That's true. Maybe she just likes to live dangerously. Anyway, what's the deal on Mickeen at Rosedene?'

220

'He's arrived and Charles Bellamy has everything in hand. He and Jordan fell into each other's arms and are enjoying lunch together at Rosedene as we speak.'

'So everybody's happy?'

'Until Ferguson surfaces. God help us all then. I've booked your flight plan for three hours from now at Belfast City. Over and out.'

Dillon leaned back. 'Three hours to lift off. Say farewell to beautiful Ulster.'

'If you're worried about Ferguson, I really meant it when I said I'd pay for the air ambulance,' Holley told him.

'After an initial roaring when he hears of it, Ferguson will calm down. The department will pay. It's a matter of honour.'

'Actually, I don't see why they should. Mickeen isn't in the employ of the Secret Intelligence Service. He just had an accident. It's you who've used your position to cause things to happen, helped by my promise to pay. Strictly speaking, I doubt whether Mickeen has any right to be in Rosedene.'

'Damn you and your logic, but I suppose you're right. Okay, I'll just have to pay for it myself.'

'Can you afford it?'

'To be honest, I made a great deal of money back in Nineteen ninety-one, payment for a spectacular, and we won't say what it was. The money's sat in a numbered account in Switzerland ever since. Over eighteen years, I believe it's trebled.'

'You old bastard,' Holley said. 'Is there no end to you?'

'So that's Mickeen taken care of. I'm going to have a nap.' Dillon inclined his seat back and closed his eyes.

Jack Kelly, sitting opposite Justin in the study, told him about the scene at the Green Man.

Justin was angry. 'What was my mother up to, creating such mayhem in Collyban?'

'She told me she simply wanted to express her sympathy to Paddy O'Rourke. She's known Flynn for years, always buys petrol from his garage.'

'So she was there just by chance when Dillon and Holley turned up. Really?'

'It seems so. And it was she who insisted they go to the Green Man to celebrate the deal. Unfortunately, Curry's man objected to Dillon, and matters got out of hand.'

'Unfortunate,' Justin shrugged. 'Well, if all that's true, I suppose there's really nothing to worry about. After all, she hasn't the slightest idea who Dillon and Holley are.'

'I can't see how she could,' Kelly said.

'Good. Then let's have a drink on it.'

9

Other things had been happening the previous evening, too, while Dillon and Holley were racing to make their flight to Belfast.

After the death threat from 'number one man', Kalid Hasim had felt extremely nervous. His friend, Sajid, was still in St Luke's Hospital with the broken arm. Omar, who had swum into the darkness of the Thames, had vanished. Alone, he felt very vulnerable.

But he was no coward, and he soon got restless. Tired of staying in the furnished room he rented, he ventured out at seven-thirty in the evening and went to his usual gym for a training session, a baseball bat in the long sports bag he carried, just in case.

It wasn't particularly busy and there was no one to spar with, so he just worked out for an hour, then showered, dressed and left, unsure of where he was going to go. There was a lamp shining down from a bracket about ten feet above the end of the narrow street, the beam causing a reflection of his image in the shop window, so that he was aware of the other image merging into his own, a gun in its right hand.

'I told you you were a dead man,' the voice said from behind him. 'Now keep walking and turn into the alley on the right. The canal's at the end. Very convenient, that, I'm sure you'll agree.'

'Just give me a break.' Hasim half sobbed for effect as he said it, then stumbled, dropped the bag, the baseball bat in his right hand, and swung wildly against the man's left thigh.

'Number one man' cursed and stumbled, the silenced pistol discharging. Hasim dropped the baseball bat at the sound, and ran out into the road blindly, dodging through traffic. He stopped in the safety of the far side, pedestrians around, and stepped into a doorway from where he could observe the alley. When a figure emerged, he gave himself away by carrying Hasim's sports bag in one hand.

He must have assumed Hasim was running for his life. Hasim had not been able to get a good look at his assailant on the street, but now he stepped back into the darkness of the doorway and watched him. The lights on a silver Mercedes down the street came on – must be a remote control. Hasim found a pen in a pocket of his tracksuit and wrote the licence plate number across the palm of his hand.

The man drove away, and Hasim stood, thinking. There was no point going home. That would be the equivalent of committing suicide. He had twenty-five or thirty pounds in his pocket. A limited future indeed, whichever way you looked at it. 'Number one man' was obviously serious about killing him, and it only gave him one choice. He waved down a cab, got in, and told the driver to take him to the Dark Man on Cable Wharf. It was time to talk to the Salters.

Harry and Billy Salter were in the corner booth, Dora serving them with two plates of sandwiches. 'Ham and pickles,' she said, 'and salad for the vegetarian teeto-taller.'

'So kind, Dora.' Billy reached for one. Harry said, 'Well, look what the cat's brought in.'

Hasim stood uncertainly just inside the door, and Joe Baxter went and grabbed his arm. 'Shall I give him the heave-ho, boss?'

'Just listen to me, Mr Salter,' Hasim pleaded.

'Why should I?'

'The guy I told you about who's just a voice on the phone?'

'The one you'd never met?' Billy said.

'He just tried to shoot me.'

There was complete silence, then Harry said, 'Now why would he do that?'

'After you gave me the money and told me to find my friend, I took him to the hospital. He's still there. The man I'm talking about called me. He said I'd shot my mouth off to you. He added that you now knew it was connected to Al Qaeda and it was my fault and I was a dead man.'

'And he's had a go?' Billy demanded.

Hasim described exactly what had happened when he'd left the gym in Camden.

'What a bastard,' Salter said. 'We can't have this. Let's have a look at your palm.' He examined it, turned to Billy, and read off the licence plate number Hasim had written there. 'Roper should take at least five minutes to trace this bleeder on his computer, wouldn't you say?'

'Absolutely.' Billy was already on his mobile, calling Holland Park. He got up, walking away as he talked to Roper.

Harry said, 'You look half starved. Have a sandwich. There's salad there. I know you Muslims don't go for ham.'

'Actually, I'm rather partial to it, so if you don't mind.' Hasim helped himself. 'There are Muslims and Muslims.'

'You'd better stay here for a bit while we sort this out,' Dora said as she brought him a drink. She ruffled his hair. 'Can't have a nice young lad like you running round in fear for his life.'

'God help us, she'll be adopting you next,' Harry

said. 'But she's got a point. Go on, have another sandwich, build yourself up.'

The licence plate number was the key that unlocked everything.

'His name's Selim Lancy,' Billy said when he returned to the booth. 'An interesting geezer. His father was an English seaman, his mother's Muslim. She's got cancer and she's a patient at St Luke's at the moment.'

'Just up the bleeding road,' Harry said. 'Bit of a coincidence.'

'Not really. They live in an old house on Tangier Wharf. That's no distance at all.'

'What's he do?' Harry asked. 'Has he got any form?'

'Not the kind you mean,' Billy said. 'A corporal in 3 Para. Couple of tours in Afghanistan, badly wounded, discharged. Roper's even got the amount of compensation he received from the Ministry of Defence. Seventeen grand.'

'Well, I think we should do better than that for our gallant lads,' Harry said. 'That isn't going to keep him for the rest of his life, is it?'

'He's bought a second-hand Mercedes and is a licensed private chauffeur.' Billy shrugged. 'It's a living, I suppose.'

'More than a living, I'd have thought,' Harry said. 'What's more glamorous than a war hero in a good suit driving a silver Mercedes? Those posh birds that go shopping to Harrods or Bond Street will lap him up. I bet he's making a fortune.'

'Which still leaves us with the Al Qaeda connection,' Billy said, and turned to Hasim, who'd been listening intently. 'What's that all about?'

'I honestly don't know,' Hasim said. 'He only mentioned the name Al Qaeda once, like I told you, when he sentenced me to death.' And then he frowned. 'I think he takes his religion seriously.'

'In what way?' Billy asked.

'He paid me and my friends once to smash up a shop selling anti-Muslim literature; then on another occasion to do the same to a place selling pornographic magazines.'

'Did you do that often?' Billy asked.

'We torched an old shop somebody had bought with the intention of turning it into a massage parlour. He told me over the phone that the people involved used young girls and that his boss thought it an offence against Allah.'

'Well, I agree with him there,' Harry said. 'But who was this boss he mentioned?'

'I haven't the slightest idea,' Hasim said. 'That was the only time he said such a thing.'

Harry turned to Billy. 'What do you make of this?'

'It fits with the Al Qaeda attitude,' Billy told him. 'They follow the teachings of the Koran, they're moralists, and these joints Hasim and his pals turned over were purveyors of filth.'

'All very well, my old son, but the attack on the Dark Man was nothing to do with Allah or the Koran, and everything to do with some personal vendetta against all of us,' Harry said.

'I agree,' Billy told him.

'Then I suggest you do something about it, like getting your arse over to Tangier Wharf, grabbing Lancy by the scruff of his neck and bringing him back here where I can put a few pertinent questions to him.' Harry looked grim. 'I mean, Muslim morality is one thing, but he's got questions to answer. Take the boys as backup if you want.'

Billy nodded to Baxter. 'I'll take Joe as driver, and Hasim might be useful. I'm just going to check my laptop. Roper was putting an identity photo through from army records.'

Harry said to Hasim, 'Do you feel okay about this? He sounds like a bad bastard.'

'Yes, I think he is.' Hasim looked tired, but shrugged and tried to smile. 'It's as Allah wills, Mr Salter. I made a bad mistake getting involved with this man. I will do anything to get rid of him.'

Billy returned wearing a dark single-breasted raincoat. He produced a silenced Walther from the interior pocket, checked it and replaced it.

He said to Baxter, 'You tooled up, Joe?'

'In the car,' Baxter told him. 'A selection.'

'That's it then.' Billy put a hand on Hasim's shoulder. 'Let's get it done.'

*   *   *

Selim Lancy had been visiting his mother in the oncology department at St Luke's. An operation for her skin cancer seemed to be working and they'd assured him the treatment had stopped the spread. He'd taken her flowers and sat with her for a while. She was a kind and simple person who divided her time between keeping the old Victorian flat on Tangier Wharf spotless and offering whatever services were required at the mosque.

She was overwhelmed by what seemed to her the luxury of her private room at the hospital, and Lancy had spent time assuring her that they could afford it. Except for pocket money, he'd always put everything into her deposit account, including the largesse from the Preacher, a total in excess of fifty thousand pounds. The dangerous game he had chosen to play carried the chance of instant death at any time, so it was his way of making things as simple as possible by leaving her everything in advance.

When he'd had enough, he kissed her hand and said to her in Arabic, 'Sleep well, Mother, Allah and all the angels protect you.'

Her eyes already closing, she murmured something and he eased out.

Turning from the busy right lane traffic of Wapping High Street into the gloom of Tangier Street was like a journey back in time, the old warehouse buildings, several storeys high, rearing up into the night, obviously waiting for the developer.

The streetlights were museum pieces, many of them originally gas lamps from the look of them. There was a strange, brooding air to the place, as if it was waiting for something to happen, as Joe Baxter cut his engine and coasted down over the cobbles to the Thames below.

'What a bleeding place to live,' Billy said. 'You'd only need the cameras to make a Jack the Ripper film.'

'It gives me the creeps,' Hasim said. 'I'm already imagining a bogey man waiting to jump out at me.'

They coasted silently down to a Victorian tower-like rookery about five storeys high, the wharf below it creating a basin of deep water where ship and barge traffic had been able to ply their trade. A gateway, its gates long gone, gave entrance to a courtyard, and the only light came from a lamp bracketed over the main door. A rotting sign said: 'Tangier Wharf, Hart & Son, General Shipping, 1852'.

'Christ,' Billy said. 'It's like Charles Dickens is writing the script.'

There was a modern sign at one side of the entrance, advertising a development of apartments and offices the following year with unsurpassed river frontage.

'I don't care what they do,' Hasim said, 'this place would still give me the creeps.'

'Never mind that,' Billy said. 'The important thing is there's no sign of a silver Mercedes in the courtyard, so we'll go and suss out the situation. Joe, just put the car across the street in that turning, so that it's out of sight.' Baxter switched on for a moment and turned into the yard across the way, then killed his engine again.

Billy opened the glove compartment and took out a Smith & Wesson revolver. 'Have you ever fired one of these?'

'Never,' Hasim said.

'Well, you've been to the movies, so you know what to do.' Billy replaced the weapon in the glove compartment. 'You know where it is if you need it. Stay here and keep your eyes open. We'll check where he lives.'

They moved across to the courtyard and Baxter tried the front door, which swung open. There was a tenant listing beside the door, most of the slots blank, and Billy read it quickly.

'They've all gone, except for Mrs Lancy. She's on the top floor.'

'And she's in the hospital, isn't she?' Baxter said.

'She certainly is, so let's get up there and see if we can arrange a surprise for her son when he returns home.'

Hasim sat there, not enjoying himself at all. The whole atmosphere of the place was threatening, and sitting in the Mercedes he felt claustrophobic, so he took the Smith & Wesson from the glove compartment, opened the door, got out and stood looking down at the river.

A boat passed, lit up, the sound of people and music echoing across the water, and then the muzzle of a pistol was rammed into the side of his head and the Smith & Wesson torn from his hand.

'Now then, you young bastard,' Selim Lancy said. 'Let's have some answers. What the hell is going on here? Don't try lying to me. I know who Salter is, and I recognize the geezer with him from my visit to the Dark Man when you dropped me in it. You've been doing it again.'

'Come off it,' Hasim said. 'I didn't know your name, never mind your address, until they picked me up.'

'And how did they know where to find you?'

'Salter had a look at my Social Security card when they turned me over that night at the Dark Man.'

'And how do they know about me?'

'Salter said he had one of his men follow me a couple of times and he noticed you in the silver Mercedes. He thought it odd, so they checked your licence plate number.'

'So what are they up to now?' The muzzle of the gun bored painfully into Hasim's right ear.

'Checking on your place to see if you're at home. He said your mother was in the hospital.'

The fact that they knew about his mother disturbed Lancy and made him angry. 'The bastards,' he said. 'Bringing my mother into it. Well, we'll see if I can provide a nice surprise. Get moving, across the court-yard and straight down the left side and round the back.'

Hasim did as he was told, wondering what had gone wrong. It was, in fact, very simple. Lancy parked in a yard on the high street by arrangement with a shopkeeper. It was sheer chance that he'd walked down Tangier Street just after Baxter's silent approach and had – from the shadows – witnessed what had gone on.

Now, he shoved Hasim roughly ahead of him, and paused. The rear of the building dropped five storeys down into forty feet of water in the basin, but at the side, another ancient lamp illuminated an old goods lift, the doors long since gone.

'Get in,' Lancy said. 'It still works, so hang on at that rail. We wouldn't want you to fall out, would we?'

Hasim was desperate, but there seemed no way out of his predicament. They stopped, and Lancy shoved him out on a flat roof. There were the remains of a low wall, which in some places had crumbled already. Hasim could see only the dark waters of the basin far below, the dim glow of a lamp.

'A fast route to hell,' Lancy said. 'A good seventy feet, so behave yourself or I'll shove you over. Now put your hands on your head.'

Hasim did as he was told. There was a stairhead with a door. Lancy got out his mobile and punched the right button and it was answered at once.

'Preacher. Is there a problem?'

'You could say that. I've got Billy Salter and one of his goons trying to invade the flat at Tangier

234

Wharf. I'm hoping to ambush them, but you never can tell.'

'How much does Salter know?'

'That Al Qaeda is a problem for them.'

'And how could they know that?'

'I was trying to do you a favour and it backfired. I haven't got time to explain now. But promise me one thing, Preacher. If things go sour, see to my mother for me, all right? I hear sounds now. I've got to go.'

He put a finger to his lips, nodded to Hasim, and gently eased the door open. A short flight of stairs dropped to the top landing and he could see the front door of the apartment, a dim light above it. There was the slightest of movements, the old stairs creaking, and he took aim and waited.

Hasim pushed him with all his force, screaming, 'Salter, he's got a gun!'

Lancy cursed, fired blindly three times down into the stairhead, then turned to fire at Hasim as he ran, head down, for the edge of the roof. A bullet plucked at his sleeve and he leapt out into space and fell to the basin, arms whirling.

Lancy kicked the door shut as bullets ploughed through it, then turned and ran to the lift, jumped in and pressed the button. It descended more rapidly than it had gone up. A couple of bullets chased him, ripping through the roof, but he made it to the ground floor, crossed the courtyard and ran up the steep slope towards Wapping High Street.

Billy and Baxter were right behind him. 'I'll get after him; you see what's happened to the boy.' Billy started to run.

As neither cigarettes nor alcohol featured in his life, he was very fit and, in spite of the steep slope and cobbled street, was gaining on the other man fast. Lancy glanced back and realized he was being overtaken, those Afghanistan wounds not helping. He put everything into that final spurt and ran straight out in front of a bus in Wapping High Street.

A woman screamed, people cried out, horns sounded as traffic was halted. Lancy lay on his back, blood on his face, and the driver got out of the bus, distraught. Other people approached as a lone policeman, who'd been on foot patrol, appealed for order and dropped down on his knees and went through the motions. He shook his head and stood up, spreading his arms to herd people back.

Somebody said, 'My God, he's dead.'

The bus driver wailed, 'He ran straight in front of me,' turning in appeal to people around him, and then there were the sounds of sirens approaching, police and ambulance, and Billy turned away and went back down Tangier Street.

As he reached the Wharf, Baxter came round the side of the building and started across the courtyard. 'Did he get away?' he asked.

'Ran headlong into traffic and got mown down by a bus,' Billy said. 'What about Hasim?'

'I've been all over the roof.' Baxter shook his head. 'Not a sign. He was a brave young bastard, warning us like he did, but Lancy did a lot of shooting up there. Must have knocked Hasim over. I've been looking round the side, but he isn't there.'

'Damn it to hell,' Billy said. 'I'm going to take a look.'

'Waste of time, Billy. There are seven floors on that building!'

Billy ignored him and walked along the wharf. There were lights here and there, but the basin was a dark pool, and when he looked up at the height of the rookery, it said it all. In spite of that, he called out at the top of his voice.

'Hasim, where the bloody hell are you?' His voice echoed between the old buildings and he turned to walk away.

'Over here, Mr Salter, I'm trying to get up this ladder.'

Billy ran along the wharf, Baxter following him, and they found Hasim in the light of a single lamp, halfway up an iron ladder. Baxter reached down, managed to grasp his right wrist, and heaved him up. He was shaking with cold and Billy took off his raincoat.

Hasim tried to wave it away. 'I think I'm bleeding, I'd ruin it. He tried to shoot me, so I had to jump off the roof.'

'I can't believe it,' Billy said. 'It's a miracle you're in one piece. Get this bloody coat on and we'll get out of it.'

'He's got away, has he?'

'He was knocked down by a bus and killed up on the high street,' Billy said as they walked to the car. 'How the hell did you come to be up there with him?'

Hasim explained, teeth chattering. As he finished, he said, 'He was going to kill all of us, no question, but something else happened on the roof. He called someone on his mobile. He said he had you two trying to invade the flat. He mentioned you by name. He said that Al Qaeda was a problem for them, which I figured meant you. He called the guy he was talking to "Preacher", and asked him to look after his mother if things went sour.'

They were at the Mercedes now, and Billy felt for the wound, got out his handkerchief and bound it tightly. He pushed Hasim into the back of the car and sat beside Baxter.

'St Luke's accident and emergency, Joe. I'll take over the car when we get there and you stay with Hasim – the story is that he fell in the river and hurt himself on the ladder. When everything's okay, we'll come up from the Dark Man and fetch you.'

'You mean me as well, Mr Salter?' Hasim said.

'Who else do I mean? You're a bleeding hero, sunshine. After what you did tonight, you're a made man. Harry Salter will see to that.'

Harry was over the moon as Billy sat in the corner booth and told him exactly what had happened, Sam

Hall and Dora hanging on his every word. They were still discussing it when Joe Baxter appeared, having come down in a taxi with the news that Hasim was being kept in the hospital for a day or two.

'Hypothermia,' he said. 'And he needed a few stitches in his arm. He was more worried about that than anything else – said it would give him a problem boxing.'

Harry shook his head. 'He's got guts, that kid, to do what he did. Have a word with Chuck Green, Billy. He's opened another health club, in Wandsworth. That makes seven. We've got money in that. Get him to take Hasim on, keep an eye on him.'

'I'll do that,' Billy said. 'But I'm going to take a run up to Holland Park and report in to Roper. I'll see you later.

In West Hampstead, Professor Hassan Shah sat at the desk in his ornate Edwardian villa, thinking about everything as calmly as he could. Lancy's telephone call had set every alarm bell going. Lancy didn't do panic, it wasn't in his nature; he was a hard-knocks paratrooper who'd done his time in Afghanistan and paid the price with his wounds. More than that, he'd killed on Shah's behalf without the slightest compunction. He was a man who could handle anything, and yet he hadn't been in touch since his call from Tangier Wharf. So Shah did the obvious and called him on his mobile. After all, he couldn't be traced if someone else answered.

It rang for a long time and he simply sat there listening. He was about to give up when a woman answered. 'Grange Street Morgue.'

Hassan Shah said calmly, 'I'm so sorry, I must have called the wrong number.'

'Probably not, sir. This is the personal effects room, where we store the belongings of those brought in dead, to be claimed later, of course. Could you give me the name of the individual you were trying to call?'

Shah took a huge breath to steady himself. 'Selim Lancy.'

She answered at once. 'Oh, yes, he was brought in quite recently. Knocked down by a bus in Wapping High Street.'

'And killed,' Shah said. It was a stupid remark, but involuntary.

'Of course, sir, he's here waiting for a post mortem. You're a relative?' she asked.

'No, I employed him on occasion.'

'Could I have your name? It may be of use if there are identification problems.'

'I'm so sorry, but I suddenly feel very upset. I'll have to call you back.'

He switched off and sat there. The consequence of the business he was in was death, sometimes of a few, sometimes of many. You had to harden your heart: he had learned that a long time ago. Strange, then, that he felt genuine sadness in Lancy's case. Considering what had gone before, it was obviously not an accident. The Salters had to be behind it – them and Ferguson.

Ferguson had been a problem for too long, but he seemed to live a charmed life; it was rumoured he had even walked away from a car bomb. Perhaps, after all, the best solution was the old-fashioned way as used by the IRA for years. A silenced pistol loaded with hollow point cartridges, the bullet in the back of the head one lonely night in the rain and dark. Or in the back in a crowd, the target falling to the ground, the assassin calmly walking away.

All it required was a man with nerves of steel, and probably one who liked his work: a man like Lancy. Justin Talbot certainly liked his work, and was mad enough to take any chance. In fact, he was beginning to worry Shah, who for some time now had decided it was a good thing that Talbot did not know his identity. Perhaps the temptation of putting a bullet in the back of Shah's own head on a dark rainy night might have proved too great.

But all this would have to wait, for suddenly the most important thing in his life was an old Muslim woman in the cancer ward at St Luke's Hospital who did not know that her best beloved son had gone to paradise, leaving her alone. Professor Hassan Shah had no idea how to break the news to her, but it had to be done. It was a matter of honour, but at this time of night she would be asleep. He would leave it till the morning.

There was another matter that needed taking care of,

also a matter of honour. He made a call on his special mobile and spoke to the man who answered it.

'Hamid, this is the Preacher. I have traffic for you, starting now. A photo and address will be in your laptop in five minutes. Deliver punishment at once with extreme prejudice. Osama's blessing on you.'

There was a short pause and then the reply. 'Allah is great and Osama is his Prophet.'

It was just past midnight. Billy Salter had been with Roper for the past hour, getting filled in on the reason for Dillon's sudden trip to Ulster, and now he was driving down from Wapping High Street to the Dark Man. There were lamps here and there, three on the jetty that had the *Linda Jones* tied up to it, a few scattered around the car park. Not that there were many vehicles around at that time of night, with the pub closed since eleven, Dora's implacable house rules. There were lights on at the back of the building in the private quarters, but otherwise it was quiet and remote, with only the river noises to be heard.

He parked the red Alfa Romeo Spider, got out and stretched, for he was exhausted, hardly surprising after the events of the evening. He stood by one of the lamps at the beginning of the jetty and inhaled that wonderful river smell that was the Thames; it was where he'd grown up and it always made him feel better.

When he turned, a man was standing there, medium

height with longish hair, wearing a leather bomber jacket. 'Mr Salter.' The voice was very soft.

'Who the hell are you?' Billy demanded.

'The Wrath of Osama.'

His hand swung up, there was the dull thud of a silenced weapon, and two rounds hit Billy around the heart. The force of the blow was enormous, sending him staggering on to his back. He breathed deeply as he had been trained to do, trying to stay conscious.

The man came forward to finish him, and Billy's right hand found the silenced Colt .25 with hollow point cartridges in his ankle holster. As the man leaned over, Billy shot him between the eyes.

Billy sat up, coughing and feeling sick, then unbuttoned his coat, ripped open his shirt, and felt for the two rounds sticking in the nylon-and-titanium vest he was wearing. Finally, he got up and went to the body and examined it. The face was covered in blood and the back of the skull was fragmented. He got down on his knees and searched it, but all he found were empty pockets. There wasn't even a mobile.

He went and sat on a bench by the pub entrance and called Roper, who answered at once. 'Did you forget something?'

'I've got a disposal. Make it fast. I'm outside the entrance to the Dark Man. The geezer was waiting for me. Said he was the Wrath of Osama, then shot me twice in the heart, or thought he did. He said my name. I think it was a revenge thing. I bet the bloody Preacher sent him.'

'I'm calling it in now. You go inside.'

'God damn it, no,' Billy said. 'I'm sick of it.'

He switched off his mobile, went down to the jetty to the *Linda Jones*, and sat on the stern seat, waiting.

After a while, a dark van appeared, pulled in front of the pub, and two men in black overalls got out, produced a body bag, eased the corpse into it and closed the door. They would see to it that the inconvenient corpse turned to six pounds of grey ash within two hours.

Billy walked down towards them and the door of the pub opened. Billy said to one of the men, 'Many thanks, Mr Teague.'

'Are you all right?' Teague asked.

'Well, the bastard did shoot me twice but, thanks to the Wilkinson Sword Company, I'm still here.'

'Thank God for that,' Teague said. 'We'll be on our way.'

Billy turned and found Harry looking grim and Dora in a dressing gown behind him. Harry Salter said, 'Well, at least we know where we are with this Preacher fellow. He means business and we've got to be ready for him.'

'Harry, I couldn't bloody care less,' Billy said. 'Just lock all the doors so nobody can break in, and let me go to bed. I've had it.'

10

The following morning, Harry Miller appeared in the computer room, hair wet from the shower and wearing a track suit. It was just before noon and he was yawning.

'I thought you'd have slept longer,' Roper said. 'You don't exactly look your best.'

'I'll pull round. Any word from Ferguson?'

'Not yet, but when he does surface, wait for the fireworks.'

'And why is that?'

'Let me begin at the beginning. Night before last, Sean and Daniel took themselves off to Belfast.'

Miller was astonished. 'But what the hell for?'

So Roper told him everything. Miller sat there, mesmerized, and when the story was finished, said, 'So Mickeen Oge has just been delivered to Rosedene, and Dillon and Holley are on their way back to Belfast, after creating mayhem at Collyban which even managed to involve Jean Talbot?'

'Exactly. I talked to Sean just this morning. What will the brand-new Chairman of Talbot International have to say about his beloved mother and our gallant friends getting involved in a brawl in the worst kind of Republican pub?' Roper smiled. 'It's quite bizarre, isn't it?'

Miller was grinning; just couldn't help it. 'I don't think that's the way Ferguson will describe it. That's quite a bit of event while we were gone.'

'And that's not all,' Roper said, and told him what had happened to Billy.

Miller listened intently. 'So there it is,' Roper said as he finished. 'The existence of the Preacher is confirmed, and we now know with absolute certainty that Al Qaeda is out to get the lot of us.'

'The hit man: no further news of him?' Miller asked.

'Not a thing. It was a totally clean job. No identification, no mobile phone, the silenced Walther he was using was treated with some resin so there are no fingerprints.'

'The kind of man willing to sacrifice himself, like a suicide bomber?' Miller said.

'Yes. When Billy asked him who he was, he said he was the Wrath of Osama and then shot him.' Roper grunted. 'I feel so damn passive. We have these two mystery figures, the Preacher and Shamrock, and we're no closer to finding out who they are. We can only respond when they make a move against us. I want to make a move against *them*.'

'And we will,' Miller said and stood up. 'Meanwhile, I know one thing. We're all going to have to be bloody careful from now on,' and he went out.

A few minutes later, Roper's phone sounded and Ferguson's voice boomed out from Cavendish Place. 'Ah, there you are, Roper. I'm just enjoying my first decent cup of tea in two days. Why don't you bring me up to speed on what's happening.'

'Everything, General?' Roper asked.

'Of course, everything, man. Get on with it!'

So Roper did.

Ferguson was amazingly calm when Roper finished. He said, 'Anything to do with Dillon these days is usually so beyond belief that it can only be true. It's the only bloody explanation. I shall call in at Rosedene on my way in, and I'll discuss Mickeen Oge's situation with Professor Bellamy. Naturally, we'll do everything we can.'

'And the air ambulance?'

'I must be practical there. Budgets are tight these days for all of us. If Daniel Holley feels like taking care of it, that's fine. God knows he can afford it. As for that other adventure in Collyban, it was damn reckless of Dillon. He knows perfectly well there are plenty of people there who'd be delighted to put a bullet in his back. I'll speak to him, of course, but I don't think it will do much good.'

'Is that it, General?'

'No, we'll have a council of war later on today when everyone is available. This attempt on Billy's life worries me greatly. It's very difficult to deal with brutal, simple attacks like that, particularly when the assassin doesn't care whether he lives or dies. From now on, everyone wears his vest, everyone goes armed, and everyone must assume he could be drawn upon at any moment.' Ferguson managed a laugh. 'It's not really very funny, this war on terrorism, is it?'

Over the years, the Preacher had evolved certain rules concerning assassination. His asset, as he called him, had to be clean. No mobile phone, nothing that could identify him or the weapon he used. Nevertheless, after the death sentence had been carried out, the asset was supposed to phone in within three hours to tell him it was done. The man he had given the Salter job to had been successful on six previous occasions. The fact that he had not been in touch now could only mean one thing.

Shah had a faculty meeting later in the afternoon, but with two hours to kill, he felt for the first time that things were going wrong. He was used to being in charge, to everything running like clockwork, and now something was out of joint, and he didn't know what to do about it. On impulse, he called Justin Talbot.

Shah knew nothing about the Mickeen Oge Flynn affair or any of the subsequent events, because Talbot had chosen to leave him in ignorance of it all. The way Justin looked at it, the comatose Mickeen Oge at Rosedene had nothing to do with the Preacher.

It was raining and Talbot had been for a gallop in the downpour. He was in the stable giving the stallion a rubdown when the Preacher called. Justin stopped working and said, 'How are things?'

In her studio upstairs, his mother had kept the door permanently ajar since she had first started eavesdropping, and now stopped working to listen.

'Not too good,' Shah said. 'You remember Billy Salter?'

'Of course.' Justin lit a cigarette and sat on a bench.

'He's become what the Mafia would call a stone in my shoe. He's been responsible for causing the death of a young man I valued highly.'

'What a shame. Perhaps it's time to make an example of him.'

'I tried to do exactly that. I gave the job to one of my best assets last night.'

'You mean you gave a hired killer instructions to shoot Billy Salter?'

'Exactly. A good man, a true follower of Osama.'

Justin had an insane desire to laugh. 'Don't tell me: let me guess. He didn't shoot Billy Salter, Billy Salter shot him.'

'So it would appear.'

'Have you any idea what you're dealing with with these two, Billy and his father? In spite of his millions from legitimate developments, Harry Salter is still a gangster, and so is Billy. Sean Dillon and Daniel Holley, both Provos, for Christ's sake. Harry Miller – a living legend of Army Intelligence. Ferguson – well, his record speaks for itself.'

'So what's your point?'

'Read *The Art of War* by Sun Tzu. It's two thousand years old, but still true today. Make your enemy come looking for you, choose your own field of battle and make it unfamiliar and difficult terrain. Take Vietnam. Soldiers from the most sophisticated army in the world found themselves up to their bellies in jungle swamps chasing scrawny little peasants called Viet Cong. Remember who won?'

'Point taken,' Shah said. 'But what are you suggesting?'

'Get Ferguson and his people into the jungle, so to speak. Give them something to hunt for, something they want badly, and they'll come to you.'

'Something like what?' Shah asked.

'I'd think that would be obvious. Shamrock is the man they want to get their hands on more than anyone else. Give them me.'

Shah was shocked. 'What?'

'I understand Daniel Holley was put through an IRA-sponsored training camp deep in the Algerian desert at a place called Shabwa. His chief instructor was a man named Omar Hamza, once a Sergeant in the French Foreign Legion. I've checked him out, using contacts from my SAS days. The camp closed down for lack of business years ago, and Hamza moved on to run a trading post in the Khufra Marshes.'

'Where is that?'

'On the Algerian coast near Cap Djinet, what you might call badlands. Marsh Arabs in villages on small islands, fishermen, Berber tribesmen. It's a haven for smugglers of every description and a home to thieves and cutthroats of every kind,' Justin said quite cheerfully.

'And where is this leading?' Shah asked.

'It's very simple. Your Colonel Ali Hakim has a friendly word with his friend Malik and tells him he's heard rumours which he thinks might interest Holley. His mentor from Shabwa, Omar Hamza, is up to his old tricks, this time in the marshes – and his informants speak of a mystery man Hamza calls Shamrock. Like certain other Arab states, the Algerian Government is not Al Qaeda's best friend. Hakim could say he has been given secret instructions to take a police unit into the marshes to hunt Omar down in a covert operation. Malik is certain to report this to Daniel Holley, and I can almost guarantee you that the idea of a hunting party will appeal to Ferguson very much. What's the betting that he'll offer Holley expert assistance from Dillon and some of the others on this venture into the marsh?'

'From which they'll never emerge,' Shah said.

'I thought the general idea was to kill the bastards, right? Talbot said. 'Okay, we've no idea how many people Ferguson would send, but I'd think three or four at least. It's essential not to delay on this. You must speak to Hakim as soon as possible so that he can get the ball rolling.'

'And you think this could work?' Shah said.

'I don't see why not. Especially since I intend to go and supervise the job myself.'

Shah was shocked. 'But that's crazy. How could you disguise yourself?'

'To Marsh Arabs and Berbers, I'd be just another white face. I was in the Algerian desert four years ago with a Talbot International oil exploration team. I was very impressed with the Tuaregs – noble and aristocratic bastards who wear dark blue robes and turbans and veils. Ordinary Arabs shy away from them. I took some of the robes home as a souvenir. I knew I'd find a use for them one day.'

'So how would you get there?'

'There's an old World War Two air-force base called Fasa on the eastern end of the marshes. It's in ruins, but the runway is still viable. Talbot International has a Citation X at Frensham with full tanks, which can manage the flight to Algiers and the return to England.

I might fly it myself, but I'll take another pilot along, too, to stand guard while I'm in the marshes. With luck, it won't take more than thirty-six hours.'

'And you insist on doing this?'

'I'm bored out of my skull and I want to see some action. So I suggest you get things moving with Ali Hakim, like yesterday, unless you think he'll say no.'

'Impossible,' Shah said. 'He has taken the oath. I'll call him at once, but I'll give you his mobile number, too, just in case you need to get in touch at some stage.'

Justin returned to rubbing down the stallion, whistling to himself softly. Above, in the studio, his mother still sat on a stool by the half-open door, trying to take it all in. It had been only half of a conversation, so it was difficult to make sense of, but there'd been enough to tell her that her son was getting into something very heavy indeed. And yet she felt, as she had before, a strange kind of paralysis that prevented her from broaching the matter with him. Once again, she backed off and went down the stairs into the stable.

He turned to her and smiled. 'Haven't you finished that damn portrait yet?'

'Soon,' she said, 'I promise you. I'm going to the kitchen to make some sandwiches. Come when you're ready.'

She went out, and he eased the stallion into its stall, closed the gate and went after her.

Dillon was having coffee with Holley when he got a call from Roper. 'So you've got out of dear old Ulster in one piece.'

'Why, Roper, you sound unhappy about that. Is the General functioning, and Miller?'

'Oh yes. Ferguson's been very understanding about the whole Mickeen Oge business, though he says he'll be happy to have you pay for the air ambulance, Daniel.'

'That's very gracious of him,' Dillon said.

'Just shut up and listen, Sean. He knows about the trip to Collyban and what happened to you, and considers your behaviour ill-advised and reckless.'

'That's nice of him.'

'Yes, but while you guys were busy last night in Belfast, things were happening here as well.'

'Like what?' Dillon was frowning now.

'Like an Al Qaeda hit man shooting Billy outside the Dark Man. If you can keep quiet for five minutes, I'll give you the details.'

When he was finished, Holley said, 'So we now know for certain that Osama bin Laden's man in London is called the Preacher, Shamrock is one of his assets, and Al Qaeda is hoping to shoot the lot of us at the first opportunity.'

'Yes, isn't life grand?' Roper said. 'Ferguson is having

a council of war this afternoon. I think it's time to start going after these guys hard.'

At the same time, Colonel Ali Hakim was also on the phone to the Preacher, who explained exactly what he wanted Hakim to do.

When he was finished, Hassan Shah said, 'Are we clear?'

'Of course. Actually, it shouldn't be that difficult. That old ruined air base at Fasa is on the edge of the desert and about ten miles from the west side of the Khufra marshes. We keep two police launches there, and there is a coastal village called Dafur, which also has an old runway from the days of the Afrika Korps. It's still used in emergencies.'

'Do the police go into the marshes frequently?'

'Not really. It's a place for bad people to hide in. Omar Hamza is an old friend of mine. He acts as a government supply agent. To be frank, I have a financial arrangement with him. He will do as I say, I assure you, and that will include welcoming this Shamrock.'

'It is essential that you do. Ferguson wants him badly, and Shamrock is the bait in the trap to make them come. What about the Ministry in Algiers?'

'You can leave that to me.'

'And the police to crew the launches?'

'Blackguards to a man. The men I'll use are thoroughly corrupt – and they don't take prisoners.'

'Excellent,' the Preacher said. 'Speak to Malik now. Time is of the essence.'

He switched off. Hakim sat there for a moment, then called Malik at his villa. When Malik answered, Hakim said, 'My dear friend, how are you? I was wondering if I could call round for a coffee.'

'Of course. You know I'm always glad to see you.'

'I have something I think you might be interested to hear.'

They sat on the terrace drinking Yemeni Mocha coffee, and Hakim told him everything he thought Malik needed to know. 'Things have got out of hand in the Khufra. This Hamza used to be a good man, but now he's a bad man. Who this individual is he calls Shamrock, I have no idea.'

'It was always a haven for scoundrels,' Malik said.

'Yes, well, the days of the honest thief are over, especially the way the drug traffic has increased. Our friend Hamza has operated under several false names over the years and made a living running a trading post on Diva Island, right in the centre of things. We knew it was him, and decided to let it go as long as he behaved himself, but the cocaine and heroin smuggling can't be overlooked. There's a fortune in that white powder!'

'Disgraceful,' Malik said. 'It must be stopped.'

'Oh, I intend to do that. I'll go in with two launches

and elite police and lay hands on Hamza, if it's the last thing I do. Mind you, it won't be easy, but I'm old-fashioned, my friend.' He stood up and put on his cap. 'Duty and honour. If you are talking to Daniel, give him my best – and if he needs assistance from me in any way, you can give him my number.'

Daniel Holley and Dillon were deep in conversation when Holley's mobile sounded. Malik said, 'Where are you? Can you talk? I've something interesting to tell you.'

'What is it?'

'You were asking where Omar Hamza had got to. I've discovered where. Those damn Khufra marshes.'

'What's he doing there?' Holley asked.

'Well, I've just been talking to Ali Hakim and it goes like this.'

When Malik finished Holley said, 'That's very interesting, Malik, very interesting indeed. I'm glad you called.'

'The good Colonel said I could give you his personal number if it would be useful and you wanted a word.'

'It certainly would,' Holley said, and inserted it into his own mobile as Malik gave it to him. 'Thanks, you've done me a real service.'

When he hung up, Dillon said, 'What was that all about?'

Holley gave him the gist of it in a few terse sentences, and Dillon said, 'Do you know this place, the Khufra marshes?'

'No, I've never been. The occasion just didn't arise.'

'Well, I have. Billy and I had a hell of a time there about three years ago, chasing a guy who was involved with the murder of Hannah Bernstein, Ferguson's personal assistant.'

Holley said, 'What did you make of the place?'

'Well, the town was pretty wide open, but the back country is wild and treacherous, with water reeds twenty feet high. The villagers and fishermen live pretty much as they have done for centuries. A good place if you want to drop out of sight.'

'Do you think Ferguson would be interested in what Malik's told me?'

'I'd say you can count on it,' Dillon said. 'If it's all true, it's the only really positive lead we've got. It can't be ignored.'

'But what would Shamrock be doing there?'

'I can remember when it would have been the most natural thing in the world to come to Algeria in search of revolutionary training camps,' Dillon told him. 'Both of us did it.'

'That was then, this is now,' Holley said.

Dillon nodded, 'But if he is there, even just passing through, there must be some purpose to his visit. And I intend to find out what.' As he stood up he said, 'Before facing Ferguson, I'd like to call in at

Rosedene and check on Mickeen Oge. Is that okay with you?'

'Be my guest,' Holley said. We'll go straight there.'

The moment they walked in to the lounge at Rosedene, the Matron, Maggie Duncan, appeared and greeted them warmly.

'How is he?' Dillon asked.

'Much as expected, Sean, but Professor Bellamy just looked in to see a few patients. I'm sure he'll be with you soon. There is one thing. You can't go into Mickeen's room without supervision. He's all wired up, as it were. A very delicate balance. You can go and have a look at him through the viewing window. Room Nine down the corridor.'

They stood together, peering in at the dimly lit room. Mickeen was festooned with cables leading to electronic equipment, tubes into his body from several bottles of fluid. His sleeping face was very pale, no colour there at all.

'He's just like a waxwork,' Holley said.

'More like a corpse, poor devil.' Dillon shook his head. 'A living death is pretty terrible, when you think of it.'

'But if he doesn't know what's happened to him,' Holley shrugged. 'They say that some people waking up from this state have no idea of all the time passed.'

'That's right.' Professor Bellamy came up behind them. 'This condition is one of the strangest known to medical science. He could wake up at any moment or he could languish in the comatose state for months, occasionally even longer than that.'

'So we're keeping him alive with the help of modern electronics and drugs?' Dillon said, and he sighed heavily. 'God help me, I don't know what's right and what's wrong any more.'

Bellamy patted his shoulder. 'At least he's here, Sean, getting the very best of attention. It could have been much worse. Anyway, I must finish my rounds. I'll see you again. By the way, are you aware of what happened to Billy Salter last night? You've been away, of course.'

'Yes, and thank God for the vest,' Dillon said.

'It certainly saved his life, but two forty-five-calibre rounds delivered to the heart area at a range of ten or twelve feet has not left him in the best of conditions. I've released him, but he needs to take it easy for a while. He's not fit to play any of your usual games, Sean.' Bellamy took off his spectacles and rubbed an eye. 'You're his friend and I'm appealing to you.'

'You can rely on me, I promise, Professor.'

'Excellent.' Bellamy walked away.

'Shall we?' Holley asked.

'Yes, let's go and see the old sod and get it over with.' He followed Holley across the hall and out of the front door.

ALGERIA

—

THE KHUFRA MARSHES

11

Holley drove and Dillon called in to Roper, who cut in on him instantly and said, 'I thought you'd be coming straight here. The General's been asking for you.'

'Do we get blasted out of the water for being naughty boys?'

'I don't think so. He's dark and sombre. I can't remember seeing him in such a black-dog mood. There's a kind of despair there because we aren't making progress, and the attempt on Billy's life last night greatly worried him.'

'So it should,' Dillon said. 'We've just been talking to Bellamy at Rosedene. He released Billy, but he's not happy about his health. I gave him my word that we wouldn't get Billy involved in anything active for a while, and I mean to keep it. Bellamy's put him together again more than once. He can't keep doing it.'

'How was Mickeen?'

'Comatose is the word they're using, and that sums it up. But listen, Roper. Something seriously important's just turned up from Malik in Algiers. I'm handing you over to Daniel, who'll fill you in.'

When Holley was finished, Dillon cut in. 'What do you think? It could give Ferguson a shot in the arm.'

'It's an interesting prospect, to put it mildly,' Roper said. 'But we shouldn't discuss it without the General present. I'd get here as fast as possible if I were you. I imagine he'll bring that council of war forward.'

Ferguson, catching up on paperwork at his desk in Cavendish Place, was galvanized by Roper's call.

'What incredible news. I'm just finishing the Peshawar report for the Prime Minister, then I'll come straight round. Have everybody there. This might be some sort of breakthrough for us.'

Harry Miller was already on the premises, enjoying a workout in the gym, which left the Salters. Roper hesitated, then thought, well, there was no harm in having Billy in on the discussion, as long as they didn't send him out into harm's way. He contacted Billy and found him at the Dark Man, told him Ferguson had called a meeting and wanted everyone there.

Billy sounded subdued. 'What's he up to now?'

'That's for him to say, but it's important. Are you okay?'

'Of course I am.' Billy was irritated. 'Why wouldn't I be?'

'Only asking,' Roper said. 'We'll see you then,' and he got to work researching Omar Hamza and the Khufra marshes.

It was an hour later when Ferguson arrived at Holland Park to find everyone waiting for him in the computer room. He was full of energy, and it showed.

'I don't know how much you all know about why we're here, so let's start from scratch. Daniel, just go through the conversation Malik had with you.'

Which Daniel did, ending with an observation about Hakim. 'I've known Ali Hakim for years; he's probably Malik's best friend. A Military Police Colonel, highly regarded in government circles, a specialist in anti-terrorism. I don't need to tell you that Algeria has problems with fundamentalists just like other countries in the Middle East, and the government don't like Al Qaeda.'

It was Harry Salter who made the obvious point. 'But what would Shamrock be doing there in the Khufra?'

'We don't know. Hakim's informant simply mentioned a mystery Westerner staying with Omar Hamza who called him Shamrock.'

'I've had a thought on that point,' Roper said. 'There

265

has been more than one bombing in Algeria during the last three months, by a jihadist group thought to be linked to Al Qaeda. They've tended to go for police barracks. The most recent one caused eighteen deaths and forty-seven wounded. Perhaps Shamrock has a link with all that.'

'That's just supposition again and it doesn't help in the slightest,' Ferguson said to Roper. 'Let's go to the source. You have Hakim's personal mobile number. Get him now and put him on speaker. Everybody else, keep quiet.'

'Colonel Ali Hakim?' Roper said in Arabic. 'I have Major General Charles Ferguson for you.'

'A great pleasure,' Hakim said in English.

'I won't beat about the bush, Colonel,' Ferguson told him. 'We've heard about the conversation you had with Hamid Malik regarding Omar Hamza, and mentioning the name of Shamrock.'

'Ah, yes, but I'm afraid I can't help you there. That name has only just come to my attention as someone Hamza is involved with. Apparently, he could be British. He certainly isn't Arab. I don't even know how far his involvement with Hamza goes. He is an unknown entity to me.'

'Well, not to me,' Ferguson said. 'Tell me, how would you go about your expedition into the Khufra?'

'There is a small fishing village on the coast, called

Dafur, with a population of only seventy or eighty. It has two good jetties that Rommel's people constructed in the war. There's even a crumbling landing strip for aircraft, which the coastguard can use in emergencies. I have two large police launches and fifteen thugs in uniform who just love those who say no to them so they can knock them down.'

'I should imagine that's what you'd need in a place like that, but let me be completely frank with you. Shamrock is a very bad man and I want to lay my hands on him more than anything else in the world. You'd be doing me a great favour if you allowed me and my people to join in.'

Hakim did 'shock' very convincingly. 'But, General, this would be completely out of order.'

'Would it make a difference if Daniel Holley were involved? He's an Algerian citizen.'

'That's true,' Hakim said, 'Daniel is highly regarded, but my arrangements are firm.'

'You mention a landing strip. We could fly direct from the UK and land there.'

Holley waved at Ferguson and gave him a thumbs-up and mouthed 'Falcon'. Hakim said, 'It would be most irregular.'

'Not in a Falcon owned by Malik Shipping and piloted by Daniel Holley.'

Hakim now did a good performance of accepting defeat. 'I suppose in such circumstances, it would be all right.'

'Excellent,' Ferguson said. 'I'll call you back.'

Roper cut the call. 'Who's going, then?'

Ferguson said to Holley, 'How many does the Falcon take?'

'Two pilots in the cockpit, six passengers.'

'We could all go,' Ferguson said.

'No, we couldn't,' Dillon told him. 'We can cut out Billy, for starters.'

Billy was indignant. 'Who says so?'

'Charles Bellamy,' Dillon told him. 'He made me promise to make sure you stay out of things for a while. The vest saved your life, Billy, but two forty-five-calibre rounds at short range to the heart takes time to get over, and he warned you.'

Harry Salter turned to Billy. 'You didn't tell me.'

'So what, it's no big deal,' Billy told him.

Harry looked at Ferguson. 'That's it, he's out of it.'

'Yes, I understand the situation—' Ferguson began, but Dillon cut in on him. 'And you're out of it, too. You've been a great soldier, Charles, but to use military terminology, Peshawar was a bridge too far. Any idea of you penetrating a pesthole like the Khufra marshes is ridiculous. Think Vietnam. The average age of those Yanks in the Mekong Delta was nineteen.'

Ferguson's face was pale. 'God damn you, Dillon. Yes, I'm an arrogant bastard, but I'll have you know I'm still as good a man on the ground and in the air as anyone else here.' He appeared to be trying to get a grip on his emotions. 'But that said, you're right. My role is here and yours is in Algeria. Roper, call Hakim back and finalize the arrangements.'

Hassan Shah was in West Hampstead, working at his computer, when Hakim contacted him.

'It worked. Dillon, Holley and Miller are leaving in four hours' time to fly here. They're as good as dead.'

'Just those three?' Shah frowned. 'I'd hoped for Ferguson. What about young Salter?'

'Who knows? The death of these three alone will be an enormous coup. It will cripple Ferguson. When will Shamrock leave?'

'I'll call him now to tell him the whole thing is a go, and get back to you.'

His call found Justin Talbot in the study, having a drink and reading *The Times*. 'It's on,' Shah said. 'Dillon, Holley and Miller are leaving in four hours. They've arranged with Hakim to land on the old German runway at Dafur to join him for a dawn invasion of the marshes. It seems Ferguson is not going.'

'I didn't think he would,' Justin said. 'And what about Omar Hamza?'

'He expects you, and Hakim will inform him when he knows you're on your way. When will that be?'

'Sooner than you think. I got moving on my preparations yesterday. I arranged for one of my pilots, Chuck

Alan, to fly the Citation X over yesterday evening. It's owned by a Swiss company and untraceable. It's at Belfast City now and Chuck is standing by, waiting for my call. I'm already packed, too, so I'll get straight off. I'll be in Belfast in an hour.'

'But what about your mother?'

'She's gone into Newry to get her hair done. I'll leave her a note pleading urgent business. She's used to it.

'Good. Now take this down. Hakim gave me Hamza's mobile number.'

Justin did. 'I'll get moving then.'

'May the blessing of Allah go with you.'

'Nonsense,' Talbot said. 'He gave up on me long ago.'

He switched off, went to the writing desk, jotted a note to Jean and left it in a prominent place. Then he dashed upstairs, found his flying jacket and the bag he'd packed, went down to the front door, and was in the Mercedes and driving away just ten minutes before the maroon Shogun turned into the drive.

He got his mobile out one-handed and called Chuck Alan. 'Hi, old buddy,' he said. 'I'm on my way, so get moving.'

Alan said, 'Will do, boss.'

A little while later, Justin's mother called. She didn't argue, simply said, 'Couldn't you have said goodbye?'

'Sorry about that. Something urgent came up, a company matter. It's a last-minute thing.'

'No, it wasn't. I took a call from Frensham when you were out yesterday afternoon. They were checking to see if everything had gone well with the Citation at Belfast. You knew in advance you were going to make this trip.'

'Come on, love, it's no big deal.'

'Secrets and lies, Justin, so many of them. I don't know where I am any more. You're as careless as a young boy; your conversations on that wretched mobile echo round the house, or half of them do, and that's enough to frighten me, because so much of it seems to concern itself with death. I even know where you're going now – Algeria. I hear the name Al Qaeda mentioned many times, as well as Sean Dillon and Daniel Holley, the men I met in Collyban. I know what they are and I'm so, so frightened.'

'Maybe you've been listening when you shouldn't,' Justin told her. 'That's always very unwise, because when you only get part of a story, you don't get the truth.'

'Oh, go to hell, Justin,' she shouted at him, and threw her mobile across the room.

Hassan Shah called Hakim. 'I've spoken to Shamrock. He'll be airborne before they are.'

Hakim said, 'You gave him Hamza's number?'

'Of course.'

'Good, I'll have them alert me as soon as he lands. Hamza will be on a small island called Diva in the centre of the marshes: that's where the trading post is. It's about ten miles from Fasa. People use small boats to get around in there, mostly with outboard motors. I'm sure Hamza will pick Shamrock up himself.'

'Amazing,' Hassan Shah said. 'You and your men have no intention of invading the Khufra to flush out the thieves and vagabonds. The only purpose of the entire operation is to kill Dillon, Holley and Miller.'

'But of course. That's what you wanted, wasn't it? My units on patrol in the Khufra learned a long time ago that it was better to leave well enough alone up here. It's like keeping animals in a zoo. The people who are penned up in the marshes are the scum of the earth, so we leave them to get on with it as long as they don't venture outside. Omar Hamza rules with a rod of iron, on my behalf.'

'I assume you take your share of the drug trade and so on?'

'A man must live, Preacher.'

'Take care you never reveal such matters to Osama. He would not approve.'

'It's a hard and disgusting world from a policeman's point of view. I do my best to protect good people and the weak, but I am past apologies.' Hakim sounded weary. 'We will talk again when I confirm the arrivals.'

At Holland Park, Dillon, Holley and Miller went through the wardrobe room and settled on green fatigues with no camouflage markings and crumpled green jungle hats. One outfit to wear, another as a spare, in the bottom of a dark green holdall, with T-shirts, a toilet bag and military items. Their usual weapons, the Walther and the Colt .25 in the ankle holster, were backed up by an AK47 each, and some fragmentation grenades.

Dillon went out carrying his holdall. He put it down while he spoke to Roper, who said, 'Very dashing. I'm not used to seeing you in uniform.'

Miller joined them and said, 'That's because the Provos never wore one.'

'Now that wasn't fair,' Roper mocked.

'Remember what President Kennedy once said,' Dillon shrugged. 'Anyone who expects fairness in this life is seriously misinformed.'

'I love that,' Holley said, as he joined them. 'Seriously misinformed. It has a ring to it. Rolls off the tongue.'

Sergeant Doyle came in. 'I'm ready, gentlemen.'

'No fond farewells from the boss?' Dillon said. 'Ah, well, we who are about to die salute you.'

'Oh, get out, Dillon,' Roper said. 'I'll start to cry.'

'That'll be the day,' Dillon said, and led the way out.

They reached Farley Field in forty minutes and discovered Ferguson and the Salters standing beside the Daimler, talking.

'There you are,' Ferguson said. 'We thought you'd got lost.'

'No, that's what happens when we try to find Algeria,

General.' Dillon shook hands all round. 'Keep the faith. We'll see you soon.'

'It would seriously inconvenience me if you didn't,' Ferguson told him.

Holley and Miller got in, and Dillon paused. 'Keep an eye on Mickeen Oge for me, Billy.'

'You can count on it,' Billy called, as the door closed and Dillon moved up to take his seat beside Holley.

Ferguson and the Salters moved back to the Daimler and stood watching as the engines fired and it started to move away.

'What do you think?' Harry Salter asked.

'I don't know: a funny one, this.' Ferguson looked up as the Falcon lifted. 'All up to Dillon, I suppose.'

'Well, there's nothing new in that,' Harry said.

The Citation had taken off two hours before the Falcon. Chuck Alan, a former US Navy pilot with a DFC who had served in Iraq and Afghanistan, was familiar with Justin Talbot's vagaries, but with the fabulous salary he was paid, never complained. Cruising at thirty-five thousand feet, he put the Citation on automatic pilot and went over their route.

'Should be easy,' he said. 'We'll pass over the Irish Republic, Bay of Biscay, Spanish mainland, and across the sea to Algeria and this Khufra place. Presumably there's a decent landing facility? You said we'd speak about that.'

Justin produced a photo text he'd obtained from the

computer. 'Just there on the edge of the Khufra marshes is a desolate old airfield the Germans built in the Second World War. The buildings are ruins, but the runway can still take traffic.'

'You didn't mention that,' Chuck said. 'Is this an illegal drop?'

'No, it's part of a covert operation run by Algerian Military Police, which I'm assisting in. I should return in twenty-four hours. You'll be safe by the plane. I'm carrying a spare AK47 in my bag just for you.'

'That's a bit outdated,' Alan said.

'Not at all. It's the perfect weapon for swamp country. Vietnam proved that. You can bury one for years, dig it up, load it and it will fire instantly.'

'I don't know about this,' Alan said. 'Maybe I won't be able to land.'

'If you can't, I will, but after Iraq and Afghanistan, I'm willing to bet you a bonus of fifty thousand dollars that you can put this baby down at Fasa.'

Chuck Alan brightened considerably. 'You're on!'

'Good,' Talbot told him. 'Just turn off the automatic pilot and let's see some real flying. I'll go and get some coffee.'

Which he did and also called the Preacher. 'Thirty-five thousand feet up, cloudless blue sky and we're on our way.'

'You should be a couple of hours ahead of our friends when you land.'

'Not that it will make any difference to the final outcome,' Justin said, and switched off.

He had his coffee and a whiskey in it, thinking of what lay ahead, but his thoughts also turned to his mother. He brooded for a while, considering whether to call her, but decided on Jack Kelly instead. He found him in the estate office.

'I've gone away in rather a hurry for a few days,' he said. 'I'd like you to keep an eye on my mother.'

'I've seen her already, and she's distraught. Hannah found her weeping in her bedroom.'

'We didn't exactly part on the best of terms.'

'What on earth are you up to?'

'The problem is, it appears that she's taken to listening in to my phone conversations, and since she can only hear half of them, she seems to have come to the wrong conclusions about what's going on.'

'From what she's said to me, I'd say she's got an excellent idea – and it's scaring her to death. This Algerian trip, what the hell is it all about?'

'Al Qaeda business. A way of sorting out the Ferguson problem. I came up with a good idea and the Preacher approved.'

'What is it?'

Justin told him and, when he was finished, said, 'Quite clever, though I say it myself. What do you think?'

'That you're a raving bloody lunatic, Justin Talbot. You're Colonel Henry's grandson, all right.'

'Don't you dare say that to me.' Justin flared up at once.

'You do realize that the men you are going up

against are extraordinary by any standards? Dillon and Holley, two of the most feared enforcers the Provisional IRA ever produced, and Major Harry Miller, who did our movement more harm during the Troubles than any other individual. Frankly, it's Hakim and his fifteen crooked coppers I'd be worried about in that swamp.'

'The difference is, I'll be there waiting for them.'

'Well, I'd take care, Justin, great care, that's all I can say. Watch your back. You'll need to.'

After he had gone, Justin opened the holdall which contained his Tuareg clothing. It would work, the whole thing, he told himself: had to. He checked and loaded the weapons, putting an AK47 to one side for Chuck and the other in a military rucksack, together with a few assorted grenades and extra ammunition, three field-service wound packs and some penicillin. He returned to the cockpit and eased into the second seat.

'Everything okay?' Chuck asked.

'Go have a coffee or whatever. I'll take over.'

He sat there, flying the plane; normally he enjoyed it, but not this time, and he knew why. It was what Kelly had said. *A raving bloody lunatic. You're Colonel Henry's grandson all right*. It was what he'd been afraid of for most of his life. It would take more than consigning his grandfather's portrait to the bonfire to make it go away.

* * *

The call came in while Miller and Dillon were in the cabin eating sandwiches. Miller took it and switched it on to speaker.

Roper said, 'Check your laptop, Harry. I've just sent you a couple of better photos I managed to run down of Ali Hakim and Hamza. I know Daniel's familiar with them, but they should be of use to you, too.'

'Thanks for that,' Miller told him. 'How is everybody?'

'Billy's gone to Rosedene to see Bellamy, and Harry insisted on going with him. He's taken the situation very seriously. I believe he thinks Billy might die on him.'

'And Ferguson?' Dillon asked.

'Just after seeing you off, he got a call from your pal, good old Henry Frankel, the Cabinet Secretary. The PM wants one of those one-page reports that he can use during Question Time. The worst problems facing the Secret Intelligence Services at the moment, blah blah blah. Naturally, Ferguson asked me to come up with a quick answer, but I doubt it's the kind of thing the PM wants to raise in the House of Commons.'

'Let me guess,' Dillon said. 'Number one, Muslim fundamentalism. Two, the rise of the Russian Federation. And three, the fact that, since the Peace Process in Ulster, what was the PIRA has become a criminal organization that's bigger than the Italian Mafia.'

'Got it all, Dillon. Hardly worth my writing it down. The Russians have sixty-two thousand in the GRU.

Compared to that, British Military Intelligence is a joke. With the Muslims, Al Qaeda is only one of an exponentially growing number of extreme jihadist organizations.'

'And the Provos?' Miller said. 'They blew up the centre of Manchester and made a fortune out of rebuilding it, at least that's what many people think. It's a funny old life.'

'Well, I don't think you'll find it funny when you plunge into that wilderness at dawn tomorrow,' Roper said. 'Take care.'

He switched off, and Dillon said, 'I'll go and spell Holley.'

He went into the cockpit and Holley came out, got coffee from the kitchenette and joined Miller. 'There's something I meant to mention to you and Sean.'

'What's that?' Miller asked.

'I learned Arabic when I was in that training camp – became pretty fluent. Hamza told me it was a good idea to keep quiet about it.'

'Why did he say that?'

'Because people give themselves away when they think you don't understand. Once I was given a job to handle a consignment of guns to County Down and deliver fifty thousand pounds in a suitcase. The fools in the boat's crew discussed which way they would murder me, in Arabic of course.'

'What happened?'

'I shot a couple of them dead – to encourage the

others, you might say. It did the trick. You speak a little Arabic, I understand?'

'Military short course. Very basic.'

'And I know Dillon speaks it very well. Ali Hakim knows about my ability, but he doesn't know about you two.'

'You'd rather Dillon and I keep quiet?'

'I think it would be a good idea.'

'So that we can hear them discussing how to murder us?'

'Absolutely,' Holley said. 'One thing I learned during my five years in the Lubyanka was how frequent it was that totally absurd and impossible things turned out to be true.'

'I take your point. Dillon and I don't speak Arabic.'

'Exactly,' Holley said in perfect Arabic. 'So if you would pass me the sandwiches, I would be very grateful.'

'Sorry, old man,' Miller replied in English, 'I don't understand a word you're saying.'

In the heart of the marshes was the small island of Diva. Hamza's house and trading post were substantial, and built on firm land, but with extensions all around, wooden shacks supported by pilings driven into ground below the water. There were seven or eight of those, with boats ranging from canoes to inflatables with outboard motors tied up to them. One old sport fisherman was painted dark green, and Hamza, who wore a sailor's peaked cap, jeans and a reefer coat, was sitting in the stern having a beer when his mobile buzzed.

'Omar Hamza, this is Shamrock. Half an hour to go.'

Talbot spoke in English, and Hamza replied in the same. 'You've come a long way. Let's hope you find it's worth it.'

Hamza climbed a short ladder to the jetty above and ducked into a large dark room with rough tables, chairs and a long wooden bar. Bottles of every description were crammed on the shelves, and an open archway revealed a shop crammed with goods.

A drunk was sleeping in the corner, mouth open, while three Arabs in soiled white smocks and battered straw hats played cards at one of the tables. A young woman in black, her head covered, but her handsome olive face revealed, came in from the store and spoke to him in excellent English.

'Was that him, this Shamrock you are expecting, Father?'

'So it would appear, Fatima. I'll go get him.' He sounded grim and shook his head.

'You're not happy?'

'I've involved myself in this matter because of my position here and also because of you. This is a favour for Colonel Hakim, so I can't say no. I want things to remain as they are, nice and stable. If the police ever decided to come down heavy on us, and we were forced to move on, it would be a tragedy at my age. Your mother, may she rest in peace, would have understood this.'

'And you think I don't? Hakim is all right, and he likes me. Ever since his wife died, I have known this.'

'You are too young for him.'

'One is never too young for an older man with money and social standing. But we are wasting time. I will go with you and take the wheel of *Stingray* while you handle the pole.'

The salt marshes were like a green miracle sprouting out of the desert, saltwater channels flushing through great pale reeds up to fifteen feet high. Chuck Alan had taxied the Citation right up to the edge and stood there looking at it. He picked up a stone and hurled it into the marsh, and immediately birds of every description flew up, creating pandemonium with their noise as they called to each other.

Behind him, Justin Talbot emerged from the cabin. He wore the dark blue turban and face veil of a Tuareg, and a three-quarter-length dark blue robe open to reveal a khaki shirt and trousers. He had a belt round his waist carrying a holstered Browning, an AK47 slung over his left shoulder, and held the military rucksack in his right hand. He made a hugely dramatic figure.

Chuck Alan said, 'Jesus, boss, are you going to war or something?'

It was extraordinary how Justin seemed to fit into that landscape, everything shimmering in the intense heat.

'I think I hear an engine,' he said, and was right.

There was a movement in the reeds, and the boat emerged, Hamza in the prow clutching a long pole. *Stingray* came to a halt, the front easing up on the sand. Justin looked up at the woman at the wheel high above. She said something in Arabic.

'Sorry, no can do,' Justin said. 'English only, I'm afraid. Comes with all those years of Empire, you see.'

He was the English public school man to the life, and Hamza roared with laughter. 'You sound just like a man I met in the French Foreign Legion many years ago. He'd been cashiered from an English Guards regiment.'

'What rotten luck.' Justin turned to Chuck. 'Off you go, old son.'

'I'll be waiting, boss.'

Alan went back to the plane and climbed into the cabin, pulling the airstair door up behind him. Justin turned and said, 'Omar Hamza?'

'That's me, and this is my daughter, Fatima.'

'Charming,' Justin said, 'nice to meet you.'

She looked uncertain, as if not knowing what to make of him, and he climbed on board and moved to the stern, where he put down his rucksack and the rifle. He looked up at her at the top of the short ladder as she switched on the engine.

'Can I join you?'

'If you want.'

As the engine started into life, Hamza climbed over the prow rail and shoved off. They reversed, pushing into the curtain of reeds, and then turned and ploughed forward, emerging into a waterway which was only as broad as the boat itself.

'An amazing place. How long have you lived here?' Justin asked.

'I was a child when we came, twenty years ago. My father had problems in the desert so we moved here. He has the trading post, so we have a good living, but it's hard. My mother died last year. There are many people here for whom it is the final stopping place.'

'It's certainly striking, and some of the flowers are incredible,' he said.

'It also has snakes of many types in the water, and the bite of some bring instant death. Not to mention the malaria and other diseases.'

'But you still stay. Why?'

She shrugged. 'Because there is nowhere else to go.' The boat emerged into the lagoon, revealing Diva Island and the trading post and the shacks on pilings; they coasted in, and a small boy caught the rope Hamza tossed and tied it up. Fatima said, 'I'll take you in and show you where you will sleep.'

He followed her up the ladder and into the trading post, and Hamza, still on the boat, was speaking to Hakim. 'Well, I've got him. He was waiting by the plane dressed as a Tuareg, turban, face veil, the lot. Took me back to my days in the legion in the deep Sahara. Just looking at them frightened people to death. What news of the others?'

'I had a call from Holley saying they should be landing in an hour.'

'So they'll spend the night with you at Dafur and the police incursion in the launches will start at dawn. Wouldn't it be simpler to cut their throats while they're sleeping?'

'No. In the world's eyes, they must have died at the hands of the bandits who infest the Khufra, especially Holley who, on paper at least, is an Algerian of some importance.'

'Malik will be desolate to lose him. I understand he looks on him as a son.'

'Well, he'll have to get over it.'

'I liked Daniel. A born killer, and one of my finest pupils.'

'Everyone's time comes sooner or later, so stop moaning. Tell Fatima not to get close to this Shamrock. They take liberties, these Westerners. No morals.'

'As you say.'

Hamza went into the trading post. There was no sign of his daughter or Justin and then she emerged from the rear sitting room, went behind the bar and found a bottle of whiskey and two glasses.

'So he wants a drink?' Hamza said. 'He'll have to remove the veil. Tuaregs aren't supposed to drink. It's an offence against Allah.'

'Then you've been offending him all your life. He's unpinned his veil at one side. He is quite handsome, actually,' Fatima told him, and grinned. 'As you can see, I've got you a glass, too. Come.'

285

She led the way into a back room that was quite spacious and carpeted, with large stuffed cushions scattered around and a low Arab-style dining table. There was a bed in one corner and another archway showed a further bedroom.

Justin sprawled on a huge cushion, smoking a cigarette, the veil hanging down one side. He looked astonishingly dramatic and was excited beyond belief, the brief trip through the marshes had seen to that. Omar Hamza and the whole atmosphere of the place was everything he had hoped for. Fatima was just a bonus.

She half filled a glass for him and for her father, and, when Justin smiled, there was an edge of wickedness that excited her. 'To your bright eyes, my dear.' He toasted her, then half turned and said in excellent French to Hamza: 'And to you, *mon brave*, and good hunting.'

12

As the Falcon descended on its approach, Holley, at the controls, said, 'Since the runway is parallel to the shore, I'm going to go straight in and have a look at the place first.' He went down to four hundred feet and roared in.

At Dafur the river emerged from the marsh; there was a surprisingly large stone jetty, another legacy of the Afrika Korps and Rommel, with two large launches alongside. Men in uniform gazed up, shading their eyes, but nobody waved.

'A cheerful bunch, aren't they?' Dillon said.

Miller, leaning over between Dillon and Holley, said, 'So it would appear. Did you notice the machine gun mounted on each launch?'

'I certainly did,' Dillon said.

It was a typical Arab fishing village, boats pulled up on the beach, nets, a range of flat-roofed houses painted a grimy white, most of them in various stages of decay. Poverty was very definitely evident and, from the look of the twenty or so villagers in shabby clothes who had turned out to watch the plane come in, it looked as if it was a daily companion.

The Falcon swept round, and landed, turned, taxied back to the village and stopped. Holley turned off the engines and Hakim came forward, followed by half a dozen policemen in khaki uniforms.

'That's our man,' Holley said.

'I know,' Dillon said, 'I saw his photo. I don't think much of his friends. An ugly bunch. They look as if the only thing they have on their minds is rape and pillage.'

Miller dropped the airstair door and Holley went out first. Hakim embraced him, and his men came to a halt, watching.

'The greetings of Allah, Daniel, my friend,' he said in Arabic. 'It has been too long.'

'To see you again, Colonel, is always a pleasure.' Holley kissed him lightly on each cheek. 'And how is Malik?'

'Missing you as always. Naturally, I've not informed him how far this business has gone. He's a worrier where you are concerned. Much better to achieve a successful conclusion and then tell him.'

'I agree completely.'

Hakim's men seemed to be surprised at Holley's fluent exchange with Hakim and were muttering amongst themselves. Holley now said, 'But my friends, Major

Miller and Mr Dillon, don't speak Arabic. You must excuse them.'

Hakim moved into English. 'Gentlemen, a sincere welcome to Algeria. If my men can help you with your equipment in any way, you only have to ask.'

'Actually I could do with something to eat and maybe a drink,' Dillon said. 'But I suppose alcohol would be a difficulty.'

'Not at all,' Hakim said. 'We can handle that. Allow me to escort you to my boat.'

'That's fine,' Dillon said. 'You carry on, Daniel, I need Harry to help me with the controls. We'll catch up.'

He turned back to the Falcon, and went through the airstair door into the cabin, where Miller found him in the cockpit.

'What's going on?'

'Just killing a little time.' Dillon watched Hakim and Holley go. Several of the policemen were still hanging around the Falcon, looking it over and talking amongst themselves.

'I just wanted us to get away from Hakim and Holley. I don't like the look of that bunch of gorillas. They look all bad to me and I wonder why that should be.'

'I admit they don't seem very prepossessing,' Miller said.

'Which is a posh way of saying they look bloody awful,' Dillon told him. 'And as they've now been told we don't speak Arabic, I think it might be interesting to hear what they say about us.'

'Okay, let's test the water. I suggest we each take an AK47 loaded for bear, as they say.'

'Now you're talking,' Dillon said, and went and unpacked the holdalls.

When they emerged from the Falcon and went down the steps, Dillon closed and locked the airstair door, turned and smiled at the policemen hanging around, then said to Miller, 'Shall we go, old man?' He turned to the men, 'Where is Colonel Hakim?' He spoke rather slowly, as if to fools.

'That is the British for you,' one of the policemen said. 'Stupid and arrogant, Nadim, as if we were idiots.'

'What you say is true, but be patient: every dog has its day, and that day has come as far as these two are concerned.' Nadim, who was a Sergeant, pointed in a direction and said to Dillon, 'Hakim.'

'Thanks very much,' Dillon told him.

As he and Miller started to walk, another of the men said, 'The AK47s they've got are the fully automatic version. A very dangerous weapon.'

'Do not be afraid,' Nadim said. 'A knife in the dark can be just as effective.'

'And the small man carrying it doesn't look like much,' another said.

'Cut it out,' Nadim told him. 'Remember what Colonel Hakim said: these are dangerous men. You must be very careful. Remember the proverb. It is the cat which bides its time that catches most mice.'

They moved away, and Hakim appeared on the jetty

and waved. 'So what do you make of that?' Miller asked.

'Well, it could just have been some Muslims shooting their mouths off. They don't like us much these days.'

'Dillon, I only speak a certain amount of Arabic, but what I could understand, I didn't like. You speak the language fluently, so for God's sake, you little Irish bogtrotter, tell me what you think.'

'Well, to put it inelegantly, I'd say we're in deep shite,' Dillon said. 'You are carrying?'

'Armed to the teeth, which includes my underwear if you count the vest.'

'Excellent. Let's go and enjoy Hakim's hospitality and see what unfolds. It intrigues me, the thought that the police could turn out to be our problem.' Dillon shook his head. 'Now why would that be? It would put Hakim on the other side, a man whom Daniel has known for years and respects, a government man.'

'Yes, well, life does have its little surprises.' Dillon waved to Hakim, who was standing in the stern of the launch with Holley. 'Join us for champagne,' Hakim called. 'You see we have everything. Then we'll go to the village café where they are preparing a meal – it's better than you would imagine.'

An orderly in a white jacket came forward and offered a tray, and Dillon and Miller accepted a glass each. 'To the friendship of our two great countries,' Hakim said. 'And especially to Daniel, who more than anyone has built the bridges that unite us.'

'Isn't that nice?' Dillon said. 'You have a way with the words, Colonel.'

Sergeant Nadim came along the jetty and stood waiting. Hakim said, 'Excuse me a moment.' He went down the short gangway to speak to him.

Dillon took the last glass from the tray, the orderly went below, and Miller said, 'You were saying how sensible it would be to keep quiet about being able to speak Arabic.'

Holley's face betrayed nothing. 'Tell me the worst.'

Which Dillon hurriedly did. 'It all sounded pretty menacing to me.'

Holley frowned. 'It's not that I disbelieve you. But he's been a friend for years.'

'Let's just stay alert and prepare to cope with whatever comes up,' Miller said.

Hakim returned. 'Excuse my bad manners, but I was just discussing your quarters with Sergeant Nadim. You'll be staying on the second boat, *Evening Star*. He'll command the boat with six men. He is very experienced in the ways of the Khufra, so he'll lead our little invasion, and I will follow, half an hour later, in *Fortuna*. General Ferguson expressed a wish for you to take part in the action, so I thought my plan would please you.'

'It certainly does,' Miller said.

'So, you will leave at dawn. Four in the morning, gentlemen. But for now, the Café Bleu awaits.'

As they went over the side to the jetty, Dillon murmured, 'I thought the French left this country years ago?'

Holley said, 'Just shut up, Sean, you never know. Maybe you'll get a surprise.'

Which they all did. It was a house slightly larger than the others, a terrace open to the sky and looking out to sea. Sergeant Nadim and four men armed with small Uzi machine guns stood guard, menacing and watchful.

There was French wine, Chablis, cold from a deep well where it had been hanging suspended by string. There was a roast lamb to be carved, mounds of rice, peppers of various kinds and onions that had been cooked with the lamb.

Afterwards, drinking more wine, Hakim said, 'I am sorry if the presence of guards has spoiled the meal, but there are those out there in the marshes, possibly even watching us now, who would kill me without compunction.'

'There is no need to apologize. Life is the most precious thing we have,' Dillon said. 'One must be willing to do anything to preserve it. Sometimes, however, even the guards are not enough.'

'Then what is, my friend? If we were sitting here, as we are now, and brigands from the Khufra rushed in to overwhelm us, what would you do?'

Dillon took a pineapple fragmentation grenade from his pocket, pulled the pin and held the release bar tight. 'I would point out that if I released the bar, I might kill myself, but also every person within a fifteen-metre radius.'

The four men with Nadim cried out and backed away

hurriedly. Nadim stood firm and Dillon smiled. 'A brave man, your Sergeant, but we'd have died together.' He replaced the pin and put the grenade back in his pocket.

'My friend, you must be insane.' Hakim was horrified.

'Ah, well, I'm from County Down, and they say we're all a bit crazy there.' Dillon turned to his friends. 'I'll need to get a few things from the plane, Harry. If you'll help me, we can leave Daniel to chat on for a while.'

'Of course,' Hakim said, 'but I insist Sergeant Nadim and his men accompany you.'

Dillon said, 'A good man, the Sergeant. I'm sure he'll take care of us perfectly.'

There was a half-moon and a slight breeze as Dillon and Miller walked ahead, Nadim and his men behind.

'There was a purpose to your utterly mad act and now this?' Miller said. 'I'm right, aren't I?'

'Of course you are, but let me listen, Harry.'

They walked in silence, the murmur of conversation behind them, and reached the Falcon. Dillon found the key, opened the airstair door and led the way in. He reached for the weapons bag and opened it. 'I'll get an AK47 for Holley: he's going to need it.'

'Why?' Miller demanded.

'One of the cops asked Nadim why they couldn't cut our throats in bed while we were asleep on the launch. Nadim said it was necessary for us to die in action in the Khufra. He said Hakim had told him it would look better.'

'Anything else?'

'Oh, yes. One of the other guys tried to argue, and Nadim told him he had taken the oath from Colonel Hakim. You know what the oath was, Harry? To put his life on the line to serve Al Qaeda and Osama bin Laden. What do you think of that?'

'I learned a long time ago not to be surprised at anything in our line of work, Sean. It'll be terrible for Holley when we tell him the man who's been his partner's best friend since youth, is what he is. Do you think there's any chance Malik has gone the same way?'

'No, I honestly don't, for all sorts of reasons,' Dillon said. 'The most important thing here is that we've been sold a pup. Clearly, the purpose of our being here isn't to try to get our hands on Shamrock.'

Miller nodded. 'The whole thing has been a ruse to get us here so we could be executed. They were probably hoping that Ferguson and Billy would come along for the ride, too. So there's no Shamrock waiting with Hamza on Diva Island.'

'That's the crazy thing,' Dillon told him. 'It seems Shamrock actually did come in on a plane shortly before we did. He landed at some place called Fasa on the other side of the Khufra. Hamza and his daughter picked him up and he's with them now at Diva. Hamza has been in touch with Hakim, and everyone is very puzzled.'

'And why would that be?' Miller asked.

'It seems he talks like a Brit, but is disguised as a Tuareg, wearing dark blue robes, face veil, the lot!'

Dillon smiled wolfishly. 'Wouldn't you say that's a trifle bizarre?'

'I could say a lot more than that,' Miller said. 'What's our next move?'

'To get back to the *Evening Star* and check in with Holley, who's going to get a bit of a shock. If Hakim is with him, have your AK handy, just in case.' Dillon picked up the weapons bag. 'Let's get moving.'

They left the Falcon, he locked the airstair door again and walked along the beach to the jetty, Nadim and his four men following. Hakim's boat, *Fortuna*, had five policemen lounging around it, smoking and passing a jug of wine from hand to hand. The second launch, *Evening Star*, was tied up at a point where the river was swallowed up in a wall of fifteen-foot reeds.

There was a small hut to one side, a large door open to reveal a range of army cots. Two policemen lounged there, smoking in slung hammocks. Nadim and his men joined them and, as Dillon and Miller went on board, Holley and Hakim appeared together, walking along the beach from the Café Bleu.

'Ah, there you are,' Hakim called. 'We thought we'd lost you.'

'No chance,' Dillon replied. 'Come and have a nightcap. I've brought a bottle of whiskey from the plane, unless it would give you a problem.'

'Not at all, a delightful idea, and over a long life I have discovered that one thing is absolutely for certain. Allah is merciful and understanding of the frailties of men.'

'Excellent,' Dillon said. 'So come on board. Let's go below. The midges are beginning to bite.'

'But of course,' Hakim said amiably.

They went down to the saloon, sat on the benches on either side of the table, and Dillon put four glasses down and poured. He picked one up and toasted them. 'To friendship.'

'To friendship,' Hakim answered.

'Good, I'm glad we've got that over with.' Dillon took out the Walther and put it on the table. 'What would you say that is?'

Hakim laughed. 'A Walther PPK, the new silenced version.'

'Exactly,' Dillon told him. 'And the automatic AK47 which Major Miller is holding across his knees is also silenced, a rare model. He could open a porthole, stick the barrel out and have a very fair chance of knocking off Sergeant Nadim and those six men before they knew what hit them.'

'I'm sure he could, but why would he do such a thing?'

Holley said, 'Come on, Sean, the grenade was bad enough, but this is going a bit too far.'

'Really?' Dillon carried on in excellent Arabic. 'As you can see, we haven't been honest with you. Even Major Miller speaks some Arabic. Your men have been loose-tongued, discussing in our hearing how they would murder the stupid Englishmen. Of course, they got that wrong, as I'm Irish.'

Holley turned to the Colonel and said in Arabic, 'Tell me this is not true.'

Dillon poured himself another whiskey. 'He's our man in Algiers as far as Al Qaeda and the Preacher are concerned. Nadim and his boys have all taken the oath at his hands. They were talking about it as we were walking to the Falcon.' Hakim's face had turned ghostly pale; he was consumed with uncertainty about what was going to happen next. Dillon added, 'It would seem obvious to me, Daniel, that he's been using his friendship with your partner, Hamid Malik, to no good purpose. This whole thing was an Al Qaeda sting, a ruse to draw us all in for summary execution.'

'So no Shamrock?' Holley said.

'Oh, yes, he landed in a plane on the far side of the Khufra, shortly before we got in, at a place called Fasa. He's with Hamza on Diva now, a puzzle to everyone. He speaks like a Brit and is disguised as a Tuareg.'

'You bloody sod,' Holley said to Hakim. 'I should kill you myself.'

'Don't let's be hasty,' Dillon said. 'He still has his uses.' He picked up the Walther and cocked it. 'If I shot you now, Nadim wouldn't hear a thing, so be sensible. Who is the Preacher?'

'The most powerful man in Europe. If I did know his name, which I don't, and told you, there would be no place to hide. He's the Preacher, a voice on the phone. It's impossible to trace the source of his calls.'

'There's no such thing as impossible,' Dillon told him.

'I thought that, too, and had experts try.' Hakim tried to make it sound convincing. 'They all failed.'

'You bastard,' Holley said bitterly. 'All Malik's years of friendship meant nothing to you.'

'Osama bin Laden meant more.' There were tears in Hakim's eyes. 'You must see this, Daniel. He is the greatest hope for the Arab world since the Prophet himself.'

'Strange,' Holley said. 'All I see are the never-ending bombs, the bodies in the streets.'

'Okay, let's move on from that and discuss what's going to happen.' Dillon was still holding the cocked Walther and smiled amiably at Hakim. 'I am prepared to kill you at any given moment. Your friends outside won't hear a thing. The only way you stay alive is by doing exactly as you're told.'

'So what do you want?'

'We'll go on deck and you tell Nadim you've changed your plans. You've decided to take command here on *Evening Star* and he can follow in *Fortuna*. Tell him to leave his six men as arranged. It might puzzle him if you didn't. Tell him you want to handle the situation yourself; say that you might go in earlier, but stress that he keep half an hour behind you.'

'And what do you intend to do?'

'Why, push our way through to Diva and get our hands on Shamrock.' Hakim frowned slightly. Dillon put the muzzle of the Walther between Hakim's eyes. 'This is your moment of truth. I could kill you now, and I'll certainly kill you on deck if you don't do as I say. Once we start on that, Major Miller will start spraying your men, and you know how destructive the automatic version of the AK47 is.'

'Only too well,' Hakim said bitterly. 'So let's get it over with.'

'When you speak to him, make it in Arabic,' Dillon said. 'That way I can hear exactly what he's saying about me without him realizing. Another thing.' He held out his hand. 'Your mobile phone.'

Hakim took it from his breast pocket, put it on the table, turned and went up the companionway, Dillon and Miller following. There were strange birds calling, cicadas, the voices of the marsh and the croaking of bullfrogs. The men were playing cards beside a coal brazier, two armed guards by the prow of the launch, a small fire glowing. Nadim was watching and smoking, and turned as they appeared, and Hakim called him over. He told him exactly what Dillon had told him to say.

'You think this wise, Colonel, exposing yourself in such a way? These people need handling with care, especially Dillon. I wish you would allow me to dispose of them for you. What is to be gained by this farce concerning the man Shamrock? What is he here for? It was not necessary.'

'He wants to have a hand in the killing,' Hakim said, 'so obey me in this. Make the change now, and have one of the men bring me my night robe and toilet bag from the *Fortuna*.'

Nadim glanced at Dillon, his expression giving nothing away, then turned, moved to the fire. He outlined the change of plan, then went into the hut. He came out five minutes later with his peaked cap on, carrying a holdall, and walked to the *Fortuna* at the far end of the jetty.

'We'll wait for someone to bring those things you wanted,' Dillon said. 'Have a cigarette, it will calm your nerves.'

Hakim did as he was told and offered one to Daniel, who said, 'Never again. I don't trust myself not to kill you now.'

The policemen playing cards retreated inside and made ready for bed, leaving just the two on guard. An orderly came running along the jetty, saluted Hakim, handed over the robe and toilet bag, and retreated.

'Time to go below,' Dillon said. 'You lead the way.'

Hakim did as he was told. In the saloon, Dillon took the toilet bag from him and emptied it while Miller checked the robe.

'Did you really think I might have a spare in there?' Hakim asked.

'Plenty of people do,' Dillon said. 'Now go and get your head down for a while and behave yourself.'

Hakim went and settled himself in a bunk in one of the stern cabins, and Dillon and his friends had a drink and discussed the plans. 'I'd like to see us move out at a different time than Hakim arranged,' he said.

'That was four o'clock in the morning,' Miller pointed out. 'Any earlier, it would be dark.'

'Would you think there was any kind of chance of slipping away without those six policemen?' Dillon asked.

Holley said, 'We could dispose of the sentries easily enough. There's that long pole on deck for punting the boat when in difficulty in the reeds, so you could float the boat some distance away before turning the engine.'

'And that would be enough to wake the dead.' Holley shook his head. 'That's no good at all. When we did the low approach in the plane, there were a few other boats further upstream from here. I think I'd better go for a walk and take Hakim with me. You two stay and keep the sentries happy.'

Ali Hakim, instructed to come for a stroll and smoke a cigarette, did as he was told, and Holley found what he was looking for a hundred and fifty yards along a path beside the river. A shack with the door padlocked and a small jetty just above the water. There were two plastic orange inflatables with both outboard motors and oars. Each inflatable was capable of carrying five or six people. Holley had brought a lantern from the launch and examined them closely.

'Who owns these?'

'The coastguard service, but they hardly ever come.

Local people frequently use them illegally, that's why you can smell the petrol. I've travelled in them myself.'

Holley gave him the lantern. 'Check them out.'

Hakim did. 'As I thought, somebody's been using them: both tanks are quite full. It's a push-button engine. Shall I show you?'

'I'll take your word for it. Let's go back.'

They sat at the table in the saloon and discussed it. Holley said, 'That would be the way to do it as far as I can see. It would be suicide to keep to Hakim's time. Omar Hamza would blow us out of the water. With these boats, you can cut the engine and approach with oars.'

'Just the two sentries to dispose of,' Miller said.

'No problem in that,' Holley said. 'And I've been thinking about the earlier start. The sky's clear and there's a lot of light from that half-moon. I say we go.'

'That's it then,' Dillon said. 'Back to your bunk, Hakim. I suggest we all get some shut-eye. Three o'clock it is.'

Earlier on Diva, Justin, Hamza and Fatima had been drinking coffee when Hamza received a call. 'This is Sergeant Nadim. How is everything?'

'We are ready and waiting, but I haven't heard from Hakim and his phone isn't answering.'

'I suppose he could be sleeping.'

'It's certainly an early start.'

'Perhaps earlier than you think. He changed plans a couple of hours ago. Told me he was going to take command of our lead boat, *Evening Star*, and relegated me to *Fortuna*.'

'Why did he do that?' Hamza asked.

'I've no idea. He's acting it up with our friends. I think he's enjoying himself, but that's playing with fire. He even said he might want to go in even earlier.'

'Than four o'clock? He must be mad. It will be dark, for one thing.'

'Yes, but getting lighter. I thought I'd better speak to you, as I know your strange friend is anxious to deal with them.'

'To a certain extent, that's true.'

'Wouldn't it be ironic if he got knocked off himself? This Dillon man is a maniac.'

'Well, that should make it interesting,' Hamza said. 'If Shamrock gets his way, there won't be much left for you and me. I'll see you in the morning.'

'What was that all about?' Fatima asked.

Hamza told them, and Justin yawned and said, 'I suppose I'd better get a couple of hours' sleep. What about you, Omar?'

'Gave up sleeping years ago in the Legion. They taught you how to do that. I only doze.'

'Was the Legion everything they say?'

'And more. Muslims, Jews and Christians and every colour under the sun and every race. Everyone was equal. Nothing like it anywhere else in the world. You'd have to go back two thousand years to the Roman legions to find anything similar.'

'I guess I missed out on that one.'

'What about you?'

'Grenadiers and SAS.'

'A formidable combination. You should do well in the morning. I'll see you then.' He went in his room and closed the door.

There was a kind of silence except for the marsh sounds, and it hung heavy between Fatima and Justin. She said calmly, 'Would you like to make love to me?'

He gave her one of his dazzling smiles. 'I'm not really in the market for that.'

'Are you of the other persuasion sexually?'

'Good heavens, no.'

'I see, so I am not attractive to you?'

'You are immensely attractive, Fatima. It's just that I wouldn't be good enough for you.'

'Do you mean in bed?'

'That's only about one per cent of any relationship. I'm not good enough for you or any woman: I'm a bad man. I spoil things and that includes relationships. I have a very, very wonderful mother and I spoil it for her, too.'

'I think that's the saddest thing I ever heard,' Fatima told him.

'I'm inclined to agree with you.'

She walked out and he sat there for a while, then

pulled his rucksack over, produced his AK47, took it apart then put it together again effortlessly.

Dillon came out of a catnap and found Holley standing by the other bunk, his face – beneath the crumpled jungle hat – already darkened. 'Come on, Sean, ready to go.'

He moved out, Dillon pulled on his hat, grabbed his weapons bag and AK47 and followed him into the saloon, where he found Miller already geared up. Hakim was sitting, waiting, and Holley was slinging his weapons bag across his body to the left. He picked up his AK47 in his right hand.

Dillon took some camouflage cream from a tin on the table and rubbed it on his face. 'What about the sentries?'

'I've taken care of that,' Holley told him. 'Shot them both.'

Hakim looked sick as Dillon said, 'That's all right then. Let's get out of here.'

They left the launch very quietly, everything still in the darkened shack, and moved along the path of the marsh in line, Dillon leading the way, Hakim next, then Miller, with Holley at the rear. When they reached the boats, they examined them quickly.

'I think we should take both,' Dillon said. 'Holley and Hakim in one because of that "special relationship", and Miller and me in the other. It means we've got backup.'

'I'll buy that,' Holley said. 'We'll row for a couple of hundred yards before starting the engines and, with luck, they can coast along on a very low rumble.'

'And remember the mobile phone,' Miller said. 'It'll be useful in this kind of terrain if you stray.' He said to Hakim, 'Get the oars out then, you bastard, and show us what you can do.'

The Colonel did as he was told. They led the way and Dillon and Miller followed, the Irishman at the oars. The reeds were alive with life in the pale moonlight as they floated past, wings beating and muted cries as they disturbed the birds.

After a while, Dillon said, 'I've had enough of this, so I'm shipping my oars and starting up.' His thumb on the button produced a gratifying growl, which he turned down until it balanced out to a pleasant throbbing. Hakim achieved the same results and they nosed into a sort of small lagoon, the reeds towering above them, the half-moon still glowing in a dark sky that was already clearing. They floated there together.

'Where are we?' Holley asked Hakim. 'How far to Diva?'

'Perhaps a mile,' Hakim told him, and pointed. 'From here, think twelve o'clock as you look ahead, and Diva is ten o'clock.'

Way behind them in the distance, there was the sound of an engine. 'It's one of the launches,' Hakim said and stood up.

There was the crack of a rifle quite close by and he

was struck in the left side of his chest, spun round and went into the water. Holley reached over and got him by the collar and half turned the boat, towing Hakim behind.

'Get out of it, for God's sake, and into the reeds as quickly as you can,' he called. He crashed the boat through, came to a halt, switched off the engine and realized he was alone, except for Hakim in the water.

So often in life, the most careful plans are disrupted for the simplest of reasons – in this case it was due to a police officer named Abu, one of those sleeping in the shack. Awakened by a bad stomachache, he had taken a torch and visited the outside latrine. He had noticed the absence of the two sentries and, on investigation, had found one of them in the water between *Evening Star* and the jetty. The further discovery that there was no one on the launch had sent him on the run to alert Nadim. The Sergeant's more thorough check had discovered the second sentry also in the water.

It seemed absurd to deduce from what had happened that Ali Hakim had been party to the murder of two of his own men, and the only plausible explanation was that the others had been responsible. As a quick search failed to discover Hakim's body, Nadim could only conclude that Dillon and his friends had taken him with them. But what for? He called Omar Hamza on his mobile.

Hamza listened to him, and Fatima and Talbot, awakened by the disturbance, awaited an explanation. Hamza said into his phone, 'God knows what's happened, but I suggest you come into the marsh heavily armed. I'll stay put in the trading post and greet them with a machine gun if they turn up here. Get moving.'

'What's going on?' Talbot asked.

Hamza told him. 'It doesn't make a lot of sense to me.'

'Well, it certainly does to me.' Justin was actually smiling. 'What bastards they are, Dillon and Holley. They know what we're up to. Don't you see, they've got Hakim with them, who's probably shot his mouth off, and he's leading them to me.'

He was full of energy, went back in the other room, hooked up his veil, slung his weapons bag across his chest and picked up his AK47.

'So what are you going to do?' Hamza asked.

'Go hunting, give them a nice surprise. What about you?'

'I've got an old Browning machine gun. I'll set it up on the jetty and await events.'

'Fort Zinderneuf?'

'Ah, you've read *Beau Geste*?' Hamza smiled. 'An Englishman named Wren wrote that book. He actually served in the Legion.'

'Very interesting, but that was then, this is now. These men who are coming are killers of the first water.'

'I know this, my friend, if only because I trained Daniel Holley myself. I can only wish you luck.' He turned to Fatima. 'What about you?'

'I think I'll go with him. You know what you're doing, he doesn't. He thinks he knows everything, this one, but he doesn't know the marsh and he could get lost. We'll take *Stingray*.'

'You're worse than your mother was.' Hamza shrugged. 'As Allah wills.'

Talbot followed her outside and looked down at the *Stingray*. 'Is the sport fisherman the sensible boat to use? I'd have thought an inflatable with an outboard.'

'The reeds are fifteen and sometimes twenty feet high, so they'll conceal the upper deck, but at the same time, standing at that wheel, I can peer over occasionally and see where we are and what's going on.'

'That makes perfect sense.' He dropped down to the deck and she followed. 'I'll be guided by you, so let's get moving.'

She cast off and went up the ladder to the wheel, and Talbot followed and stood beside her, the AK cradled in his arms. It started to rain; as they drifted out, she switched on the engine and kept it down to a low rumble. There was the grey light of dawn now, and a curtain of mist floated in.

'When we have the heat of high summer and unexpected heavy rain, it produces the mist,' she told him.

'At least it makes it easier to play hide and seek,' he said.

310

They nosed into the reeds. Suddenly, wildfowl lifted in a cloud some little distance away, the birds angrily calling, and Fatima cut the engine.

'Something caused that. Keep your head low, but we can look with caution.' She produced a pair of Zeiss glasses from the map compartment and focused them. 'Ah, a flash of orange.' She nodded and turned to him, handing the glasses over. 'And another. Two of them. Inflatables with outboards.'

'Can we get closer?'

'Not without making a noise. I'll try using the pole. You stay here watching.'

She went down to the stern and commenced, and Talbot watched cautiously as the reeds parted and *Stingray* floated through; some distance away to the left he could hear the sound of an engine.

'What do you think?' he called down to Fatima.

'It sounds like two engines. I think Nadim has probably brought both boats.'

'How many men?'

'Sixteen or so. Each boat has a machine gun mounted. There's nothing those bastards like better than sweeping the marshes with those things, shooting everything in sight like schoolboys playing with toys.'

'The next thing you'll be saying is: that's men for you. Just a little closer, if you will.' She did as he asked, and everything happened in a hurry.

'There they are, two small orange inflatables in a waterway. Two men to each boat. I can't see who it is because they're wearing jungle kit and their faces are black, but here goes.'

He took deliberate aim and fired twice, saw his target fall into the water. 'Did you get him?' Fatima called up.

'Oh, yes.' Talbot smiled in triumph and, for a moment, forgot to keep low. Sean Dillon, with an uncertain glimpse of the Tuareg who was Shamrock, took a snap shot. It drilled Talbot's left side, and he staggered back awkwardly, dropping the AK and sliding down the ladder.

Fatima was on her knees. 'Merciful Allah, how bad is it?'

'Well, I wouldn't know, would I?' He managed a smile. 'You'll have to take a look. I've got a medical kit in my rucksack. You must find the morphine. When you're first shot, the shock kills the pain, but not for long.'

The engines of the approaching launches sounded louder now. 'They're coming fast,' Fatima said.

'Yes, well, let's keep our heads down and stay out of it. Just let them get on with it. If you look in my rucksack, you'll find half a bottle of Cognac, too. Get me that first.'

Holley had dragged Hakim out of the water, and the Colonel lay there groaning, soaked to the skin, blood oozing through. He was obviously in a very bad way. Holley had been aware of the return shot and called out.

'Dillon, Miller, where are you?'

There was no reply, so he took out a spring knife and cut open Hakim's tunic. He knew just how bad it was straight away, and Hakim moaned, 'I'm going to die, Daniel.'

'Shut up and lie still,' Holley said. 'This isn't exactly the best place for medical treatment.' He took two morphine ampoules from his bag because he figured one wouldn't be enough, jabbed them in, tore open a pack containing a wound dressing, and applied it.

Hakim shook his head. 'A waste of time. This is Allah's punishment on me for my betrayal of you and Malik, the most shameful thing I have ever done in my life.'

'Don't worry about it,' Holley told him. 'I understand. Osama, Al Qaeda and the Preacher really had you in their clutches.'

Hakim clutched at Holley. 'But at least I can make amends before I go.'

'And how would you do that?'

'To others, the Preacher is just a voice on the phone, but not to me. I gave the special mobile he supplied to an electronic genius. He managed to break into the system.'

'And who is the Preacher?' Holley said, suppressing his excitement.

'He's a British-born Muslim named Hassan Shah. He lives in Bell Street, West Hampstead, I've checked. He's investigated war crimes for the British Government and is a Professor in International Law at the London School of Economics.'

'Good God almighty,' Holley said. 'We've got the bastard.'

'Yes, I believe you have.' Hakim's hand tightened on Holley's jacket, he convulsed, and his head fell to one side.

Holley sat there looking at him for a moment, wondering about his next move, but he was not given a choice. Small waves rippled though the reeds as the speed of whichever boat was approaching increased, and then the boat's heavy machine gun sprayed recklessly through the reeds and there was coarse laughter.

The inflatable rocked violently as the launch passed, and Holley took a fragmentation grenade from his bag and lobbed it over blindly. There were cries of dismay, followed by a violent explosion. He eased out into the channel and saw the *Evening Star* well alight. Two men with their uniforms on fire jumped into the water. Holley took another grenade out and lobbed it after the others, which seemed to finish the boat and the entire crew.

But there was still the *Fortuna* somewhere out there; Holley could hear the engines and the sound of its heavy machine gun firing into the reeds at random. He called Dillon on his Codex.

'What's your situation?' Dillon demanded.

'Hakim was hit by a sniper. Never saw who, but he's dead.'

'The sniper was Shamrock in his Tuareg get-up. I fired back and he definitely went down.'

'I got the *Evening Star* with two grenades and watched them die. Where are you?'

'Not far away at all. We'll move closer to the boat and find you.'

'Well, one other thing I must tell you, in case I get knocked off myself. It turns out that Hakim knew the name and address of the Preacher.'

'Jesus, Mary and Joseph,' Dillon said. 'Tell me.' Which Holley did, and Dillon said angrily: 'The bastard. I can just see him now, standing in the dock at the Old Bailey claiming his human rights.'

There was another burst of obviously haphazard machine gun fire not too far away. 'So what are we going to do?' Holley asked.

'Do you still have Hakim's body?'

'Sure I do. I didn't know what to do.'

'We're only yards away from the *Evening Star* and it's burning nicely. Start calling out and we'll call out, too, and see if we can get together before the *Fortuna* turns up. If Nadim's still on it, he won't be pleased.'

A hundred yards or so away, the machine gun fired again, so Holley started up, shouting, and could immediately hear Dillon and Miller calling. In a few minutes, they connected.

'Now what?' Holley asked.

'Hakim did us nothing but harm in life,' Dillon said, 'but I've got a use for him in death. Don't waste time, because the *Fortuna*'s coming up fast. We'll dump your inflatable next to what's left of the *Evening Star* with Hakim sitting up in it, the perfect ambush.'

Nadim was at the wheelhouse of the *Fortuna* as it broke out into the channel and saw the smoke and what was left of the *Evening Star* still burning. His men cried out angrily as bodies floated by, and then Nadim saw the inflatable and Hakim propped up in it. There were cries of rage from the men.

Nadim cut the engine and came out. 'Get the pole and hook him in.'

Three men started to do that. There were only the marsh sounds in the rain, smoke drifting, the fire crackling as they lifted Hakim up on to the deck.

Nadim had never known such rage. 'Dillon,' he roared out in Arabic, 'I will cut you to pieces, and feed you to the fishes when I find you.'

'Over here,' a voice responded in Arabic.

The grenades bounced on deck, two at the same time, then a third that rolled against Hakim. It was the last thing Nadim saw on this earth.

Somewhere nearby in the rain, there was the sound of a plane taking off, but in the mist there was little to see.

'Are you thinking what I'm thinking?' Holley asked Miller and Dillon.

'I definitely shot the Tuareg,' Dillon said.

'Well, let's do the sensible thing and go see your friend Omar Hamza,' Miller said to Holley.

As they emerged at the side of the lagoon, they saw the sport fisherman, with Fatima at the wheel, moving towards the trading post. Holley checked through his binoculars. 'Hamza's sitting beside a Browning machine gun,' he said, and called loudly across the water. 'It's Daniel, let's talk.'

Fatima got out of the sport fisherman and tied up and turned to look at them all. Hamza shouted, 'Okay, come over.'

He was drinking beer and sitting there beside his machine gun when they arrived. Fatima leaned in the doorway, arms folded, watching them closely.

Hamza said, 'So you've been killing again, Holley? How many?'

'All of them except for Ali Hakim. Shamrock shot him twice.'

'So he's dead?'

'He lived long enough to tell me a few interesting things. Was that Shamrock flying away?'

'So it would appear,' Hamza said.

'I thought I'd shot him,' Dillon said. 'He shot Hakim.'

Fatima nodded. 'So you did. You hit him in the left side and the bullet came out through his back.'

'And you patched him up?' Dillon asked.

'He had a military kit. He told me what to do. I gave him morphine.'

'And then took him to his plane?'

'Yes, his friend was waiting.'

'What kind of plane was it?' Miller asked.

'I have no idea.'

'He was English, I believe, not an Arab.'

It was her father who said, 'That's enough. Go, Daniel, and don't come back.'

'Just one more thing. He was in reasonable health when you left him. You gave him the penicillin in the kit, and soon?' said Dillon.

'Oh yes, I did everything he told me – not that it will do him the slightest good. He's obviously going to die and I think he knows it.'

She went inside, leaving a stunned silence, and Hamza said, 'That's it, on your way.' He patted the machine gun. 'Unless you want to argue with this.'

'Whatever you say, old friend,' Holley told him. 'I think you can take it that we won't be back.'

'You weren't even here, as far as we're concerned,' Hamza said. 'I imagine that's the way the authorities in Algiers will look at it. After all, an Al Qaeda operation is the last thing they'd want to have anything to do with.'

The heavy rain kept what little life there was in Dafur indoors. They dumped the inflatable in the creek, walked down to the runway where the Falcon stood, silent and waiting. Holley took the controls and, within five minutes, they were taking off. Dillon found himself a drink and Miller called Roper on his Codex.

'That was quick. Did you finally come face to face with Shamrock?'

'In a way, I suppose. The whole thing was a sting.'

'What do you mean?'

'Ali Hakim turned out to be Al Qaeda's man in Algiers.'

'God in heaven,' Roper said.

'You can imagine what a shock it was for Holley. The story about Shamrock having dealings with Hamza was just bait for us to go and get knocked off. They'd hoped Ferguson would be there, too.'

'So no Shamrock?'

'No, he turned up. Apparently, he wanted to enjoy dealing with us personally.'

'Just start at the beginning, so I can make some sense of it,' Roper said.

Which Miller did, and when he was finished, said, 'So there it is. Shamrock winging his way back to wherever he came from, with the pilot who flew him in and waited for him.'

'Badly wounded and dying, according to this Fatima girl.'

'She's a strange one, but that's what she said.' Miller was repeating himself now. 'Dillon shot him in the side and the bullet went straight through.'

'And he's making a flight to we don't know where, which could take hours. He's committing suicide.'

'Well, that's the story and it's obviously not finished yet.'

'It's incredible. You've certainly had an extraordinary outing this time. God knows what Ferguson will make of it.'

'He'll be over the moon about one thing. We now know who the Preacher is. Imagine, a Professor of International Law at the London School of Economics, and he's moonlighting for Al Qaeda in London.'

'If you wrote it up, nobody would believe it,' Roper said.

'I would: my father knew Kim Philby at Cambridge,' Miller told him. 'Anything been happening while we've been away?'

'There hasn't been time, Harry. You've hardly been away. Take it easy. I'll see you soon.'

LONDON

NORTHERN IRELAND

13

By the time the Citation X was winging its way across Spain to the Bay of Biscay, Chuck Alan was beginning to worry. When Justin Talbot had returned to the plane at Fasa, he had seemed very hyper and full of nervous energy. He'd insisted on taking the controls on take-off and only handed over during the second hour when Chuck had suggested the autopilot.

'Excellent idea,' Justin said. 'I don't think I had a wink of sleep while I was away. I'll get my head down.'

Two hours later, when Alan checked him, he was still asleep, his forehead damp, so Alan returned to the cockpit, considerably concerned.

At the same time, the Preacher, having heard nothing from Hakim and no response when he tried to call him, contacted Hamza.

'What's happened to Hakim? I don't seem to be able to contact him.'

'Well, you wouldn't,' Hamza said. 'He's dead. In fact, his people are all dead. Dillon and his friends don't take prisoners.'

'Merciful Allah! And Shamrock?'

'Where did you find that guy, the Arabian Nights? He was really something in his Tuareg robes. God knows what he was here for. He only managed to shoot one person, and that was Hakim by mistake. Dillon shot him in return.'

'Are you saying he's dead?'

'No, badly wounded, but fit enough to have flown back out of this cesspool. My daughter did her best for him with his medical kit.'

'So he's going to be all right?'

'Not according to her. She thinks he's a goner and she's usually right about things like that. Where did you get my mobile number from?'

'Hakim.'

'Well, don't call again. I'm not afraid of Al Qaeda, and neither is anyone else that I know around here. After this cock-up, your new motto should be: Stay out of the Khufra.'

He cut off and Shah sat there thinking about it, and then called Talbot, who came awake with a start, the phone ringing in his breast pocket.

'Hamza's told me everything. What a debacle, and not helped by you indulging in your usual theatricals. So you've managed to get yourself shot?'

'Yes, and I don't exactly feel at my best. When I hit

Belfast, I should book in at the Seaton – when it comes to gunshot wounds, Belfast hospitals are the best in the world; the Troubles gave them forty years' practice – but I don't know. They'll report me. What's the point in that?'

And Shah, angry and immensely irritated, said, 'You bloody fool, you're dying. Hamza's daughter said so.'

'Did she? Well, there you are then. She was a nice girl. You know your trouble, Preacher? You don't listen. I told you Dillon and his friends were hell on wheels, but you wouldn't have it. Your stupidity has ruined everything.'

'My stupidity?' Shah said. 'Damn you to hell, Talbot. I'll destroy you.'

'If I'm dying, it won't make any difference, so why don't you go fuck yourself?' Justin told him and cut off.

In his study at Bell Street, sitting behind the desk, Hassan Shah quite suddenly felt utterly helpless for the first time in years. Everything was slipping away from him. The consequences of the fiasco in the Khufra would undoubtedly affect his position in Al Qaeda when word reached Osama bin Laden. Once, he'd had the power to ruin Justin Talbot by just reaching for a telephone and making an anonymous call to any major newspaper, but that was no threat to a dying man. He frowned suddenly as a thought struck him: As long as he did die, of course.

*　　*　　*

325

Roper informed Ferguson of everything while the Falcon was still on its way, and Ferguson was astounded. 'This is one of the most sensational coups in the history of my department.'

'Do you envisage repercussions, General?'

'No. Algeria is not well-disposed towards Al Qaeda, and Hakim was notorious for his deeply secret covert operations where no questions were ever asked. I think this will simply be regarded as one that went badly wrong and in one of the worst places in the country. The whisper of an Al Qaeda connection will kill it stone dead. It never happened, Major.'

'Tell that to Shamrock, flying off into the blue with Dillon's bullet in him.'

'And dying, if that young woman is right,' Ferguson added thoughtfully.

'Which leaves us with Professor Hassan Shah,' Roper told him. 'What's to be done there? Do we arrest him?'

'Not at the moment. We know how badly things have gone wrong – and so will he by now. Al Qaeda's tentacles spread far. Call in Billy right now. Tell him he's to stick to Shah like glue.'

'Should I put out a red code travel restriction so he can't leave the country?'

'No. I'll rely on Billy, and also Shah's confidence in his social and governmental position.' Ferguson shook his head. 'You know what really gets to me? He's the kind of eminent lawyer you would have expected to get a life peerage.'

'I see your point, General. I suppose he'll have to make do with a thirty-year sentence for high treason instead.'

'Exactly,' Ferguson said. 'But give Billy his orders now.'

The Citation X landed at Belfast City just after noon, Chuck Alan sitting alone in the cockpit. He parked as instructed, went in the cabin and opened the door. He found Justin dozing. He shook his shoulder lightly and Justin's eyes opened. He seemed puzzled for a moment, as if unaware of where he was, and the sweat on his forehead was more obvious.

He smiled suddenly, 'Hi, old buddy, are we there?'

'Belfast City,' Alan said. 'You don't look too good.'

Justin sat up, reached for a napkin and wiped his face. 'I'm good, Chuck, just fine.' He reached in the rucksack, found the medical kit and the morphine pack. He extracted a phial and jabbed it in his left arm.

'What in the hell are you doing?' Chuck Alan demanded. 'What's going on, boss?'

'Morphine's going in, Chuck, it kills the pain, which is good if you've been shot, which I was back in that stinking marsh.' Justin was obviously light-headed now.

'Look, I don't know what I've been involved with or what happened back there this morning. I don't think I've heard machine gun fire like it since Iraq, but I think you should probably be in the hospital.'

A man in ground-crew overalls peered in. 'We've

brought your Mercedes from the VIP car park Major Talbot. They presumed you needed it.'

'Well, that's damned nice of them.' Justin picked up his rucksack with his right hand and said to Alan, 'You should be at Frensham.'

Justin went down the steps carefully, like a drunk, and walked to the Mercedes, where the ground-crew man held the driver's door open for him. He put the rucksack on the passenger seat, slid behind the wheel, switched on the engine and lowered the window.

'Bon voyage, old buddy, happy landings.' He drove away, was waved through security without a search, smiling and calling hello to various officials who knew him well. A few minutes later and he was part of the busy city traffic of Belfast.

Chuck had to hang on for another hour for his departure slot, and waited in the private lounge, drinking black coffee and going over it all in his mind. He finally did the right thing and called the house number he'd been given for Talbot Place. A man's voice answered.

'It's Chuck Alan, Mr Talbot's pilot. I was hoping to speak to his mother.'

'I'm afraid she's out. I'm the estate manager, Jack Kelly. I thought you were in Algeria?'

'We've just got back.'

'Is there something wrong? I know Justin was up to no good.'

Chuck hesitated. 'Look, this is my boss we're talking about.'

'Just tell me the worst,' Kelly ordered.

Which Alan did, and when he was finished, said, 'I know it sounds difficult to believe—'

Kelly cut him off. 'Not where Justin's concerned. I'm going to change your orders. You do have your Talbot credit card?'

'I sure do.'

'Cancel your departure, put the Citation in for a flight check, refuelling and so on, and then go down to the Europa, book in and await further instructions. I don't know how this business is going to turn out, but you could be needed. Understand?'

'Perfectly, Mr Kelly, I'll get moving on that at once.'

Jean Talbot had been up the mountain again with Nell, hoping that the strong wind blowing in from the Irish Sea would clear her head of the dark thoughts that had filled it since Justin's departure. She was surprised to see Kelly's old Morris driving towards her on the lower track. It stopped. Kelly got out and came towards her.

She knew it must be trouble of a sort, and hurried to meet him. 'What is it? Justin?'

'Get in the car out of the wind and I'll tell you.'

She took the passenger seat, Nell scampered in the back, and Kelly got behind the wheel as it started to rain.

'Jack, what's going on?' And then the thought hit her and she turned pale, 'Oh, dear God, he's dead?'

'No, but I understand he's been shot.'

'Then where is he?'

'It would appear he's driving down from Belfast.' Kelly started the Morris and coasted down to the road below.

She took a deep breath to pull herself together. 'What's been going on, Jack? I've heard half of everything for too long. Who is my son, really, what kind of man?'

'I don't think he's ever known that,' Kelly told her. 'The little Protestant bastard who was really a Catholic bastard, a boy who had to survive a bigger bastard, Colonel Henry Talbot. But forget all that. The serious trouble he's in started after he left the army and went to Pakistan and Peshawar.'

'Why was that?'

'He and our happy band of brothers from Kilmartin were selling illegal arms over the border to the Taliban in Afghanistan. Selling arms became also agreeing to train people in their use. Al Qaeda, discovering what he was doing, blackmailed him into working for them.'

She said, in horror, 'You're asking me to believe he would go along with that?'

'He didn't have a choice, Jean, and certainly not at first. The trouble is he found he liked it. Action and passion are everything to him. You know your own son.'

She nodded, calmer now. 'Just how bad is what he's done?'

'He's led a Taliban group, some of them including British Muslims, in battle against American and British forces.'

'And killed people?'

'A great many, I'm afraid.'

'This can't be happening.' She shook her head. 'Why hasn't he been arrested?'

'The authorities don't know who he is. I do, because the other year he confided in me. He's controlled by a man in London called the Preacher, and Justin has a codename, Shamrock. Dillon and Daniel Holley, whom you met, are working for General Charles Ferguson of British Intelligence, trying to find out who Shamrock is.'

'So where does Algeria come in?'

'False information was fed by Al Qaeda sources to Ferguson that Shamrock was known to be in a pretty unsavoury part of Algeria. Justin devised the plot, which was to draw Ferguson's people to hunt for him, unaware that they were the hunted themselves.'

'And this is what he's back from – and with a bullet in him? Where is he?'

'Like I said, he's on his way from Belfast City Airport, driving his Mercedes SL.'

They were on the coast road now and she seemed to have recovered. 'What do you suggest? Do we go looking for him or do we just wait for him to turn up?'

The problem was solved, for Jack's mobile sounded at that moment. It was Hannah. 'The strangest thing,

Jack. I went down to the pub for a few things and noticed Justin's Mercedes by the church lych-gate.'

'Is he in it?'

'No, I found him sitting on the bench beside Sean's grave.'

'But it's raining, for Christ's sake.'

'I know. Could he be drunk?'

'I wish he were, but I'm afraid not. We're on our way, I'm with Jean.' He explained what was happening and put his foot down so that they were there in fifteen minutes. They found Hannah with a raincoat over Justin's shoulders and Father Cassidy holding an umbrella.

'Justin, dear, what are you doing?' Jean said.

'Hello, Mum, just paying my respects to Sean and all the brave young men. A bloody sight braver than I could ever be, eh, Jack?' And then he started to cry, slow and bitter tears.

She cradled his head for a moment. 'It's all right, love, it's all right, just let's get you home.'

He nodded and reached for Kelly and grabbed him by the coat. 'Only no hospital, Jack. This is good old Ulster, where all gunshot wounds must be reported to the police. You're the expert, you know that.'

'Don't worry yourself, boy,' Jack Kelly eased him up and, as Justin groaned, said, 'Where are you shot?'

'Left side and straight through. I don't know how the hell Dillon did it. It was dawn light, so it was appalling visibility and pouring with bloody rain, just like this. A snap shot was all he managed, but it was enough. The man's a bloody marvel. He's done for me. Natural justice, in a way, when you think what I did to his uncle.' He started to laugh helplessly.

They got him into the back of the Morris, Jean holding him. Hannah joined her husband in the front and called Dr Ryan on her mobile, then alerted Murphy at Talbot Place. He was waiting anxiously at the front door and, seeing the situation, got Colonel Henry's wheelchair out of the cloakroom. He and Jean crowded into the lift and took him up to his bedroom. Kelly and his wife followed upstairs, and Hannah got bath towels and spread them on the bed so they could lay him out.

Justin seemed quiet now, and Jean panicked. 'What's wrong?'

Murphy said, 'He's passed out, his pulse is weak, but it's there. Dr Ryan is on his way, so just leave me to do my job. I'm the nurse here. Go and have a cup of tea or something.'

He produced scissors and cut open Justin's battle blouse and eased him out of it. Fatima had used two wound packs and they were swollen with blood.

'Oh, my God,' Jean said.

'Just take her away, Jack, until the doctor gets here. You stay, Hannah,' Murphy said.

Kelly tucked Jean's arm firmly in his. 'Let Murphy do his job. During his years as a nurse in Belfast, he worked on more gunshot wounds than most battlefield surgeons.'

He took her down to the study and gave her a brandy in spite of her protests. 'Drink it down, it will help.'

She did as she was told, the warm glow steadying her, but refused another. 'Tell me what Justin meant when he said that what Dillon had done to him was natural justice.'

Kelly was caught and it showed in his face. 'Oh, he was just rambling.'

'Come off it, Jack, you're hiding something. It can't be any worse than what I've heard already, so spit it out.'

'Mickeen Oge Flynn's mishap . . . I was with Justin that night, he was out of his mind with rage about everything after the funeral. Dillon had been on the phone from London to Mickeen, and Paddy O'Rourke overheard. It was mentioned in PIRA circles and the news passed to me. I told Justin because, in his circumstances, I'd no choice.'

'And what did he do?'

'Insisted he and I go and speak to Mickeen, which we did, and found him under the car and working. Justin just lost it. He was shouting at Mickeen, demanding to know what Dillon had been talking about.'

'And there was an accident?' Jean Talbot sounded so weary.

'Exactly, the jack was raised, Justin was—'

'Stop it, Jack,' she cut in. 'What happened to that old man wasn't any accident, you know it and I know it.'

Kelly couldn't help himself and blurted out, 'All right then, but Dillon believes that it was an accident. Mickeen's had serious brain surgery, he's in a coma. Dillon's had him flown over to a private hospital in London, but there's every chance he'll never regain consciousness.'

'And that's supposed to be good, is it?' Her face was white and strained. 'So it lets Justin Talbot off the hook, is that what you're saying?' She shook her head. 'What kind of world has it become when I'm surrounded by deceit and lies at every turn?'

She turned, wrenched open the door, ran out, and found Dr Ryan just being admitted at the front door by Hannah.

It took Larry Ryan only fifteen minutes to examine the wound; they all waited for his verdict.

'No question, the bullet's passed straight through, which is fine, but he should be in the hospital.'

Jack Kelly said, 'How many times did you say that to PIRA volunteers who went to you for help in time of trouble, Larry – and we were grateful to you.'

'That's a kind of blackmail, Jack. I'd remind you I could get struck off.'

Jean said, 'Please, Larry, anything you can do.'

He sighed heavily. 'Damn Justin, he was always a wild man, but just for you, Jean.' He turned to Murphy, 'You're as good as I am at handling wound trauma. Keep a close eye on him. I'm going back to my place to pick up everything we'll need to set up a hospital bed.'

He went out and Murphy said, 'Why don't you all go and have a cup of tea, pull yourselves together so we can sort everything out when Doc Ryan's back.'

'Oh, I don't think so,' Jean began.

'He's right, Mum,' Justin murmured. 'Sorry about all this. I always was a bloody nuisance.'

The Falcon had landed at Farley an hour and a half later than the Citation X had in Belfast. On the way in, Dillon stopped by Rosedene to check on Mickeen.

Professor Bellamy wasn't there, but Maggie Duncan was, and had a bit of news as they stood looking in at Mickeen through the window. He looked exactly the same as when Dillon had last seen him, lying very still with all the paraphernalia attached to him.

'He's moved a little, according to the staff on night duty. A line in his saline drip was pulled out, and they've reported sounds.'

'What kind of sounds?' Dillon asked her.

'Nurse Perry said she's heard long, low sighs in the middle of the night.'

'What does Bellamy think?'

Her practical Scottish nature came to the fore. 'Wee signs of hope, Sean, that's all he will say. It could be worse, though.'

'Absolutely.' He kissed her cheek. 'I'll be seeing you.'

At Talbot Place, Justin's bedroom had been adapted as much as possible to hospital standards. His double bed had been replaced by a single to facilitate the nursing. He wore a hospital smock and there was a saline drip on the pole beside the bed, a portable machine on the other side measuring heart and pulse rates. Ryan had stitched both the entry and exit wounds, assisted by Murphy, and Justin, heavily bandaged around his waist, was propped up, the top of the bed inclined behind him.

Ryan had used local anaesthetic for the stitching, and Justin sat there, drinking glucose through a straw and looking surprisingly well. Murphy was sitting beside his bed when Jean came in.

'Go and get something to eat. I'll spell you,' she said, and Murphy got up and left.

She leaned down and kissed Justin's forehead. 'It's not so sweaty,' she said. 'Larry's done a first-class job on you.'

'Don't worry, I'll see he's taken care of.'

It was a careless and throwaway remark and in a way typical of him. 'He's taking a great chance, Justin. It's a criminal act in the eyes of the law. He could be struck off, his career ruined.'

'Okay, Mum, I take your point. Dammit, he did enough for men on the run during the Troubles, so now he's doing it for me.'

'When I hear you talking like that, I think I never really knew you. You use people, Justin, then throw them away.'

'That's a nice turn of phrase.' He smiled. 'Don't tell me you're turning against me, too? I mean, here I am, the wounded hero—'

She cut right in on him. 'Don't give me that, *Shamrock*, because I only see the young British and American soldiers you've killed – and for what? Because Justin Talbot enjoys war in all its blood and gore more than anything else in this life. When I look at you, I see the body count, and if that wasn't enough, I see Mickeen Oge Flynn lying under a car and that car collapsing on him.'

'It was an accident,' Justin said.

'That was no accident.' She shouted the words, carefully spacing them. 'I've spoken to Jack.'

A moment later, the door burst open and Murphy came in, Jack Kelly behind him. 'Is everything okay?' he said.

'No, it's not. Apparently, you've been shooting your mouth off, Jack,' Justin said to Kelly. 'We can't have that. I think you're maybe forgetting your place.'

'Justin, for God's sake,' Jean said. 'After everything Jack's done, to talk to him like that.'

'It's all right, Jean,' Kelly said. 'I always worried there

was too much of his grandfather to him. He was Colonel Henry to the life for a minute there.'

He went out. Justin said, 'So now you'll go after him and say sorry? Well, I'm damned if I will.'

She took a deep breath, turned and went out, leaving the door swinging. Justin reached and opened the locker on his right side and found his rucksack. The pain on his left side was intense. He cursed, found the half-bottle of brandy and turned the cap with his teeth.

Murphy had closed the door and stood watching. 'You were dying when you got here and Doc Ryan's done a marvellous job, just about pulled you back from the brink. You could still die – I'd be failing as a nurse not to tell you that – but one thing is certain. Drink that stuff and you might as well order your coffin.'

'Is that so?' Justin Talbot said, and swallowed deep.

Murphy showed no emotion. 'Like they say, it's your funeral, Major. I'll go down to the kitchen now and see what they've got for you to eat.'

In London, Shah was methodically going through the newspapers when the text light blinked on his mobile on the desk. He picked it up at once and his world turned. The message said: *The winds of heaven are blowing and you must fly with them as does the Eagle. May Allah go with you.*

It was advice he had hoped never to receive, and from the highest level of Al Qaeda, the word that meant the game was up and his cover blown. If there was no escape for him, the only alternative was death. He thought quickly. He had three passports under different names. Many Muslims used the airports in Yorkshire or Lancashire, he'd blend in better there. At least he could try.

He quickly packed a holdall with basic requirements: the passports, a toilet bag, a Koran and a couple of law books. He had always kept two thousand pounds in the zipped base of the holdall, had never touched it, so that was all right.

He looked around him. So this was how it all ended. The house in which he had been born, in the West Hampstead street where he had played as a boy, in the great city with one of the finest universities in the world where he'd been privileged to work. He suddenly felt incredibly sad, as if all this couldn't be happening.

He shook himself out of it, let himself out of the front door and went to the Toyota saloon parked in its usual place. He opened the driver's door and got in, but when he started it up, the car wouldn't move. He got out and saw the case: all four tyres were flat. As he stood there looking at the car, Billy Salter got out of a red Alfa, one of a line of cars parked on the other side of the street. Shah recognized him instantly.

Billy called, 'Have a nice day,' then produced his mobile, called Roper, and Shah went back in the house.

Roper said to Billy, 'Did you hear anything to make you think he was going to try to leave the country?'

'No, I checked him out, chatting up people in the local newsagent and café. He never uses his car since he had a bump a year ago. He's a taxi man. I just thought it would be a good idea to make the car useless to him, just in case.'

'And he saw you?'

'Too damned right he did.'

Ferguson's voice boomed. 'You've forced my hand, of course. We'll have to lift him now. Stay there, make sure he doesn't try to sneak out of the back.'

Shah sat at his desk as despair overwhelmed him. For the first time, he realized the price he was going to have to pay, his eminence as a lawyer, his professional standing. He had come to this: someone to be despised. And for what? It was all Talbot's fault, the fiasco of the Khufra affair. Damn him! A complete loose cannon. He thought back to what the girl, Fatima, had said. If she was right and Talbot's life hung in the balance, it would be nice if somebody gave him a nudge. Shah thought he had the very man.

Jack Kelly was in the estate office at Talbot Place, angrily clearing his desk, for what had passed between him and Justin had been hard to take. 'Jack Kelly,' he barked.

'Why, you sound angry, Mr Kelly. You should be,

after Justin's role in the Algeria debacle. He's not well, I understand. I gather Sean Dillon put a bullet in him.'

'Who the hell is this?' Kelly was aghast.

'Talbot knows me as the Preacher.'

Shah's front doorbell rang. He got a pillbox out of a small drawer in his desk, took what looked like a lozenge out of it and slipped it into his pocket. He walked to the bow window, taking the desk phone, looking through the glass at Ferguson, who was standing there with Billy and Harry Miller.

Kelly was shouting, 'Answer me, damn you, what's going on?'

'Well, I've just looked out to see Major General Charles Ferguson at my door with two henchmen. I fear my end is near.'

'Does he know that Justin is Shamrock?'

'Not that I'm aware of, but I haven't time for a prolonged discussion. I just wanted you to know, as an old PIRA hand, that Major Justin Talbot lied to you and your friends at Kilmartin, lied to his own mother. Many years ago, he moved from the Grenadier Guards to the Twenty-second SAS at Hereford. He took part in more than twenty covert operations over a number of years.'

'You're lying,' Kelly shouted.

'Come now, Mr Kelly, why would I lie? June the third, Nineteen eighty-nine, an ambush at Kilrea. Eight members of the PIRA were killed. It was known as the Kilrae Massacre. I believe Justin killed four of them himself.'

342

'Damn you,' Jack Kelly said.

'Already taken care of.'

Shah dropped the desk phone on a coffee table, took the lozenge from his pocket and kept it in his cheek. The doorbell rang again and he opened the door as Ferguson led the way in, followed by Billy with a Walther in his hand, and Harry Miller.

'Ah, there you are,' Ferguson said. 'I presume you know who I am?'

'I do indeed, General.' Shah turned to walk to the sofa.

Billy said, 'Where do you think you're going?'

'To sit down,' Shah told him. 'I might as well die comfortably.' He bit hard.

'No,' Ferguson cried and reached out, and Shah fell back, face contorted, gave a terrible moan, jerked to one side, his legs shaking, and rolled on to the floor. There was a strange and pungent smell and Miller dropped to one knee.

'See the froth on his lips? The only good thing about it is it was quick.'

'What a stink,' Billy said. 'What was it?'

'Cyanide capsule,' Ferguson told him. 'A favourite of high-ranking Nazis when they lost the war.'

Miller had gone to check the desk and found Shah's open mobile which he'd left there. He read aloud the text: *The winds of heaven are blowing and you must fly with them as does the Eagle. May Allah go with you.* He handed it to Ferguson. 'Maybe some kind of warning?'

'We'll never know, but I'll give it to Roper to ponder over.'

'What do we do now, send for the disposal unit?' Billy asked.

'I think not,' Ferguson said. 'Leave him to be found as what people believed him to be. An eminent Professor of a great university.'

'Christ, you are being kind,' Billy said.

'No, Billy, just charitable. He can't harm us now, so let's go, shall we?' And he led the way out.

Jack Kelly, totally distraught, sat with his head in his hands at his desk, trying to come to terms with what he had been told. That the Preacher, faced with the prospect of being lifted by Charles Ferguson, was choosing death, made perfect sense to Kelly. On the other hand, in such circumstances, why would the Preacher lie about anything? So Justin had served with the SAS, hunted down and killed members of the PIRA. The real problem was it didn't really surprise Kelly. It fitted with everything else about Justin. He'd had a kind of madness since boyhood, and Kelly saw that now.

He took a Browning he'd used in his wild days out of a bottom drawer, always kept loaded from force of habit, put it in his right-hand pocket and went out. He went up the stairs in the Great Hall slowly, aware of the weight of the Browning in his pocket, feeling like an executioner again, for he had been here before in similar situations, a bullet being the only way to deal with traitors and informants.

When he went in, Justin was sitting up, his head slightly to one side, eyes closed. Murphy was reading a book. Kelly said, 'Go and have your tea break. I want a word with him.'

'Not for long, he gets tired,' Murphy said and went out.

Kelly stood at the end of the bed. Justin opened his eyes. 'There you are again. I was out of order before. I apologize.'

'I've got news for you from the Preacher.'

Justin frowned. 'You've got what?'

'He called me on my office number. He said he only had a few minutes because Charles Ferguson and two of his men were at the front door demanding entrance.'

'What was he going to do, make a fight of it?'

'No, kill himself, but he told me that he thought I ought to know a few things. Like that you lied to all your friends in Kilmartin about your army service during the Troubles. That you served on more than a score of covert operations with the Twenty-second SAS, including the Kilrea Massacre in June eighty-nine.'

Justin tried to brazen it out. 'Are you telling me you'd take the word of a man like the Preacher against mine?'

'The word of a dying man,' Kelly said. 'He seemed very well informed to me. That girl in Algeria said you were dying and it would be the best thing for you. When this gets out, you're finished in Kilmartin. I wouldn't be surprised if someone wasn't able to resist the temptation to shoot you.' He produced his Browning. 'You've no idea how much I'd like to use this.'

Justin leaned down, picked up his rucksack, put it on the bed and produced a Walther. 'You could always try.'

'You bastard,' Kelly said. 'According to the Preacher, you even lied to your own mother.'

'What did you expect me to do? Worry her to death every time the SAS handed me another death warrant? Anyway, it would have made life for her and the old man impossible.' He smiled. 'I've always thought the world of my mother. I do have my good side.'

'I doubt that,' Kelly said.

'Ask her, if you like. She's been trying to make some sense of my clothes in the dressing room. You launched your attack too soon, didn't give me an opportunity to tell you she was there.'

The half-open door next to the bathroom opened, and Jean entered. She wore jeans and a white shirt, her hair tied back, and her face was incredibly calm.

'Sorry about the guns, Mum, I'll put mine away if he'll pocket his. He's caught me out again: more of those secrets you keep bumping into where I'm concerned. You'll have heard what Jack's had to say, and I'm afraid it's all true. I deceived you for years, and it was so easy to do. Covert operations with the SAS are as secret as anything could be. I was thinking of what was best for you.'

She was instantly aware of what he was trying to do, trying to clear her name of any blame in the matter against what would happen when the news spread; for this was Ireland, and spread it would. So she lied in a sense and said to Kelly, 'I can see his point, but obviously you and the villagers will have a different attitude.'

'Not where you're concerned, but as for this one, here goes . . .' Kelly shook his head. 'I lost one son at nineteen, Justin, and you were the closest I came to replacing him, but if Sean was alive today, he'd spit on your grave.'

'Well, I'm not in one yet, so be a good chap and clear off.' Justin cocked the Walther and pointed.

Kelly walked out of the room and Justin said to his mother, 'So the Preacher's gone to a better place. That's something to be grateful for, anyway.'

'I wouldn't know about that,' she said. 'In fact, I don't know about anything much any more.' And she too went out.

14

On the way back, Ferguson called on Roper and filled him in on what had happened. 'Do you think I've done right?' he asked.

'Oh, yes, although it could well give his cleaning lady a heart attack when she finds the body. If we'd used disposal, it would have left an ongoing mystery about what had happened to him. If we'd gone through the motions properly and arrested him, the show trial would have damaged everybody, including the Cabinet Office for having employed him.'

Harry Miller cut in. 'I agree. The Secret Intelligence Service wouldn't have come out of it very well for not spotting him.'

'Well, the Prime Minister's private army has done it again,' Roper said. 'I think he'll be pleased. Another notch on your gun, General.'

'All very well, but Shamrock, the mystery man, is still floating around out there.'

Dillon and Holley had just turned up at the computer room, and Roper gave them the news. 'It's fantastic when you think of it,' Holley said. 'A man like that, one of the most eminent in his field, academic degrees up to his armpits, and yet he chooses the path of violence.'

'Ever since Robespierre in the French Revolution, the big movers and shakers have always been intellectuals,' Roper said. 'I seem to remember you got first-class honours in *your* degree,' he told Holley.

'Which is absolutely no help at all when some bastard's trying to shoot me.'

Ferguson and Miller walked in. The General was in an excellent mood. 'Billy rather pushed things with Shah and I must admit I was annoyed, but in the circumstances, I'm glad he did. He's following us in his own car.'

'A hell of a coup,' Dillon said. 'You could get a promotion with this one.'

'Don't be silly, Dillon.'

Billy joined them and Dillon said, 'You did well. Sometimes you need to take a chance on doing the wrong thing in the hope it will get the right result. You were on the button with this one.'

'I can't really take much credit,' Billy said. 'The truth is, I had it in for Shah for getting me shot.'

'Well, there you go,' Dillon told him. 'Anyway, we've got a lot to celebrate tonight. Are you going to line something up for us, General?' he asked Ferguson.

At that moment, Roper took a call on speaker, and Maggie Duncan's voice boomed out. 'Hello, Major Roper, have you got Sean there?'

'What is it?' Dillon asked.

'We've had movement with Mickeen, lots of groans and moans and vigorous stirring. I've phoned Professor Bellamy. He's at Guy's Hospital. He's going to come straight round when he's finished, but he's suggested you come now if you're available. In this kind of case, a result can come right out of the blue.'

'I'm on my way,' Dillon told her.

'One thing, Sean, I don't want a crowd here, it wouldn't be good for him. Just you, and one other person if you like. I'll see you.'

'Fantastic news,' Ferguson said. 'You must get moving straightaway.'

Dillon said to Holley, 'Will you come with me, Daniel? After all, you and I are the only ones here who've visited the scene of his accident. My Mini Cooper's outside. You can drive it. I'm too excited.'

'How could I refuse?' Holley said, and they hurried out.

At Rosedene, there was a certain excitement, Maggie Duncan at the window peering in, a couple of nurses looking over her shoulder. When Dillon and Holley appeared, she chased the other nurses away. An older nurse was sitting at Mickeen's bedside.

'Mary's there to control him if anything happens in a hurry. A patient can get panicked when he awakens out of nowhere.'

As she said that, Mickeen opened his eyes, raised an arm and reached out at Mary. She took his hand. He looked thoroughly bewildered and then spoke very hoarsely.

'Who are you? Where am I?'

'You're all right, Mr Flynn,' she said. 'You've been ill.'

He panicked then. 'What's going on? I don't remember you!'

He shrank back, pulling out the line to his saline bag, and another line to the machines monitoring his vital signs. Maggie Duncan opened the door and rushed in to assist Mary.

Mickeen was shaking, crying desperately, and Dillon stepped in the room, leaned over the bed from the other side and took his hand. 'Mickeen Oge Flynn,' he said in Irish. 'It's me, your nephew Sean Dillon, come to help you in your hour of need. Be still now, for you have not been yourself.'

Maggie, Mary and Holley didn't understand a word, but Mickeen did. 'God save the good work, Sean, is it indeed you?'

'And none other.' Dillon smiled and touched his face.

'But shall we speak English now, for it is only good manners with the ladies not understanding.'

The old man nodded slowly and said to Mary in English, 'And who are you, my dear?'

'Staff Nurse Mary Hanson, Mickeen, and this is the Matron, Maggie Duncan. You're in hospital in London.'

He looked puzzled. 'London, you say? I haven't been to London in years.' There was alarm. 'How did I get here – and who's that?'

Dillon glanced up and saw Bellamy standing in the door, excited and fascinated. 'This is your doctor, Professor Bellamy.'

'Now then, Mickeen, you've been on a long journey. Can you remember it?' Bellamy connected the electronics line and Mary the drip.

Mickeen frowned. 'I don't recall,' and then he looked up at Dillon. 'I remember you, Sean, phoning me from London about the funeral.'

'And which funeral would that be?' Bellamy asked, and murmured to Mary, 'A cup of tea I think, and chocolate biscuits; all nice and normal.'

She withdrew and Mickeen said, 'Which funeral? Old Colonel Henry Talbot's. He was a bad man. A real bad man.'

He was wandering now, and Dillon said gently, 'So you went to the funeral?'

Mickeen's face seemed to light up. 'I did that, but they were stopping people going in.'

'Who?'

353

'The Provos from Kilmartin. Justin didn't want outsiders to go.' His face became vacant as he looked at something he alone could see. 'That's right, I went back to Collyban and Paddy had left Father O'Grady's car up on the jack. His exhaust was damaged, so I thought I'd take a look and I got underneath and they came.'

There was a stillness in the room now. And Bellamy said, 'Who came?'

'I could only see their feet so I put my head out to look up. It was Jack Kelly from Kilmartin and Mr Justin Talbot. He was angry and asked me why I'd tried to go to the funeral, and then he said he knew you'd been on the phone to me, Sean, and asked what was it about.'

'And what did you say?' Dillon asked.

'That you were family, had just called to say hello.'

'And what happened then?'

'He said there must have been more to it than that. He lost his temper. Then he started kicking at my face and the car fell down.' He shook his head, puzzled. 'Or did it?' He smiled a little, like a child in a way. 'I only remember one word after that. Someone said, "Shamrock." A strange thing to say, surely?' He looked around. 'Where am I? How did I get here?'

Daniel Holley said, 'Sweet Jesus, now we know, Sean.'

Dillon's face was very dark. 'So it would appear. I should have remembered the old Sherlock Holmes quote: "When you have eliminated the impossible, whatever remains, however improbable, must be the truth." Justin

354

Talbot's war record speaks for itself. He's simply been carrying on, except that he's been doing it for the Taliban and Al Qaeda.'

Mary returned with tea and biscuits and Bellamy said, 'Now then, Mickeen, settle back and enjoy yourself. Do you like sugar in your tea?'

'I do indeed. Three sugars, and those chocolate biscuits look grand.'

'We'll leave you now with Mary to enjoy yourself and we'll be back in a little while.'

Mickeen was already trying a biscuit. 'You won't go, Seaneen, without telling me?'

'Now why would I do that?' Dillon reached over and kissed him on the forehead. 'The terrible scare you gave me. Enjoy your tea.'

They sat in the lounge and Maggie said, 'I'll get some tea on the way,' and went into the kitchenette.

Bellamy said, 'I never cease to marvel at the human spirit. The journey that old man has been on is a miraculous one. So much to learn from it, so damn much.'

'I agree, but it's his past that's important now,' Dillon said. 'The events leading up to all this.'

Bellamy nodded. 'A bad business, I agree, a matter for the police, I'd say. My confidentiality goes without saying, but obviously the name of Talbot is very familiar to me.'

'And to a lot of other people,' Holley said.

'Is what he said about Justin Talbot beyond doubt?'

Daniel Holley said, 'Yesterday he murdered a man in my custody in Algiers.'

'I fired back and shot him in the left side,' Dillon said. 'We've returned by private jet and, I believe, so has he. He has a house in County Down. I expect to find him there.'

Just then, two things happened at the same moment. Maggie Duncan emerged with the tea tray and, down the corridor, the alarm bell sounded, an ugly and frightening sound. Maggie dumped the tray, went off on the run, Bellamy following her. Dillon and Holley went after them.

The crash team had swung into action, working desperately on Mickeen, and through the window, Dillon could see the flat line on the heart monitor. The team worked in a frenzy, but it was fruitless. Finally, Bellamy gave the order to switch off.

'Time of death, two o'clock, Matron, agreed?'

She nodded, wiping her eyes, and went back down the corridor. Dillon stood there, looking through the window. Holley put an arm about him for a moment.

'Come on, Sean, let them get on with what they've got to do.'

They went back to the lounge and Bellamy found them ten minutes later. 'There's absolutely nothing I can say except that the reaction of coming back to life, as it were, obviously put an enormous strain on his entire system, which was weakened already by the brain surgery.'

'I've absolutely no complaint, Professor. This is a remarkable hospital, as I know more than once from my own experience. If you couldn't save him, no one could.'

'I believe you are the only relative?' Dillon nodded. 'So I presume you'll want everything done right, a Catholic burial and so on? Everything above board – not like some of the cases that have come my way from you and Ferguson in the past?'

'Of course.'

'Then that means a post mortem, and a coroner's inquest. Obviously, this would take some time. And it would require that proceedings be brought against Justin Talbot in a court of law.'

'That's how I see it, too.'

'Perhaps you should discuss it with Ferguson?'

'He will want to do what's right for him. I want to do what's right for Mickeen.'

'I understand how you feel, but I really think you *should* talk to Ferguson. When I start handling this in the way you wish, I don't want to find any roadblocks waiting for me, if you know what I mean.'

'I do, but I intend to have things the way I want them this time, and Ferguson's going to have to accept that.' He got up and shook hands. 'Many thanks, Professor, but we'll be on our way.'

Holley drove again on the way back and Dillon just sat there, gazing out at the traffic. Roper called and said,

'A terrible business, Sean. Bellamy's been in touch and filled us in.'

'What do you think of the Shamrock affair now?'

'It's so unlikely that it must be true. There's an imbalance in the man, a kind of madness – there must be, for someone who has everything to risk losing the lot.'

'Maybe it's because he's decided that in having everything, he's got nothing. Then there's the whole relationship with Al Qaeda to explain,' Dillon said. 'Is Ferguson there?' he added.

'He's been called to a Cabinet Office meeting with Harry Miller, and then he's on the list to see the Prime Minister. Told me to tell you he'll see you both early evening.'

'And Talbot?'

'When I raised the matter, he said that since there was absolutely nowhere in the world that Talbot could hide, there was no rush. He's probably right. The way I see it, with all that Talbot money, they'll have a phalanx of the finest barristers in the business working for him. He's a decorated war hero, wounded in Afghanistan – imagine what the psychiatrists will make of that.'

'To hell with the barristers and the psychiatrists – Talbot's mine.'

'If he's still alive, I want to lift him,' Dillon said. He was sitting in the computer room with Roper and Holley at Holland Park. 'Everything according to the law. I want his arrest, a post mortem, a coroner's inquest and, most of all, I want to see him standing in the dock of the Old Bailey. I owe it to Mickeen.'

'I've crossed him off my guest list,' Roper said. 'He deserves everything they can throw at him, but the way things look, you aren't going to get it. I remember during the Cold War, if you arrested a Communist spy, he never ended up in the dock because they wanted to turn him.'

'Are you saying that's what Ferguson wants to do with Talbot?'

'No, Sean,' Roper said. 'What I think is that this might go way beyond Ferguson. We're talking politics here, and on an international level.'

'And you agree with that?'

'Don't insult me, you daft bastard. Just listen, for once in your life. What do you think it's like sitting here year after year in this wheelchair, knowing what's right and not being able to do anything about it because of the system?'

Dillon said, 'I'm sorry, Giles, this business has really got to me.'

Roper reached for his bottle of Scotch, poured a large one and tossed it back. 'Here's the bad news. Ferguson's already been told by the Cabinet Office to invoke the Official Secrets Act when Mickeen's death is put before a special crown coroner. The coroner will give a closed court order. No jury necessary. They'll issue a burial order, and that's it.'

'To whom?' Dillon said. 'Mr Teague and the disposal team?'

Roper ignored him. 'It all takes place quickly. I'd say about a week.'

There was a silence between the three of them, and it was Roper who said, 'You know, I did some checking. Talbot International has a Citation X. In the past couple of days, it's flown from Belfast to Algeria and back again. Landed today, just after noon, in Belfast.'

Holley said, 'A great plane that some say is the fastest commercial jet in the world.'

'And the pity of it all,' said Roper, 'is that I haven't been able to tell Ferguson about it.'

'Why not?' Dillon asked.

'I can't go breaking in on him when he's at a Cabinet Office, can I? Or when he's with the Prime Minister?'

'So what are you saying?' Holley asked.

Roper looked up at the clock. 'Twenty to three. It's half an hour to Farley, and you could make Belfast in one hour. If there happened to be, say, a Mercedes waiting, you could be at Kilmartin at five o'clock.'

'How the hell did you manage to arrange all this?'

'It's better you don't know.' Roper reached into his desk. 'Here's a copy of the warrant authorizing you to take into custody Major Justin Talbot wherever he may be found. You've got your MI5 warrant card, Sean, but here's one for you, Daniel. I took it for granted you wouldn't mind using the plane.'

'I wouldn't miss it for anything.' Holley turned to

Dillon. 'Let's get going, then.' They rushed out. Roper put the weather chart for the Irish Sea up on the screen. A nice summer afternoon, nightfall about eight o'clock, possibility of showers later. Ah, well, that was Ireland for you. He wondered how Ferguson was going to take it and discovered that he didn't really care, and he was laughing as he poured another Scotch.

At Talbot Place, Justin had spent much of the day dozing. His forehead was damp when Larry Ryan dropped in for the second time that day to see him. It was four-thirty, the sky clouding over, a rumble of thunder in the far distance.

Jean greeted the doctor and accompanied him to her son's bedroom. She stood with Murphy while Ryan examined him, and Justin said, 'Here we are again, Larry, well done thou good and faithful servant.'

'Shut up, Justin,' Jean said.

'Only joking, Mum.'

Ryan said, 'You always did, Justin. I might call in again later.'

He went out, and Jean and Murphy followed him. 'How is he?' she asked.

'Not good, his temperature is a hundred and three and the pulse is racing. The heart's under great strain in my opinion. I really do think he needs not only hospital, but intensive care.'

'But you and Murphy have done so much for him.'

361

'I'm not certain it's enough, Jean. If that fever really erupts, it will be the death of him'.

'He's determined to tough it out,' she said. 'What can I do?'

'There's not much left but prayer, I suppose. Has Father Cassidy been to see him?'

'Justin refused to speak to him.'

'That's a shame. I saw the old boy myself earlier. He told me he'll be asking people to pray for Justin.'

Jean said, 'I doubt he'll appreciate it.'

Ryan said to Murphy, 'He can't bathe or shower, because I don't think it wise to disturb the dressings. Just give him a body wash and fresh garments of some sort.' He kissed Jean on the cheek. 'Take care, and I want you to know you can rely on me, Jean. I'll call back this evening again around seven.'

She went back in the room and found Justin arguing with Murphy. 'He wants to give me a body wash, as if I were a bloody schoolboy.'

'Shut your mouth and do as you're told.' She reached behind him, untied the ribbons on his bed smock. 'You'll feel better when Murphy's washed you down and dressed you, so don't be stupid.'

'All right, but you'll have to go out. I'm not a little boy any more.'

She went downstairs, found Hannah and Emily the cook and young Jane, dressed in their best and putting their coats on.

'You remembered we were going to six o'clock

Mass,' Hannah told her. 'Murphy promised to go with us.'

'He's just giving Justin a wash and change, but he won't be long. Is Jack going?'

'Not if he can help it, if I know him. To be honest with you, he's putting his time into sorting the office out just in case he leaves.'

'He's not thinking of going after all these years?'

'He doesn't need it, Jean, he's got the pub. And I've got to be honest with you, because I love you. He feels betrayed. I doubt it will ever be the same again between him and Justin.'

Jean gave her a kiss, for she was obviously very upset. 'I'm sorry about Justin, Hannah, and the way it's turned out. I don't know what to say. I'll go and send Murphy on his way.'

'We'll hang on.'

Jean went up in the lift and when she entered Justin's bedroom found him wearing a navy blue track suit. He was sitting in the bedside armchair while Murphy fitted a pair of white sneakers on his feet.

'That's great,' Justin said. 'I feel a hundred per cent better. Prop up the pillows on the bed and I'll lie back.' Which Murphy did, assisting him back up on to it.

Jean said, 'Off you go, Murphy, the ladies are waiting to take you to Mass.'

'I'll see you later,' he said, and hurried out.

There was, for her at least, a slight, awkward silence. 'Can I get you anything?'

'I don't think so.'

'Then I think I'll just go to my studio for a while.'

'Still working on my portrait?'

'No, I decided I'd gone about as far as I could get.'

'And are you happy with it?'

'I think it says what you are and it tells the truth. When I was a student at the Slade, my professor said the most important thing was that your subject was so perfectly realized that it was as if the individual was saying not "this is me", but "this is what I am".'

'And does mine do that?'

'Oh, yes, I think so.'

'Then you must put it over the fireplace in the study.'

'No, I couldn't do that.'

'Why not?'

'I'd always be afraid that somebody would put it on a bonfire.'

She went out. He lay there thinking about what she'd said, then reached down for the rucksack and put it on the bed beside him. It hurt like hell, so he rummaged amongst the things inside and took out the half-bottle of brandy and swallowed some. It burned all the way down and he remembered what Murphy had said, but he was past caring, so he swallowed some more.

It was almost six when Holley drove through Kilmartin, people going into church and organ music clearly heard. Dillon kept his head down as they passed the pub and moved along the approach road to Talbot Place, which loomed ahead through beech trees, and then they were at the entrance to the drive.

'How do we play this?' Holley asked.

'I'm remembering that Jack Kelly is the estate manager,' Dillon said. 'They must have an office for him. All these great estates do. Just follow your nose.'

Which Holley did, and then they saw the main entrance porch to the house and at the same time noticed a sign board saying 'Estate Manager', an arrow pointing. There was a Shogun and a Mercedes and they parked their own car with them and walked round to the courtyard and found the office, opened the door without knocking, and walked in.

Jack Kelly was arranging files on a shelf and received a severe shock. He moved to his desk fast, got the drawer open and took out his Browning.

'Put it away, Jack,' Dillon told him. 'We haven't come for you, we've come for Justin.' He took out the national security warrant and put it on the desk. 'Read it.'

Kelly did, his face troubled. 'On whose authority?'

'MI Five's.' Dillon showed him his warrant card. 'Daniel's got one, too.'

'Bloody traitors, the both of ye.'

'You're entitled to your opinion,' Holley said. 'But don't tell us he's not here. His plane is at Belfast City Airport, and since his pilot happened to be in the staff canteen, we took the opportunity of interviewing him. He was most revealing.'

'So we know he's here and in a poorly way,' Dillon said.

Kelly still tried to bluster. 'And what is it he's supposed to have done?'

'If you'll take us to him, you'll discover that. Now where do we go?' Dillon demanded.

Suddenly, it was all too much for Kelly, and he said despairingly, 'Christ, there's no way round this, is there? The silly, stupid, mad young idiot. He's going down and taken the entire house of Talbot with him. Even Colonel Henry couldn't do that. Come on, follow me.'

He brushed past them and led the way out.

They went up the stairs together, and it was Kelly who knocked on the door and led the way in. Jean was sitting in an easy chair by the old fireplace, Justin still propped up on the bed.

'Yes, Jack, what is it?' Jean asked, and then Dillon and Holley moved in on either side of him.

'Justin Talbot,' Dillon said. 'We're from MI Five, here to take you into custody.'

'You can't do that.' Justin was surprisingly calm. 'You should have police with you.'

'We dispense with that on special occasions.'

'So what's the charge?'

'There will be many. Your exploits as Shamrock have been better than the midnight movie, you know. And by the way – it wasn't one of us you shot in the Khufra, it was Colonel Ali Hakim.'

Justin laughed out loud. 'You don't say. I think that's really very funny.'

Holley said, 'Hakim also told me the identity of the Preacher before he died. It's Professor Hassan Shah of the London School of Economics – if you're interested.'

'Oh, I am, but it's a pity I didn't know it earlier. I believe he met a bad end.'

'Cyanide poisoning,' Dillon told him.

Justin turned to his mother and said, 'Just like Heinrich Himmler.'

'For God's sake, Justin,' Jean said. 'This isn't funny. They're here to arrest you.'

'I'm afraid I'll have to disappoint them.'

'What do you mean?'

'I'm planning to go down to Drumgoole and fly away in my Beech Baron.'

She was incredibly distressed. 'Justin, this is madness.'

'But I am mad, just like Colonel Henry said. I've always known it.'

His hand went into the rucksack and Holley drew his Walther. Justin produced the half-bottle of brandy, waved it at him and drank deeply. Holley dropped his hand, holding the Walther against his leg. Justin replaced the brandy bottle in the rucksack, pulled out a Browning and shot Holley and Dillon in the chest.

Kelly cowered, raising his hands, and his mother screamed, 'No, Justin.'

He laughed wildly. 'Your lucky day, Jack, I'm out of here.' He pushed Kelly to one side, pulled open the door and lurched out, making for the stairs, reaching for the banister to support him on the way down.

Jean, almost demented, dropped on her knees beside Dillon, but found him taking one deep breath after another, and then already sitting up.

'Body armour,' he gasped. 'It's like being kicked by a mule, but a lot better than being dead.' He was panting, his voice hoarse, but Holley was already stirring in the same way. As Kelly helped him up, Jean turned and ran out.

Justin was making slow progress getting down the stairs, and she caught up with him as he reached the door.

'It's no use, love, there's nowhere to go.'

He knocked her hand away. 'Yes, there bloody well is.' He went down the steps and made by mistake for the Mercedes that Dillon and Holley had parked there.

As he got the driver's door open, it started to rain, and there was thunder in the distance. He got in and she pulled open the passenger door and scrambled in beside him. By chance, Holley had left the key in the ignition.

'Justin, please darling, think again,' Jean said.

'Oh, no, none of that, Mum. I told you where I was going and I meant it.' He switched on the engine and drove away.

Dillon, Holley and Kelly came down the stairs together. 'Are you okay?' Dillon asked Holley.

'I'm more angry than anything else. Imagine falling for a cheap trick like that.'

'So thank God once again for the nylon-and-titanium vest,' Dillon said, and asked Kelly, 'What about Drumgoole?'

'It's a small flying club just off the coast road. When he flies over from Frensham, he uses a twin-engine Beech Baron. Drumgoole is only twenty minutes from the house, so it's convenient.'

'Well, you know the way, so you take us there,' Dillon told him. 'Only put your foot down. God knows where he thinks he can hide now, but I'd prefer to put a hand on him while we still can.'

There was very little wind, but it was raining hard now, and gloomy, as night touched the far horizon. The Mercedes turned into the small car park at Drumgoole, but the flying club was closed, not a soul about.

'Nobody's here,' Justin said.

'That's usual when there's no activity, no bookings,' she said.

There were two Archers, a Cessna 310 and the Beech Baron. 'There she is, the darling,' Justin said. 'Let's hope Regan's done his stuff and left the cabin key in the usual place.' He got out of the Mercedes, walked to the red-painted sand box hanging beside the door of the office and felt inside. He held the key up in triumph. 'There you go.'

He started to walk towards the Beech Baron, and Jean went after him, begging, 'Please, Justin, don't do this. Where will you go? Stay and give us a chance to work this out.'

'I don't think so.' He reached the plane, stepped up on the wing and unlocked the cockpit door. At that moment, Kelly's Morris appeared up on the road, paused and started down to the car park. 'Oh, dear, must go.' Justin scrambled in across to the left-hand seat.

Jean tried to follow him, stepping up on the wing as he switched on the engine. 'I'm coming with you.'

'I don't think so.' As the propellers started to turn, he shouted above the engine roar, 'Better this way, Mum,' shoved her down off the wing, slammed the door and started to move away.

The Morris braked to a halt, the three men got out and the Beech Baron was moving, Jean Talbot running alongside, pleading.

Dillon ran in, ducked and grabbed her, dragging her away, and Justin, gazing out of the cockpit window, raised his thumb. The plane swung round and rushed forward, lifting as he boosted the engines, very fast and very low, and then it started to climb and continued until, perhaps a quarter of a mile out, the engines stopped.

There was silence except for the rushing rain, and Jean Talbot screamed, as if knowing what was going to happen, and the Beech Baron dropped its nose and went straight down into the sea. There was a great fountain of foam, and she cried helplessly as she turned and buried her face against Dillon's chest and he held her.

She looked up at him, her face swollen with her weeping. 'Damn you, all of you, with your lies and deceit and endless killing. The world should be better than this.'

She started to cry helplessly, and Jack Kelly came and took her gently from Dillon and held her close. 'Let's go home, Jean, back to the Place.' He nodded to Dillon and said, 'There's a trench three hundred feet deep out there. He knew that. This is your Mercedes, I think. I'd go if I were you. Much the best thing.'

They sat in the Mercedes waiting for the Morris to leave, and Dillon got out his Codex, called Roper and gave him a quick résumé of events.

Roper seemed subdued. 'So that's it?'

'If you mean is Justin Talbot dead, you'd better believe it. I suppose recovering the plane is possible, if Jean Talbot wants it. What do you think Ferguson will make of it?'

'He rang me from the Cabinet Office, so I seized the opportunity to get it over with and I told him what you were up to. He just said: I might have known.'

'Well, God knows how he'll react to the result. I'll be seeing you.'

Holley said, 'God, but I'm sore.'

'You're alive,' Dillon said. 'That's all that counts.'

Holley nodded. 'Do you think Justin Talbot was mad?'

'Barking mad,' Dillon said.

'So really, it wasn't his fault, any of it?'

'It's a point of view,' Dillon told him.

Twenty minutes later, when they were close to the outskirts of Belfast, Roper called again and Dillon put it on speaker so Holley could hear.

'I've told him what happened.'

'And what was his reaction?'

'He said it was perfect. Justin Talbot dies in a tragic plane crash and that clears the whole thing up without a scandal. As someone else said very recently, you have a great gift for doing the wrong thing, but getting the right result. See you, Dillon,' and then he rang off.

'Right for whom?' Dillon said. 'Ferguson, the Prime Minister, the Cabinet Office?' He shook his head. 'Do you ever get tired, Daniel, really tired?'

'Sure I do,' Holley said. 'It's a mad world, Dillon, but it's all we've got.'

REQUIEM

15

By the good offices of Blake Johnson, Dillon found himself soon after on assignment to the CIA at Langley on an anti-terrorism programme. The principle was 'set a thief to catch a thief', his years on the other side of the fence providing invaluable experience for students.

It was two months before he found himself back at Holland Park, and on the first day Roper said, 'Something that might interest you is taking place tomorrow.'

'What would that be?' Dillon asked.

'Jean Talbot's the new Chairman of Talbot International. The board didn't have much choice, since she owns so much of the firm. She moved back to Marley Court and is back at the Slade as a Visiting Professor in Fine Art, and apparently she's getting an enormous number of portrait assignments. I was reading her up in *Tatler* magazine. She's got an exhibition in Bond Street.'

'That's nice for her, but what's happening tomorrow?'

'She had a Dutch salvage firm look for Justin and they found him in the Beech Baron. She's burying him tomorrow at St Mary the Virgin Church in Dun Street, Mayfair. I thought you might be interested.'

'Now, do I look like that kind of fella?'

'Actually, I think you do.'

In any event, an assignment for Ferguson got in the way, Dillon got to the church too late for the service, and things had moved out to the churchyard.

Most Roman Catholic churches in London are Victorian, and St Mary the Virgin was a charming example, with a delightfully melancholic feel to it, crowded with Gothic tombs, winged angels and effigies of children who had died far too young.

He stayed back from the crowd of thirty or forty people standing around the grave with bowed heads while the priest read the prayers for the dying. Jean Talbot looked very fine, the veil on her black hat thrown back, smiling at everyone.

She turned to move back towards the church, talking to people close to her, moving directly towards Dillon, then passing without the slightest sign that they had met.

He was surprised to realize how put out he felt, and the following day, being in Bond Street by the Zion Gallery, he went in to have a look at her collection. It was all excellent, more than interesting, but the big surprise was the portrait of her son.

It was incredibly good, a master-work. It was late in the afternoon and the crowd had thinned and he sat on a bench for twenty minutes looking at it, thinking of Lord Byron. Mad, bad and dangerous to know.

'You obviously like it, Mr Dillon.' She appeared from behind him.

'It's a very remarkable painting.'

'Of a very remarkable young man.'

He stood and turned to face her and was amazed that a woman of her age could look so incredibly attractive.

'I tried to make the funeral, but got held up and missed the church. I did manage some of the funeral, though.'

'I saw you.'

'I didn't know that.' He was lying, of course, and she knew it.

She turned to look at the painting again. 'My son was a deeply troubled man and a great deal of it was not his fault. I sometimes think I didn't really know him.'

'Oh, but I think you did,' Dillon told her.

'You think so? Justin once told me about my painting that I was not only good, but I was too good. That I didn't just go for appearance, I got what was inside. Would you agree?'

'Yes, I think so.'

'Of course if I did your portrait, I'd find a lot inside. You see, I know an awful lot about you: I've made it my business to find out. I just want to say I appreciate why you had to shoot my son in the Khufra. After all, he'd shot that wretched Colonel Hakim, so I don't really blame you.'

'That's very decent of you.'

'On the other hand, he was my son, so I can't possibly forgive you, either. So what's to be done?'

'I haven't the slightest idea,' Dillon said.

'Have you killed, I suppose. It's one of the advantages of being so incredibly rich – anything is possible.'

Dillon took a close look at her. She was serious. The woman he was looking at was not the same person she'd been in Kilmartin.

'I suppose it is,' Dillon said.

'So, you have much to look forward to.'

Dillon stood there for a moment, then glanced again at the portrait of Justin Talbot hanging on the wall.

'He was right,' Dillon said. 'You do get beneath the surface. But I just realized something.'

'What is that, Mr Dillon?'

'I thought it was Colonel Henry's mad eyes staring out at me from Justin's portrait. Now I realize they're yours.'

For the first time since he'd known her, that porcelain face cracked. 'I loved him, damn you, more than anything in this life.'

'Yes, I thought it was something like that. Well, ma'am: people have been trying to kill me in one way or another for years. I'm still here. But you're welcome to try.'

He walked away quickly, out into Bond Street. She hurried after him, furious, but when she reached the pavement crowded with people, he was already gone, vanished into thin air, as if he had never been.